The Big Fat Book of Interesting Stories

• Quizzical Tales for Inquisitive Minds •

Tickle your Mind with the Greatest Collection of Utterly Random and Futile yet
Totally Awesome Stories about Everything

Erudition Hacks

Disclaimer

Read at your own risk. This book may cause intense bouts of hysterical laughter, accidental absorption of knowledge, and in some cases even turning you into a know-it-all.

The following stories include an exploding manhole cover, sex with gorillas, and death by dance, syrup, and make-up. Readers discretion advised.

Please do not attempt to repeat the feats of awesome heroism or sheer stupidity told in this book: the world cannot take it twice.

Finally, since my editor had the brilliant idea to make me write a funny disclaimer and I failed miserably, here are my final words of caution:

- Do not read while operating a motor vehicle, watercraft, or aircraft.
- Keep the corners of the book away from yours or anyone's eyes.
- This book is not intended as a weapon, please do not throw it against your family members (after all they were nice enough to get you this as a present).

First Printing Edition, 2020
ISBN 9-798-56655-052-7

Printed in the United States of America
Available from Amazon.com and other retail outlets

Table Of Contents

INTRODUCTION

Behind every man, there is a great story. Actually, behind every man, woman, discovery, invention, and object there is a story that shaped our history and our imagination. Some are sad, some are hilarious, some are just boring but in this book you will find only interesting stories, the will leave you stunned (like the man who was struck seven times by lightning).

Whether you want to impress your date, have an entertaining conversation piece for your friends, or simply have a laugh at the absurd misshapen of history, this is the right book for you.

From little-known facts to heart-melting stories; this book is the greatest random compilation of "insane, but true" stories you will ever read.

CRAZY FUN HISTORY

I loved history in school and it was all thanks to an amazing teacher, who always found a weird history fact to spice up the long list of dates, that however much you love history, nobody finds interesting!

So, here are the most obscure and craziest stories from our distant and recent past.

Death by makeup

Once upon a time, Snow White's skin was considered the chic, sexy look of the Elizabethan English elite. Queen Elizabeth I's signature ghostly makeup typified the 16th century ideal for women, the immaculate porcelain skin representing nobility and earthly perfection. To achieve that ideal, Elizabeth I slathered her face with makeup composed mostly of lead. She also put mercury on her lips, and most likely washed her face with a mercury-based make-up remover that ate away at her flesh. As a matter of fact, the makeup may have been the cause of her death.

During the Elizabethan era, the highest standard for women's beauty was a smooth, blindingly white skin. To achieve this look, the Virgin Queen wore Venetian ceruse, a cosmetic made with vinegar and white lead. She dabbed her face and neck with this substance, hiding her pockmarked skin beyond an eerie porcelain paste that probably smelled like sour wine.
That's one surefire way to maintain your virginity!

Thanks to 400 years of science, we now know that applying led to the face on a daily basis causes very serious, and often irreversible problems like hair loss and skin deterioration, and death by lead poisoning, which in the 16th century, was pretty damn final. It may well have been the culprit for Queen Elizabeth's death, but lead wasn't the only poison in her pigments.

But as we know, Snow White's mother wished for more than a tiny ghost baby. She wished for her to have lips as red as blood on winter roses as well.
The queen's extremely expensive lipstick was made from cinnabar, a toxic mineral with a high concentration of mercury, but gave her the signature red mouth that smiles creepily at you in all those creepy paintings.
So, the two horrific poisons worked in tandem through skin absorption for years and years.

The lead slowly corroded the queen's face, leading to visible marks. In response, Elizabeth wore thicker and thicker layers of Venetian ceruse, reportedly layering makeup as thick as an inch at the end of her life.

Symptoms of mercury poisoning include memory loss, irritability, and depression, conditions Elizabeth reportedly experienced towards the end of her life.

In the Elizabethan era, nobles didn't clean off their makeup nightly. Heck, most modern women have been guilty of that at least a couple times.
After her maids carefully applied lead and mercury makeup to the royal face, Elizabeth herself wore it for at least a week.
Never mind about pore blockage, the lead penetrated into her skin, making it gray and wrinkled.

When Elizabeth finally washed away her makeup, historians suggest she might have used a disgusting concoction made with eggshells, alum, and, as you might have guessed, more mercury. Some claimed the mercury makeup remover left their skin soft, but that was only because it was literally skinning them alive one layer at a time.

As a teen, Queen Elizabeth didn't use to wear quite so much lead as in later years: not just because she was a child, but because she hadn't suffered from smallpox yet.
On October 10th, 1562, she was struck with a high fever and displayed all the hallmarks of the smallpox. Courtiers feared that Elizabeth would die within the week, but the young princess survived.

Unfortunately, the disease left her with permanent scars in her terrible 20s, when life is either a bed of roses or a pile of shit. And scars tend to stack the odds against the former.

Smallpox scars were quite a common problem in that time, which might explain the willingness of women to wear vinegary lead face. Mary Sidney, one of Elizabeth's close friends, got stuck with them too.

As Mary's husband, Henry Sidney, wrote, "the scars, to her resolute discomfort, ever since have done and do remain on her face."

Trying to survive in an atmosphere of constant bitchiness, Elizabeth I did everything she could to cover up the blemishes and keep that virginity under lock and key: anything to avoid a husband who updates people on his wife's pockmarks.

There haven't been many female rulers in English history - let's face it, in any history - a fact with which Elizabeth was all too familiar. She knew all eyes were on her, and that any scarring on her face would mark her not as a survivor, but a pariah in those eyes.

In 1586, a 50-year-old Elizabeth commented on the burden of these expectations when she addressed the parliament, "We princes, I tell you, are set on stages in the sight and view of all the world duly observed. The eyes of many behold our actions, a spot is soon spied in our garments, a blemish noted quickly in our doings."

In a bold act that foresaw Instagram filters, Elizabeth flat out forbade unflattering portraits of herself (well, it's nice to be Queen). Painters were given an opportunity to get really, really creative. They had to make her look young and supple and white, even as she entered her autumn years, which in this case, is a little too good at describing what happens to human skin after decades of lead makeup.

The inventive artists had to make the portrait recognizable as the Queen without showing her sagging skin, the scars, and probably even molten skin beneath the inch-thick mask of white lead she wore.

The famous Darnley portrait, painted in 1575, became a godsend for later portrayals, the grateful artists reused its depiction of Elizabeth's face as a model in paintings for decades.

Elizabeth's battle against the ravages of time was fierce, literally bloody, and lasted all her life.

One of her wiser tricks was to wear a wig: who knows what lunacy would have been used to dye gray hairs back then!

For a long time, it was basically like Shatner's toupee (it existed, but was never officially confirmed) until 1599, when the Earl of Essex blew that secret out of the water and immortalized it, expressing his shock upon beholding his elderly Queen's mostly bald paté, with only a thin ring of hair hanging about the ears. We can't unsee that now.

In the last months of her life, Elizabeth I refused to let doctors cure, or even examine, her. She had fallen into a deep melancholy, according to a member of the court. But still Elizabeth refused to rest.

She had come to believe that if she laid down, she would have never gotten up. So, Elizabeth stood up straight for 15 hours, with her ladies in waiting arranging pillows around her for when she would inevitably collapse.

On March 24th, 1603, Elizabeth died. Possible causes of death might have been cancer or pneumonia, but Elizabeth's use of lead and mercury-based makeup for decades in exponentially increasing doses certainly did not improve her declining health in the slightest.

After a lifetime of lead and mercury poisoning, Elizabeth's body was toxic. Elizabeth Southwell, one of the queen's ladies in waiting, claimed that Elizabeth's body burst in her coffin at her wake due to the abundance of noxious vapors.

Southwell's account has often been dismissed by historians as Jesuit propaganda but exploding coffins aren't uncommon occurrence, even today.

In fact, the phenomenon is called exploding casket syndrome: it's what happens when a corpse is sealed a bit too well.

The coffin acts as a pressure cooker for all those gases and fluids produced by the decomposing body until… well, kaboom!

There's a reason it got chalked up to bad religion.

While Elizabeth certainly suffered in her lifetime the effects of lead and mercury poisoning, her actual cause of death might have been blood poisoning.

Just a week before she passed in 1603, her doctors recommended a risky procedure.

Since the day she was crowned, for 45 years, Elizabeth wore a coronation ring. The ring began cutting into Elizabeth's thoroughly poisoned skin, and presumably, kept on cutting.

Doctors had warned her that the ring had to be surgically removed, and a week later, she died and then exploded, depending on the accounts you believe in.

Evidence of the use of lead for makeup dates back to at least the 5th century BCE. At the time of the Roman Empire, women powdered their faces with lead. By the 16th century, it had become a paste known as Venetian ceruse, or the spirits of Saturn: the Virgin Queen's favorite cosmetic.

Unfortunately for her and every other ceruse aficionado in history, it wasn't classified as a poison until 1634, approximately 40 years after her death, which it had at least one hand in, if not both. People knew what caused hair loss and skin damage, but it took a long time for us to figure out that they were literally killing themselves in the name of beauty.

How not to kill a man for 638 times

> **March 1963, the CIA is planning to kill Fidel Castro using his greatest weakness: a milkshake.**

The U.S. feared Castro's anti-American views, and according to Castro's bodyguard, the CIA plotted 638 times to sabotage him trying things like chemical powder on his boots, a bacterial-lined scuba suit, spiked cigars, and exploding cigars.

But, the closest the CIA came to killing Castro? Poisoning his chocolate milkshake at his favorite ice cream parlor. The dictator had an obsession with dairy, ice cream, milkshakes, you name it.

I mean, it gets hot in Cuba.

So, the CIA convinced members of the mafia to carry out the deadly plot. The mobsters delivered a pill containing poison to a waiter who had to slip it into Castro's milkshake.

The waiter placed the pill in the freezer until the time was right, but the pill froze to the freezer's lining and when he went to pick it up, the pill ripped open spilling poison everywhere.

So, the would-be assassin waiter abandoned the plot.

The mission failed and Castro went on to become one of the world's longest ruling leaders, arrogantly boasting, "If surviving assassination attempts were an Olympic event, I would win the gold medal."

A shipful of women

Sure, you probably know that Australia was settled by British convicts, but chances are you have no idea just how wild those convict ships could get, especially the first ship full of female prisoners. This motley crew of British women sent over by Great Britain in hopes to reform the struggling convict colony of New South Wales was made up of primarily petty thieves and sex workers. And the complexity tragedy and triumph of their story will completely blow your mind.

Ahoy, mate, it's time to hop aboard the Lady Juliana, the wild late 18th century prison ship filled with women.

Considering it was the 18th century and you couldn't exactly hop on a jet, the voyage from England to Australia lasted about 10 brutally long months.
As the ship voyage from port to port in the Atlantic and Indian oceans, the Lady stopped in places like Rio de Janeiro and Cape Town along the way. And these weren't short them stops to buy souvenirs and stretch their legs. Sometimes they'd be docked for several weeks at a time.

Often, the convicts made the most of their global tour and did one of the few jobs available to women at the time. As John Nicol, the ship's steward, euphemistically remembered in his memoir of the voyage "we did not restrain the people onshore from coming on board through the day. The captains and seamen who were in port at the time paid us many visits."
The ladies kept at least part of their earnings. Some of the ship's officers and sailors, all men, of course, allegedly even got in on the business.

Sadly, their involvement raises serious questions about the degree to which these captive women were coerced into their activities. Whether out of love, lust, coercion, boredom, or necessity, many of the women onboard the ship became the wives of the ship's officers and crew members.

Again, as the ship's steward John Nicol (one of our main sources for the journey) recalled: "When we were fairly out at sea, every man onboard took a wife from among the convicts. They loathe nothing." While these marriages were definitely not legal, they did sometimes serve a practical purpose for the convicted women.
Taking a lover aboard the ship often meant you got to sleep in a better bed.

There was, however, at least one partnership rooted in true love. Nicol, the ship's steward, seemed to have fallen in love with prisoner Sarah Whitlam.
He even intended to marry her once her term ended, but sadly the two never made it down the aisle. Nicol had to ship back to Britain, leaving Sarah and their child behind in Australia.
He tried to find her when he got back to reunite with, but tragically they never found each other again.

The lack of privacy for prisoners on convicts ships meant that crew members had access to them. And their relations and interactions could be nonconsensual, considering the age of consent in 18th century Britain was devastatingly low, 10 years old to be exact.
Some crew members had no problem taking teenage wives during the voyage.
The historian Pamela Horne identified 14-year-old Jane Forbes as one of these young wives. She was pregnant and had the baby before reaching Australia.

The women of the Lady Juliana served a particular purpose. Colonial officials hoped that a shipload of women would help civilize the budding convict colony. Considering most of the women aboard were petty thieves, maybe they were hoping these women would steal some hearts.

According to the account of a British official, the increased presence of women would promote a matrimonial connection to improve the more conducts and secure the settlement. The women were meant to marry male colonists, which would supposedly create and maintain respectable family life in the new colony.
The women's prison sentences aim to transform them into moral vessels that would enable the recreation of the British family unit abroad.
The women being transported to New South Wales on the Lady Juliana were prisoners, but their lives were upended for infractions that honestly don't seem like that big of a deal from our 21st century gaze.

Even if most of the women on board the Lady Juliana might have been prostitutes, that's not why they were sent to Australia. Sex work or harlotry was not an offense worthy of exile. As a matter of fact, most of the women on the Lady Juliana had been arrested and sentenced for various degrees of theft. Their offenses ranged from highway robbery to pickpocketing and shoplifting.

For example, Mary Hook was 20 years old when the British court commuted her sentence for stealing her employer's money and goods from capital punishment to a seven-year sentence in New South Wales.
So basically, she was almost killed just because she stole a few things from work, but instead the British government mercifully sent her to an entirely different continent.

One of the most notable convicts on the ship was Elizabeth Barnsley. She was convicted for the dangerous and heinous crime of stealing some cloth. Anyway, Liz, the fabric thief, quickly became a leader during the voyage.
John Nicol wrote about her saying, "she was very kind to her fellow convicts, who were poor. They were all anxious to serve her. She was as queen among them."
Barnsley who ended up fashioning a career as a madam, while board the ship, was instrumental in overseeing her fellow convicts economic activities at every port along the way.

Even if they were not being exiled to New South Wales for prostitution, many of the women aboard the ship might have been sex workers in addition to whatever petty crimes they committed. The harlotry economy was alive and well in 18th century Britain.
So, it's reasonable to assume that at least some of the 200 plus convicts took part in that line of work.

The women aboard the Lady Juliana came from British prisons. Though a prison reform movement began to grow in the late 18th century, the prison conditions they escaped were deplorable. Prisons were overcrowded, and disease spread swiftly. Just existing in a prison could accidentally lead to a death sentence.
While the lady Juliana was still a prison ship and the convicts sleeping quarters were just above the ship's garbage and sewage deck, this particular ship had something that their land counterparts and other prison ships didn't: consistent access to medical care.
The ship had a surgeon and his quarters were kept relatively clean.

Moreover, the women weren't chained up like the prisoners on other convict ships and they could barter for improved conditions through various "favors". The reason the passengers on the Lady Juliana enjoyed better conditions was partly because the British government oversaw it, unlike the other vessels transporting prisoners. All the other prison ships travelling to Australia were operated by Camden, Calvert, and King, the nefarious, notorious, and prolific slave trading company. Only five women perished on board the Lady Juliana compared to the 267 deaths reported by another ship.
So, while it wasn't a Carnival Cruise, at least most of the women didn't straight up die.

The vast majority of the women who embarked on the Lady Juliana were in their 20s and 30s, but no fewer than 51 of them around 22% were teenagers.

Mary Wade was one such teen who could have been as young as 11 while aboard. Scholars debate about her exact age though, Mary was certainly the youngest on the ship.

Like many of her shipmates, Wade ultimately married and had a large number of children in Australia.

While there wasn't too much trouble sailing aboard the Lady Juliana during its 11-months-long voyage, one notable issue did arise involving drunkenness leading to disorderly behavior. But come on, if you are on a ship full of cool criminal chicks, wouldn't you want to throw back a few tequila shots with your girls?

To curb her so-called rowdiness, crew members made passenger Nance Farrell wear a repurposed wooden barrel jacket to keep her from being too much of a drunk mess. When that didn't work, they resorted to flogging her 12 times.

Some of the women aboard the Lady Juliana were already mothers before the ship departed England. And so they brought their children with them. Many of the convict passengers became pregnant and even gave birth during the long voyage.

Historians generally believe five to seven babies were born on the ship, but Steward John Nicol suggested no less than 20 had been born while the ship was in port at Rio.

They were prepared for the births. The ship had received a small donation of baby linens before leaving England. This brings a whole new meaning to the concept of water births.

Once the women of the Lady Juliana arrived in their new homeland of New South Wales, they quickly discovered they could enjoy freedoms there that they couldn't in England, even though they were prisoners with few rights who were put in difficult and often dangerous positions.

Women arriving in Australia were free from certain British moral codes, even if colonial officials expected them to be vessels of morality.

English laws that marked children of unwed mothers as illegitimate, for example, were not enforced.

Though being transported to a new colony to get married and propagate British family life was no doubt a complete and total drag, many women made the most of their circumstances in Australia. Some Lady Juliana passengers became upwardly mobile once their prison terms ended and even started their own businesses.

Ann Marsh for one found success after being abandoned by her ship-husband. She got started and ran a variety of businesses, including a liquor shop and a ferry company.

While they may have had a rough and terrifying experience, it's no doubt the ship full of women made a lasting impact on Australia and changed the course of history forever.

The women of the Lady Juliana became known as the founding mothers of Australia.

Between their side hustles, the romantic bartering aboard the ship, and the prostitution rings in every port, their journey has gone down in history books as one of the most legendary.

In the search for an imaginary king in the land that never was

In 1165, copies of a strange letter began to circulate throughout Western Europe. It described a marvelous realm, blessed by the Tower of Babel and the Fountain of Youth. The ruler was non other than the letter's mysterious author: Prester John. We now know that the extraordinary ruler of this magical kingdom never existed, much like his realm. Nevertheless, the legend of this mythical land and its powerful king played a decisive role in the decisions of European leaders for the next 400 years.

The myth around Prester John's mysterious letter would start the age of exploration, influence intercontinental diplomacy, and even indirectly begin a civil war.

When Prester John's letter started to circulate, Europe was in the middle of the Crusades.
In a series of religious wars, European kingdoms campaigned to seize and colonize what they saw as the Christian Holy Land. Any faith outside of Christianity was vilified by the Church, and they targeted with particular fervor the faith of the Jewish and Muslim communities who populated the area.
The crusaders were eager to find Christian kingdoms that could serve as powerful allies in their war.
The rumors of a powerful Christian king who had defeated an enormous Muslim army in the Far East started to spread and reached the eager ears of the blood-thirsty Crusaders.
In reality, it was a Mongol horde that included converted Christian tribes that had defeated that army. But fake news are not just a modern fad, and precise information travelled unreliably back then, even without Russian bots and trolls.
Merchants and emissaries embellished the story with Biblical fragments and epic poem. By the time the story had reached European ears, the Mongol horde had been replaced with an all-powerful Christian army, commanded by a mythical king who shared the Crusader's vision of conquering Jerusalem.

When a letter allegedly signed by a certain "Prester John" appeared, European rulers were thrilled.
The letter's actual author remains unknown to this day, but its stereotypes about the East and enthusiastic alignment with the European cause are most definitely evidences of a Western forgery. However, despite the letter's obvious origins as blatant European propaganda, the appeal of Prester John's myth was far too great for the Crusaders to ignore.
It didn't take long before the European mapmakers were arguing about the location of the mythical kingdom.

During the 13th and 14th century, European missionaries travelled East, along the newly revived Silk Road. They weren't looking, of course, for the letter's author, who at that point would have been over a century old; but rather, for his descendants.
So, the title of Prester John was briefly identified with several Central Asian kings, but it soon became clear that the Mongols were largely non-Christian. As their Empire began to decline, Europeans decided they were definitely not Christians and began pursuing alternative routes to the mysterious lands even farther east and new hints to Prester John's powerful kingdom.

As other explorers went south, at the same time Ethiopian pilgrims began traveling north.
When they reached Rome, these visitors quickly attracted the interest of European cartographers and scholars. Ethiopia had been converted to Christianity in the 4th century and the stories of their homeland fit perfectly into Prester John's legend. The Portuguese explorers had scoured Africa for the kingdom and finally a mix of diplomacy and confusion finally turned myth into reality.

The Ethiopians were gracious hosts to their European guests, who were eager to do business with the ruler they believed to be Prester John. Even if the Ethiopians were initially baffled by the Portuguese's unusual name for their Emperor, they were clever enough to quickly realize the diplomatic capital it afforded them.

The Ethiopian diplomats played the part of Prester John's subjects perfectly, and the Portuguese triumphantly announced the new alliance with the fabled king, more than 350 years after the letter had started circulating and the search had begun. But this long-awaited partnership was quickly put to test, and failed to meet expectations.

Just a decade later, the Sultanate of Adal, a regional power aided by the Ottoman Empire, invaded Ethiopia. The Portuguese sent troops that helped Ethiopians win the conflict. But by this time, the Europeans had realized that Ethiopia was not the all-powerful mythical ally Europe had hoped for. After all, who can compare to someone that never existed and has been built up in the imagination of people who believed in dragons and witches?

To make matters worse, the increasingly intolerant Roman Catholic Church had suddenly decided that the Ethiopian sect of Christianity was heretical (they probably weren't white enough to be good Christians).

Their subsequent attempts to convert the Ethiopians, that they had once revered as ideal Christians to the "true" faith, would eventually start a civil war. In the 1630s, Ethiopia cut all ties with Europe.

Over the next two centuries, the myth of Prester John slowly faded into oblivion as Europeans got bored with the whole Christianity thing and decided it was easier to colonize people without any pretense and the reign of the king who made history without needing to exist came to an end.

But his story is a fundamental teaching of the fickle nature of untrue rumors used for political purpose....Ah, if only more people would study history!

The ballet that caused a riot

When we think of ballet what comes to mind are harmony, grace and elegance: hardly anything that would trigger a riot. But history is long and crazy things happen, such as the fact that at the first performance of Igor Stravinsky's "The Rite of Spring," the spectators were so outraged that their voices drowned out the orchestra. The accounts of the event reported people throwing objects on the stage, challenging each other to fisticuffs, and subsequently getting arrested...and the evening started as a sophisticated night at the ballet.

First performed in May 1913 at the Théâtre des Champs-Elysées in Paris, "The Rite of Spring" is set in prehistoric times.

The ballet's story follows an ancient Pagan community worshipping the Earth and preparing for the sacrifice of a woman, which is their annual ritual to bring about the change of seasons.

But the ballet's plot is not so relevant, despite being quite provocative in itself, as Stravinsky was much more concerned with the violent relations between humans, culture, and nature than silly things such as characters or plot development.

These themes were developed thanks to a truly disturbing production which makes use of strident music, convulsive dancing, and eerie staging.

In the opening scene the dancers awaken to a solo bassoon, playing in an uncanny high register. The ballet continues with discordant string music, occasionally punctured by sudden pauses while the dancers convulse away to the inexistent rhythm.

The frightening jerking characters enact the ballet's brutal premise i.e., they in fact sacrifice the woman (just to shatter the hopes of anyone who would think that a ballet that ended up in a riot would have a happy ending). The ballet as a whole, but specifically the brutal ending set the audience on edge and shattered the conventions of classical music. In fact, "The Rite of Spring" challenged the orchestral traditions of the 19th century in many ways, preparing the taste of the audiences to the impending monster called "contemporary classical music."

The ballet was composed just at the tipping point for the first World War and the Russian revolution, and in fact, "The Rite of Spring" is permeated by a sense urgency. This seething tension is reflected through various formal experiments, including the innovative uses of syncopation and irregular rhythms. It is also blessed by atonality and the lack of a single key, plus the presence of multiple time signatures; I suspect just to drive the musicians crazy, but apparently, the more historically accurate reason was to push to the limit the possibility of using different keys that had started with his initial experiment with bitonality in *The Firebird*.

Stravinsky spliced in the development of the music aspects of Russian folk music along the strikingly modern features: this combination was meant to deliberately disrupt the expectations of his sophisticated, Parisian audience.

It wasn't Stravinsky's first use of folk music.
He was born in 1882 in a small town just outside of St. Petersburg and Stravinsky entered in the contemporary audiences' heart with the lush ballet "The Firebird", which was based on a Russian fairytale and the whole production was influenced by Stravinsky's fascination with folk culture. But he plotted an even wilder project in "The Rite of Spring," pushing folk and musical boundaries to bring out the rawness of a pagan ritual.

Stravinsky brought this project to life with the collaboration of the artist Nicholas Roerich.
Roerich was already obsessed with prehistoric times. He had published essays about human sacrifice and worked on excavations of Slavic tombs in addition to set and costume design. For "The Rite of Spring," he drew from Russian medieval art and peasant garments to create costumes that hung awkwardly on the dancers' bodies. Roerich set them against vivid backdrops of primeval nature: a panorama of looming trees, jagged rocks, and nightmarish colors.

Along with its otherworldly sets and perturbing score, the original choreography for "The Rite of Spring" was highly provocative as well.
It was the result of the work of legendary dancer Vaslav Nijinsky, who developed dances to rethink "the roots of movement itself."

Even if Stravinsky later expressed frustration with Nijinsky's demanding rehearsals and single-minded interpretations of the music, his choreography proved as pioneering as Stravinsky's composition. He warped traditional ballet to both the awe and horror of his audience, many of whom expected the elegance, beauty, and romance that they had come to the ballet for.

The dancing in "The Rite of Spring" is convoluted and uneven, with the performers quaking, wriggling, and leaping around as if possessed. Pointedly, the dancers are not one with the music but rather do their best to struggle against it. Nijinsky trained them to turn their toes inwards and land heavily after jumps and not even on beat. In the final, frenzied scene, the sacrificial woman dances herself to death to the music of jarring strings and loud bangs. If you can actually manage to hear it to the end after reading this story, not even the final will give you respite, in fact, the ballet ends abruptly on a harsh, haunting, hollow chord.

"The Rite of Spring" remains as chilling today as it was on the date of its controversial debut, but the shockwaves of the original work continue to resound shrilly and inspire nightmarishly.

You can still hear Stravinsky's influence in modern jazz's dueling rhythms, folky classical music, and even film scores for horror movies, which sometimes still illicit a riotous audience response or at least screaming at a camera in YouTube reaction videos.

The secret weapon of capitalism

We're all familiar with Coca-Cola and its brown reddish hue. But what about clear Coke? It's said that clear Coke was a top-secret project made exclusively for a thirsty Red Russian General.

During World War II, Coca-Cola made a killing (yes, not the most sensitive joke), selling over 5 million bottles for 5 cents and, of course, boosting American troops' morale.

At the Potsdam Conference in 1945, Dwight D. Eisenhower, who had helped along the efforts to support the American troops with Coke even abroad, met with Georgy Zhukov, a Soviet general instrumental in the defeat of Nazi Germany and they became unlikely friends. Just as good friends do, he offered him a Coke, and Zhukov was hooked!

But after the war, Coke was seen as a symbol of American imperialism in the Soviet Unionand and was banned flat out.

Zhukov, who was already hooked on the sweet taste of capitalism, called up the new U.S. president Harry Truman to send him a secret stash, but to save his communist face, he asked if they could make it look like vodka. Truman agreed to help Zhukov out (possibly for some real vodka in return) and asked Coca-Cola to disguise its iconic look. They eliminated the drink's artificial coloring, but made sure the new transparent vodka look-alike still had the same classic Coke taste that Zhukov had tasted back on that fatidic day between July 17th to August 2nd 1945 (now, you have even learned the date of the Potsdam Conference, how rad is this book? Please say so in your reviews!).

So, the Coca-Cola men packaged the crystal-clear coke in straight glass bottles, capped with a red star.

According to a World War II Coke rep, 50 cases were sent to Russia. Zhukov got his fix and he was never caught with the disguised Cola. As far as we know, it hasn't been sipped or seen since.

The smelly case of the Great Stink

In 1858, centuries of dumping raw human, animal, and industrial waste directly into the River Thames came back to haunt the city of London in the form of the great stink. The smell was so bad it could cause vomiting in people miles downwind. But it would also eventually lead directly to the construction of London's first modern sewer system.

Prior to 1858, London's primitive sewer systems, to put it mildly, were in terrible condition.

Delicious raw sewage was empty directly into cesspits, large tanks, or even just deep holes in the ground. When they filled up, they were designed to overflow into the streets via crude culverts.

The culverts then emptied into large trenches, which just ran down the street even on major thoroughfares. And if that doesn't sound delightful enough, the waste in the pits would occasionally seep through the soil and find its way into the basements and foundations of homes. This created the risk of too much methane becoming trapped in air pockets, which could and sometimes did cause explosions.

But some waste did actually make it all the way to the sewer system, which was a good thing, right? Well, no, because the sewer funneled directly into the Thames river as well as several other sources of drinking water. Yeah, they were drinking their own wastewater.

This extremely disgusting situation is very likely what caused the cholera outbreaks of 1832, 1849, and 1854 in which many thousands of Londoners died.

Advances in technology are often a mixed blessing. Such was the case with flush toilets, which had quickly become a luxury among cramped city dwellers who were used to going all the way to their basements to use the bathroom. However, their proliferation put an enormous new strain on an already outdated and overtaxed sewer system. Cesspits were designed to contain an average home's waste. But the new flush toilets were also pumping water into those shit holes.

This made them more likely to flood homes, which increased the risk of various diseases. Eventually, the cesspits were connected to the city's sewer system, which, being designed to handle rainwater, emptied directly into the Thames.

So, you're probably wondering why Londoners decided to dump their dung into their drinking water. Good question. To be fair, they didn't realize they were doing it. Starting in the 1600s, the city funneled the excrement, as well as other delightful things like industrial waste and animal carcasses, into the Thames under the belief it would be all washed out to sea.

The problem was none of that actually happened.

Part of the Thames is what's called a tideway, which means that it's an area affected by the tides. Therefore, any of the waste and sewage that was dumped into the river could be carried back or forth along its length spreading in either direction. All of that waste built up in the river for centuries. And by 1858, the entire city of London was sitting on ground that was saturated with sewage. When the heat wave hit, it all bubbled back up to the surface.

As early as 1855, the problem had started to become evident. And the famous scientist Sir Michael Faraday wrote a letter to The Times of London to call attention to the dire conditions. In the letter, he described a simple experiment he had performed to test the river's opacity. On a sunny day, he went to the river with some white paper cards. He tore up the cards and moistened them so that they would sink below the surface. Then he walked along the bank and dropped some of the paper pieces into the water at every pier he came to. Again and again, the results were the same. The paper bits became invisible before they had even sunk an inch below the surface. While performing the experiment, he also observed that in the vicinity of bridges, the human waste rolled up in clouds so dense that they were visible at the surface. Faraday noted that the stink was common to the whole river, which was basically just a giant open sewer at that point. Emphasizing that his descriptions weren't exaggerated or figurative in any way, he pleaded with the authorities to do something.

By 1858, the Thames was in an utterly horrific state. There had been no meaningful changes to the sewer system in years. And a rise in the population had caused an increased amount of waste to be dumped into the river. At the same time, it was still the city's main source of drinking water. No one was really making any efforts to clean it up. And even if they had, it's not clear what might have been done short of building an entirely new sewer for the whole city. Hundreds of years of human and animal waste, garbage, and industrial byproduct had turned their water thick, brown, and opaque. Only a few years earlier, Sir Michael Faraday warned Londoners that if we neglect this subject, then a hot season will give us sad proof of the folly of our carelessness. Despite his very specific warning, they would neglect the subject. And the great stink would soon prove him right.

As anyone who's ever seen a disaster movie knows, ignoring the dire warnings of a panicked scientist seldom leads to anything good. In this case, it led to June of 1858 when a heatwave descended on London, and an accompanying dry spell made the Thames river nearly stop flowing.
The summer heat cooked the fetid water. And the entire city was consumed by the stench. It was so overpowering that it was blamed for illnesses among the upper classes. And townsfolk miles away were reported to start vomiting whenever the wind changed in an unfavorable direction.

Prime Minister Benjamin Disraeli described the river at the time as "a stygian pool reeking with ineffable and unbearable horror". Man, the British are really good at beautifully articulating something that smells terrible.

It wasn't until the water dried up that it became apparent how much waste was really in it. It wasn't just sewage either. The river was clogged with industrial waste, dead animals, street runoff, animal feces, leftover parts from slaughterhouses, rotten food, and literally centuries of putrefied garbage.
The dry spell had brought it all to the top. And the heatwave had it fermenting in the sun.

The people of London tried to get around town by using scented handkerchiefs and various other measures, but they weren't effective.
Even Queen Victoria herself, namesake of the whole era, couldn't escape the stink.
On one attempted cruise of the river, she tried to mask the stench by pressing a bouquet of fresh flowers against her nose. She only lasted a few minutes before ordering the boat to be turned around and redocked so she could get off and get as far away from the river as possible.

Doctors of the Victorian era subscribed to a now debunked idea called the miasma theory.
The theory, which was rooted in thinking that went all the way back to the ancient world, held that diseases were caused by bad smells. It was on account of this belief that the city and the medical community focused most of their efforts on covering up the bad smells rather than cleaning the river itself. This was a mistake.

For many poor people in London, the Thames was the primary and often only source of drinking water. And they kept using it no matter how bad things got. That meant huge swathes of the population were regularly exposed to bacteria that caused deadly and sweeping outbreaks of illnesses spread by contact with feces like typhoid and cholera. These early attempts at tackling the problem by covering up the smell had other consequences.

For example, at one point, authorities spent a fortune to dump chloride of lime into the river, which they hoped would do the trick. Not only didn't it work, but it wound up adding to the river's toxicity since chloride of lime is, in fact, poisonous.

In something of a break for the people of London, Parliament had recently moved into their new offices at the palace of Westminster, which sat right beside the Thames. The new location meant that for the first time, lawmakers couldn't avoid smelling the river. And it's not for lack of trying. In fact, their first move was to attempt to cover up the stink by drenching the building's curtains in chloride of lime, but it didn't work. The body even considered relocating from their new home at the palace, but that wasn't practical or popular.
Letting the poor and powerless suffer was one thing. But if lawmakers couldn't avoid smelling the river themselves, something would have to be done about it.

It took just 18 days for parliament to pass a bill funding the construction of a brand-new sewer that would fix the damage done to the Thames and prevent additional pollution.

Parliament placed the task of redesigning the sewers into the hands of an English civil engineer named Joseph Bazalgette. He delivered nothing short of one of the greatest government work projects of all time and was widely credited with saving the city.
Constructing Bazalgette's entirely new sewer cost the city the modern equivalent of roughly $300 million. The system, which Bazalgette had designed two years prior, consisted of a network of sewers that ran parallel to the Thames river rather than into it.
The waste was carried east of the city before being emptied into the river at a point where it could easily flow out to sea.
The project also included the construction of water treatment stations, embankments to prevent further buildup of waste, and the development of alternative sources of fresh water.
The action was a huge success.

The Thames quickly returned to a healthy condition and deaths attributable to poor water quality plummeted. In fact, the new system was so well-designed and efficient, it's still in use to this very day.

The taming of the cat

If you are a cat owner, you might have wondered if they are truly domesticated. Well, history tells us that we domesticated them twice.

In 2001, when a group of French archaeologists travelled to the island of Cyprus, they quickly found that they were outnumbered.

With a population of about 1.2 million humans, Cyprus' largest population are cats. According to estimates, there are at least 1.5 million felines, both pets and feral cats, roaming the island. You can see them practically everywhere!

If you've ever had the masochistic impulse to give a cat a bath, you know most of them aren't big fans of water and will scratch their way out of it; so, that begs the question how did they end up on Cyprus, an island in the middle of the Mediterranean?

The closest mainland, Turkey, is about 70 kilometers away! So how did all of those cats managed to get there? We know they didn't swim!

Well, the French archaeologists with whom we started the story might have actually found the answer.

While they were excavating the site of an ancient settlement, they discovered something quite astonishing: the grave of a man who was buried alongside offerings of seashells, flint tools and … an 8-month-old cat.

Dating to around 9,500 years ago, the burial represented one of the oldest known evidence of human/cat relationship anywhere in the world. It predates the more famous and publicized love for cats in ancient Egypt by almost 4,000 years!

So, how did the close companionship between humans and cats begin? Who were the ancestors of the domesticated cats? And how did cats take over Cyprus and eventually the world?

To understand it, we have to dwell a bit in the complex process known as domestication.

Because despite the fact that they poop in our houses and knock stuff off our tables while we are writing a book, and sometimes pee in the laundry basket for some reason, even if we just gave them the really good canned food that costs more than our groceries, we did in fact domesticate them, even though it might not always feel like it.

The domesticated cat is its own species, known as *Felis catus* and its origin is traced back to a species of wild cats called *Felis silvestris*, which is composed of five different subspecies.

Studies on the genomes of modern house cats revealed that one subspecies, the *Felis silvestris lybica*, is the direct ancestor of all domesticated cats today.

Those *Felis silvestris lybica*, also referred to as African wildcats, can still be found in the wild across North Africa and Southwest Asia. These ancestral cats don't look very different from their domesticated descendants. They're slightly larger, and they don't have the color variations in their coats that we see in house cats. Instead, they mostly have what are called mackerel-tabby patterns, with stripes that run perpendicular to their spines. You can even find this same pattern in the cats depicted in ancient Egyptian artwork.

These wild tabby kitties are solitary creatures that don't have the same social structure that other animals display, for example pack animals, like wolves.

That's what left scientists initially baffled and led them to believe that the domestication of cats was probably a much different process from the domestication of other animals.

Unfortunately, the fossil record of African wildcats isn't great. Most haven't been preserved well enough to be used in genetic analysis, which is on of the reasons why it's been so hard to figure out how cat domestication actually came about.

Some of the oldest known fossils include specimens from Cyprus that are about 11,000 years old, and others in Turkey from around 10,000 years ago. So, how did we get from *Felis silvestris lybica* to *Felis catus*?
Well, if you have cats, you know how hard it is to get them to do stuff. Long story short, it took a lot of time!
We still don't know the full picture, but we have some theories based on the different ways in which animals can be domesticated.

A species is considered to be "domesticated" when it becomes genetically and permanently modified through human-influenced breeding. To achieve that, the animal has to be reliant on humans on some level, most often for food and shelter (or to clean out the litter box).
American archaeologist Dr. Melinda Zeder theorized that there are three pathways to domestication: the prey pathway, the directed pathway, and the commensal pathway.
In the prey pathway, wild animals are first hunted by people. Then, in order to control the hunts and the animals better, people begin to manage herds of the animals; this is the case of goats and cattle. The hunting leads to captive breeding and eventually to the domestication of the species.

The directed pathway allowed humans to put in practice the lessons they had learned from the previous attempts at domestication with the prey pathway. Horses and beasts of burden, like donkeys and camels, were most likely domesticated this way. Without the constant thought of hunting for food anymore since we had already captured the animals we wanted to eat, we fast-tracked the domestication of the animals whose abilities to walk long distances and carry heavy loads we could harness in order to have more time to eat the animals we already domesticated.

With the third option, the commensal pathway, we managed to be kinder and share our food. In fact, wild animals are attracted to human settlements by food. They go where the people go, feed off of their scraps, or prey on other animals who have been drawn to humans, like mice or rats. This eventually leads to domestication: most likely cats were domesticated this way.

For thousands of years, they stayed close to human dwellings for food, but weren't necessarily close to the people themselves. Eventually, people noticed that cats were actually pretty good at catching the pests that plagued their food stores (and were also kind of cute); so, they began to actively entice them to live in their settlements. We can observe glimpses into this process by studying the remains of ancient cats.

For example, isotopic analysis of cat remains from 5,600 years ago in northwestern China has revealed the smallest, yet noticeable amount of millet, a staple grain in the diet of the villagers at that time in China. This discovery suggests that cats were eating the mice that were feeding on stored millet, no doubt a useful service for the people who had harvested it!
The isotopic data from one such cat revealed a diet that had less meat and more millet than expected, suggesting that it either scavenged from, or was fed by, the villagers.

But what did the domestication process do that changed wild cats into house cats?
Physically, domestication has made house cats smaller than their ancestors, and resulted in new varieties in coat color and patterning. These included new variations of the tabby coat, and the occurrence of black, orange, and white colors. Most of these coat changes are fairly recent, and came about as recessive genes in wildcats became more prominent.

By the 19th century, people started to selectively breed for more variation in colors and markings.

But beyond size and color, the domestication process really didn't change the morphology of cats that much compared to dogs, which have seen major changes to their whole bodies.
This is mostly because of differences in breeding practices, as different dog breeds were bred for specific purposes.

The modern house cat also maintains more behavioral and genetic similarities with their wild ancestors than most other domesticated animals do, including behaviors related to eating and breeding. This is probably du to the interbreeding between domesticated cats and surrounding wild cats population.

But you haven't started reading this story to have a boring class in evolutionary biology 101, you read it because I baited you with the titillating fact that we domesticated wild cats twice. It is in fact the truth: we domesticated cats once in southwest Asia 10,000 years ago, and twice in Egypt, about 3,500 years ago, and the third times in my living room, since my cat is clearly not domesticated!
This is based on an analysis of the genome of modern cats (and I mean the first two domestications processes, the third one is still a matter of academic debate), which suggests that two different source populations contributed to the current gene pool in two different moments in time. We have also found archaeological evidence that supports multiple points of domestication. For example, in Egypt, six burials have been uncovered at the site of Hierakonpolis containing two adult cats and four kittens. And they date to between 3,600 and 3,800 years ago.

The smaller bones in the burials closely match the size of those of domesticated cats, and one cat's skeleton even showed healed fractures, suggesting that its human companions cured him and cared for him.
After about 3,000 years ago in Egypt, we can see these relationships becoming closer, through art and iconography that show cats alongside people.

From there, it looks like cats were brought to Rome by early Greek settlers, as well as through interactions between Rome and Egypt. As civilizations begin to expand around 2,000 years ago, especially within the Roman Empire, cats throttled along as as well. We know that ancient Romans kept felines as pets, based on historic sources, such as various artworks, like mosaics, that show cats in more domestic settings, often hunting prey. Roman cats were most likely adopted into households to catch rodents and other pests, much like they did in the early stages of domestication.

But none of this actually tells us where the story of cat domestication started: after all, if the oldest evidence of domestic cats is on the island of Cyprus, then who brought cats to Cyprus in the first place?

Well, all we know is that, at some point during the Early Holocene, around 11,000 years ago, people from southwest Asia began migrating to Europe, including Cyprus. They brought with them their dear pets: that subspecies of cat that was the ancestor of our domesticated cats. And, with cats being cats and neutering not having being invented yet, we ended up with millions of the little assh…, I mean, adorable kittens.

In modern day Cyprus, the cat population has exponentially grown to the point of being considered an infestation. Cats are often seen as vermin there, and the government tried many times to get a handle on their growing population. Luckily for the feral cats, though, there are many sanctuaries run by volunteers who try to care for every stray.

But it's not just on this island where cats have commanded such a presence.
Our relationship has been mutually beneficial enough that domestic cats have truly taken over the world.
Today their estimated overall population is 600 million: cats have officially achieved world domination.

God save the Queen!

Queen Victoria ruled Great Britain and Ireland from 1837 until her death in 1901. It wasn't easy though. During her long reign, Queen Victoria saw her kingdom through some traumatic and difficult events. She was wildly popular in England and still ranks among the most beloved and well-known monarchs in the history of the world. Along the way, the monarch would have to survive no less than eight assassination attempts by seven different individuals.

Assassin number one was 18-year-old Edward Oxford, who has about the most English name one could ever hope for. According to his own mother, Edward was prone to acting strangely, and often had random, maniacal outbursts of rage or laughter. Kind of like the Victorian version of the Joker. Though no one knows for sure, this odd behavior may have been what cost him his job at a local pub. What we do know is that a few days after joining the ranks of the unemployed, he purchased two guns and headed for Buckingham Palace. The month was June and the weather was pleasant. When Edward arrived, he waited outside the palace with crowds of onlookers hoping to spot the Queen or her husband, Prince Albert. Edward would have to wait until late in the evening. But eventually, a carriage emerged from the gates and turned up Constitution Hill toward Hyde Park. Oxford waited until the royal carriage was in range. Once they were close enough, Edward fired two shots. According to the queen's own diary, after the first shot, Albert took her hand and said, "My God, don't be alarmed." Victoria assured him she wasn't rattled. Victoria also didn't realize the shot was intended for her. After the second shot, Oxford was quickly tackled by people in the crowd who reported that he was raving about how a woman should never be able to rule England. Victoria, who was four months pregnant at the time, was praised by the British public for her bravery. Victoria, one. Assassins, zero.

After surviving her first assassination attempt, Queen Victoria likely helped nothing like that would ever happen again. But it did two years later. This time, the would-be assassin was John Francis, a cabinet maker and former actor with a criminal record for theft. Perhaps encouraged by how close Edward Oxford came to hitting Victoria, Francis ran with the same play, and tried to shoot her in her carriage outside of Buckingham Palace.

In fact, John Francis thought the plan was so nice, he tried it twice in one weekend. First, on May 29, he tried shooting the Queen on Constitution Hill, but failed and scampered off. Prime Minister Robert Peel, who apparently operated like Sherlock Holmes, set a trap for the villain, and swore to catch him. Queen Victoria volunteered to be live bait. The queen got back into the carriage the next day for another trip up Constitution Hill. However, thanks to Peel, this time, the crowd was swarming with undercover policemen.

Francis was quickly apprehended after drawing his gun. It was later determined the gun wasn't even loaded, but they charged him with treason, and sentenced him to death.

The story has something akin to a happy ending though. While Francis was awaiting execution, Victoria and Albert discussed the matter at length, and decided to take pity on the wannabe killer. Victoria personally commuted his death sentence.

Instead, he was banished from the kingdom for life, and served seven years at hard labor in Australia. Victoria with two points at three. Assassins, zero.

Assassin number three was John William Bean. Mr. Bean's father was a metalsmith who hope that John would follow in his footsteps. But it wasn't to be. John was born with a four-foot frame and a hunchback that prevented him from being able to do the job. Instead, John Bean ended up working at a newsstand. In 1842, the Bean read an article about assassin number one, Edward Oxford. The story described Oxford's life after he tried to kill the Queen, claiming that he had been confined to an insane asylum, which, for whatever reason, was portrayed as a life of luxury. Sadly though, Beam believed it. His physical deformities made him desperate, and he began to reason that if he tried to kill the Queen, he would either end up dead or in an asylum. Either one being believed would be an improvement over his day to day existence. On July 3rd 1842, a mere five weeks after John Francis made his assassination attempts on the Queen, Bean took his shot. JW Bean waited outside the palace, and then fired at Victoria as she passed by with her uncle, King Leopold of Belgium. The gun, which was loaded with papers, gravel, and bits of pipe, jammed. Robert Peel apparently burst into tears when he heard about the incident. As for Bean, he didn't get what he wanted. He was captured by the police who had started rounding up every hunchback dwarf until he was found. John Bean received an 18 month prison sentence. Victoria, four. Assassins, zero.

Surviving four assassination attempts in two years is a lot for anyone. So luckily for Victoria, it would be a good seven years before someone tried again. That someone was William Hamilton. Hamilton, then 23 years old, was an orphaned Irish farm laborer who had moved to London after the potato blight ravaged Ireland. He came to England by way of Paris where he had witnessed the French Revolution of 1848 firsthand. By 1849, he was unemployed and constantly in and out of jail. On May 19, 1849, Hamilton fired at Victoria who was returning from making one of her first public appearances after recently giving birth. She approached the palace via Constitution Hill, which at this point, you'd think they'd have renamed Assassinate the Queen Avenue. Inspired by the revolutionary spirit he picked up in France, Hamilton came packing a pocket pistol. Fortunately for the Queen, it wasn't loaded properly. Apparently, checking the gun before assassination attempts wasn't much of a thing back then. Hamilton took a shot from point blank range. And had the gun actually fired, he likely would have done some real damage. Vic, five. Assassins, zero.

Assassin number five showed up in 1850. His name was Robert Pate, and he would get closer to the Queen than anybody before him. Victoria was on her way from visiting her sick uncle's bedside when the 50-year-old ex-soldier leapt out at her, and managed to hit her on the head with an iron tipped cane. Some reports also claimed that he had a gun. Though, if he did, he didn't use it. The Queen wasn't badly hurt, but did walk away with a black eye, a welt, and a scar that lasted for years. Concerned that people would think she was seriously hurt and worry about her, Victoria made a public appearance that very night at the opera. She even called out Pate for striking a woman, and joked that at least the braver would be assassins had tried to shoot her.
As for Pate, he was exiled to Tasmania to serve, basically, the same sentence John Francis had for attempting to kill the Queen. Seven years at hard labor. Pate's motive for the attack was never discovered and remains unknown. Who's keeping track of score? Victoria is unstoppable.

Would-be assassin number six was a 17-year-old boy named Arthur O'Connor. Although he was born and raised in London, Arthur described himself as passionately Irish. He had decided to restore the reputation of the O'Connor name and join the pantheon of great Irish heroes by killing the Queen. However, he eventually changed his mind, and decided the better option would be scaring her into freeing Ireland. On February 29, 1872, Arthur waited outside Buckingham Palace for the Queen to return from an outing, as had apparently become standard for all would be assassins.
He asked a policeman when Victoria would return. And then, pushed his way to the front of the crowd near the gate she would pass through. When the carriage finally arrived, O'Connor aimed his gun, but he never got off a shot. John Brown, an attendant who had taken to traveling with the Queen after her husband died, knocked the gun out of the young man's hand. And then, grabbed him and threw him to the ground. It was later learned that the gun was never in working order. That's pretty good to assume, at this point. Victoria's bodyguard, Brown, was rewarded for his heroism with a gold medal and money.

O'Connor was sentenced to a year in prison and 20 strokes with a birch rod, which, honestly, seems pretty lenient since the other guys got seven years of hard labor. Assassins, zero. Victoria, six.

Queen Victoria's seventh and final would be assassin was named Roderick MacLean, and he was an Irish radical. At the time, the crown was under intense pressure from Ireland and Irish nationals who wanted independence. And that gave MacLean cause to hate the queen. However, MacLean also had other issues. He had previously been in an insane asylum where he had been diagnosed with homicidal mania and a bizarre distaste for the number four. We hear at Weird History kind of get it. We don't like the number one. It's the loneliest number. Whatever the cause, MacLean showed up outside Windsor Station on March 2nd of 1882. As the Queen departed the station by train, MacLean fired.

Unsurprisingly, he missed completely, and the Queen wasn't hurt. Two onlookers disarm MacLean and were thanked by Victoria on the spot.

MacLean was tried for high treason. But in a lifetime network twist, he was found not guilty by reason of insanity. The Queen, who apparently no longer felt pity for people who tried to kill her, expressed dissatisfaction with a light sentence, and urged her cabinet to create harsher laws.

You probably would have guessed that trying to kill a queen would result in an instant death sentence, but nothing could be further from the truth.

Edward Oxford was found to be insane at trial and sent to an asylum. He was released in 1867, at which time he was banished from England.

He went to Australia where he died in 1900.

John Francis was sentenced to death for his assassination attempt, but the Queen commuted his sentence, and he served time in prison instead.

John William Bean, whose gun wasn't actually able to be loaded, was charged with a lesser crime, and was imprisoned in New Gate Prison for 18 months.

William Hamilton was banished from England for seven years.

Pate was determined to be insane at trial, but the court also found he could tell right from wrong. And he was exiled to Tasmania for seven years.

Arthur Connor received 20 strokes with a birch rod, and a year in prison.

Finally, MacLean was found to be insane at his trial and was confined to Broadmoor Asylum for the rest of his life.

This outcome would move the Queen to have her cabinet establish a more stringent legal definition of insanity for future cases.

Despite the fact that Queen Victoria was one of the most beloved monarchs in the kingdom's history, not a single one of the seven men who tried to kill her were executed for their crimes.

While she did eventually try to make the laws tougher, she also recognized that the repeated assassination attempts only made her more popular.

Victoria herself has even reported to have said, "It is worth being shot at to see how much one is loved."

The clever story of an observant horse

Forget about Mr. Ed, Clever Hans was the first horse who could communicate with humans in complex ways. Well, at least that is what they thought at that time.

The story of "Kluge Hans" (which means Clever Hans in German) begins in the late 19th century with an ambitious German math teacher by the name of Wilhelm Von Osten.

He was a fervent student of phrenology, which meant that he believed that a person's intelligence, among other things, can be determined by the size and shape of their head (it was a quaint little belief that allowed people to justify slavery among other things disguising it under "scientific truths").
His other passion was animal intelligence and he believed that it was greatly underestimated by the human race.

In the pursuit of a proof for his beliefs, Von Osten decided to try and teach math to three different animals: a cat, a bear and a horse named Hans. The first two didn't turn out so well, the cat probably didn't listen, but at least he avoided being mauled by the bear and that is already a win in my book.

To his delight, the horse seemed responsive to Von Osten's mathematical tutelage. This prodigious development began with Hans simply tapping out numbers written on a blackboard. He could count any number under 10 by tapping one of his hooves the number of times corresponding to the one written on the board Von Osten had brought in his stable.
Von Osten was truly excited and encouraged by this progress, decided to test the abilities of the horse further.

He started by writing out basic mathematical problems and attempted to teach Hans to recognize simple symbols. This proved to be relatively easy for the horse and it didn't take long before he was able to provide the correct answers to a myriad of simple mathematical problems the included fractions, square roots, and multiplication.

Von Osten, recognizing the potentiality of the horse for show business, decided to take Hans on a national tour, and in 1891 he was performing free shows all over Germany.
By this stage, Hans was able to spell out names with his taps, as well as work out dates and tell the time.

Even if his accuracy wasn't 100%, Clever Hans' cleverness were impressive enough to draw large crowds, as well as attract the attention of skeptics such as journalists from the New York Times (who ran a front-page story about the horse) and, most importantly, the Germany's board of education. After all, they ought to know if they had to spend their budget on horses' schools.

They decided that they wanted to investigate Hans' abilities further and Von Osten readily agreed to it.
After all, he knew he was no fraudster and there was no scandal to be exposed; he and Hans could have only benefited from it.
The investigation team was designated the Hans Commission and was comprised of a variety of academics and experts from different fields.

More specifically the commission included a psychologist, a few school teachers, two zoologists, a circus manager, and a horse trainer.

Despite thorough investigation and testing, the commission concluded in 1904 that there was nothing fraudulent about Hans' abilities and that he really was one hell of a gifted horse.
Despite their findings, the psychologist on the commission asked another skeptical psychologist by the name of Oskar Pfungst to investigate farther Hans' supposed abilities.

With the permission of Von Osten, Pfungst picked up where the Hans Commission left off and tried some thorough and unique investigation techniques.

Firstly, he erected a tent in which the experiments would take place.
The primary purpose of this was to shield the investigation from prying eyes and the horse from outside distraction and contamination.
He then made a large list of questions to ask to Clever Hans, as well as the variables that could affect the outcome.
At first, Hans reacted to the questioning as he usually did, at least when his owner asked them.

However, things started to change when Pfungst changed certain environmental factors during the sessions. For example, he asked Von Osten to stand further away when he was asking Hans the questions. The horses' accuracy diminished, though nobody was sure why.

As a result, the psychologist decided to try some other variables. He asked Von Osten to ask Hans questions that he himself didn't know the answer to, and immediately Hans' accuracy went from being approximately 89% correct to almost 0%.
The same results would occur if Hans was questioned by Von Osten from behind a concealing screen. It seemed that to answer questions, Hans needed to have a clear view of the owner who incidentally also had to know the answer to the question itself.

The obvious conclusion would be that Von Osten had trained Hans to respond to prepared questions, but then would he then so readily agree to the investigation, especially since he had already fooled the commission?
To answer this question, Pfungst decided to continue his studies, but to switch his focus to those who were questioning and interacting with the horse.

He immediately noticed certain shifts in the facial expressions, posture, and breathing of the questioners whenever Hans tapped his hoof. Every time he tapped, their tension seemed to increase and when the correct answer had been reached, it would disappear.

Pfungst therefore concluded that Hans was using these subtle shifts in posture and facial expressions as his cue to stop. This tension couldn't exist when the questioner himself didn't know the answer to the question, which would explain why Hans had no idea what to do in that circumstance.

The most fascinating part of the story is that neither Von Osten nor any of the other questioner involved had any idea whatsoever that they were giving Hans cues. It was all done completely unconsciously.
To prove his point, Pfungst took on the role of Hans and tried to answer questions based purely off of body language.

By carefully watching his questioners, he was able to answer correctly all the questions just like Hans did, even when the questioners were aware of these cues. It seems that they weren't able to stop themselves from displaying them.

Since then, displays of unintentional cues have become known as the "Clever Hans Effect."
Despite the fact that Pfungst's investigation proved that the Clever Hans phenomenon was nothing more than an unintentional hoax, he did himself inadvertently prove Von Osten's own hypotheses regarding the intelligence of animals.

Hans might not have been able to do semi-complex math or tell you the time without a little help from the audience, but he was incredibly receptive to extremely subtle human body language. Even if it was not the kind of intellect that Von Osten was expecting from his horse, it was nonetheless quite impressive.

The sweetest ride

> At the end of World War II, the Soviets were holding Berlin under siege. In order to save millions of people from starvation, the US and the Allies decided to airlift in food. One American pilot decided to take it a step further. He decided to rain candy on the city.

Today, Gail Halvorsen is better known as the Berlin Candy Bomber, Uncle Wiggly Wings, or the Chocolate Flier. He was serving for the Air Forces and in 1948 he was assigned to be a pilot for the Berlin Airlift, also known as Operation Vittles, during the Berlin Blockade.
He was also an amateur photographer, and would go on long walks through Berlin taking pictures. One day, while he was filming the planes taking off and landing at the Tempelhof airport, Gail saw that there were some young children looking at him.

He went over to talk to them, and after a while, he came to quite a simple realization: kids love chocolate.
He knew that they had not had chocolate in the stores in Berlin for over two years. He reached in his pocket, and all he had were two sticks of Wrigley's Doublemint gum.
He broke the two sticks in half and gave them to the kids. The kids with half a stick tore off the wrapper into thin strips and passed it around to those without gum. Those who had received the wrappers put it at their nose and smelled a piece of wrapper.

Inspired by their generous disposition, he told them that in his next flight, he would drop them chocolate and candy via parachute from the plane.
They kids had suffered hardship and where weary of man giving out candies, as kids should be, so they wondered how they would have ever recognized his airplane among the others who were circling Berlin.
He promised to wiggle the wings of his airplane, just like he had done for his parents when he passed his pilot's exam.

True to his word, the next day Gail began to drop the packages, candy and chocolate delivered by little parachute made of handkerchiefs, so that the children would not get hurt by the falling candies. What started as an act of kindness by Halverson and other soldiers who began to pool their candy, became an official part of the airlift when his commanding officer got wind of it and called it Operation Little Vittles.
Halverson had started with just two sticks of gum, but eventually it turned into 23 tons of chocolate and a massive boost to the moral of the children of Berlin and the PR of the American troops.

Gail Halverson went on to become a national hero and was known in the press and to all the kids in Berlin as Uncle Wiggly Wings.

The town that dance itself to death

Medieval Europe had no shortages of super-deadly disease outbreaks that could wipe out a chunk of the population without much of an effort. But none of them were quite as entertaining as the bizarre case of Frau Troffea and the dancing plague that had over 400 people dancing compulsively in the streets, some even to their deaths.

The story of the Coachella of medieval afflictions begins on a hot July day in 1518, when German housewife Frau Troffea stepped out of her home in Strasbourg and started to get down to a boogie that no one else could hear. She danced in the streets of her small town all day, to the embarrassment of her husband, who was not himself equally compelled to dance in any way. Frau stopped dancing long enough for a few hours of restless sleep before waking the next day and tapping her toes bloody again.

A crowd began to form around this seemingly insane woman dancing to absolutely nothing, with bruised and bloody feet.

What a fun little street performance, the villagers must have thought, as this poor woman danced herself to very possible death. Soon, however, she wasn't alone.

Frau formed a whole dance troupe, with roughly 30 others catching the jitterbug and joining her in a spontaneous dance-off.

Frau soon had a full marching band worth of people dancing with her. The dancing mania, as it was eventually labeled, spread to more people in Strasbourg, with estimates as high as 400 people involuntarily joining her dance crew. It quickly grew into a full-grown crisis that the city council had no clue how to manage.

They don't teach you how to handle spontaneous raves and crisis management courses at business school. The only clear thing they could agree on was these groovy kids were not having a groovy time.

Dancers were in obvious pain, screaming in agony and begging for mercy from whatever bizarre affliction they were suffering from. As the summer stretched on and the temperatures rose, as many as 15 people a day were dying from dancing in the streets. Jeez, David Bowie and Mick Jagger made it look so fun.

Fresh out of ideas on how to handle this makeshift problem themselves, the city council consulted with local physicians to diagnose the problem and shut it down for good. After ruling out the standard astrological causes and supernatural causes, the doctor diagnosed the exhausted dancing maniacs with a probable case of hot blood, which sounds like a diagnosis from the band Foreigner.

But really, the theory was that hot blood was a problem with the balance in a person's humors. In a case of hot blood, doctors believed the brain would overheat, which in turn would cause madness. The typical remedy, it's the 1500s. So, if you guessed bloodletting, you guessed right. However, given these victims specific inability to voluntarily stop moving, physically removing any blood, regardless of temperature, wasn't a feasible course to take.

Unlike the town in Footloose, they prescribed even more dancing. They hired musicians to get the crowd hyped and brought in extras to mix up the energy of this lame party, hoping of burning out the dancers, but to no avail. This cure, like a poorly chaperoned prom, was a failure and actually exasperated the problem.

As the exhausted dancers were beginning to stumble and slow down, the musicians didn't think to play the slow jams and cool the room off. Instead, they sped up the tempo, causing the townspeople to move faster with the music. You can't play a banger and not expect the crowd to react!

Not only did these party beats fail to stop the sporadic dancing, but it also attracted volunteer booty shakers to the square, as passers-byes joined in on what was being misperceived as "fun."

The city council realized that having this giant block party to burn out the afflicted wasn't the best solution to this problem. Clearly, these poor dancing queens were not suffering from hot blood. No, no, it was obviously a curse on the city, sent as a warning to repent for their sins or suffer the consequences.

Now, acting like the town in Footloose, the police of medieval Europe liked to run a pretty tight ship to keep the sinners at bay. It's obscene, rock and roll music. If this dancing mania was a curse, sin would have to be reigned in within the walls of Strasbourg.
Gambling houses, gone. Brothels, please, not in this city. We hear you loud and clear, saints who have cursed our town with dance as a punishment for the gambling and prostitution.
The city also gathered up the "loose people" and banished them from the city: 1518 was a poor time to have a bad reputation!
They even tried to send gifts to the saints by donating a 100-pound candle to the cathedral. One candle just didn't cut it. And the dancing plague kept on hustling.

So, they went full Footloose: the town took the drastic step of outlawing dance, tacking on a fine of 30 shillings for anyone caught moving their hips to a beat. They also banned music, with the exception of string music for weddings. "But they are on their conscience not to use tambourines and drums," the municipal archive reported.
Drums were the most dangerous instrument since they allegedly triggered the strange epidemic (please, everybody knows the most dangerous instrument is the sax. It oozes sexiness, really riles up the saints.)

In spite of all of Strasburg's best efforts and bad gifts, the epidemic continued. But would you believe this was not the first dancing mania that struck Europe. In 1374 a dancing outbreak hit the city of Aachen and quickly spread across the Rhine Valley.
This was less of a free-for-all mosh pit of wild dancing and more of a hands-across-America situation. Dancers afflicted held hands in a circle and danced for hours together, in wild delirium, until at length they fell to the ground in a state of exhaustion.
Sounds like the city of Aachen was just collectively tripping balls. Aachen officials disagreed. They chalked this up to your standard demonic possession.
Exorcists were brought in to bathe the dance circles with holy water, while shouting incantations in the faces of the possessed. Honestly, it sounds like Aachen just didn't know what to do. But, of course, when all else fails, you can always blame the women.

In 1526, around 10 years after the strange dancing phenomena had tired itself out, Renaissance physician Paracelsus visited Strasbourg for a diagnosis.
According to Paracelsus forced natural dancing was an involuntary physical response, like a reflex, that could be caused if certain parts of the body were manipulated.
But because this was 1526, for good measure he also blamed the women.
He scrutinized the role of our hero Frau Troffea and saw her as a rebellious woman, who set off a dancing mania in order to avoid doing a house chore or two.
Paracelsus claimed, right before she started dancing, her husband had asked her to do something she didn't want to do.

As dancers continued to wave their hands in the air like they very, very much did not care, the city continued to search for a cure for these poor souls, at one point turning to the medieval cure-all, pray to Saint Vitus, who had been martyred as a child in the year 303 on the orders of emperors Diocletian and Maximilian.
His tormentors tossed him into a cauldron of boiling lead and tar, then tossed this lead and tar marinated child to a lion. So cruel. And isn't the lion overkill at that point?

Well, legend has it, Vitus emerged unharmed from the cauldron. And the hungry lion simply licked Vitus's yummy metallic-scented hands. He was OK and he had a new lion friend; he really earned his sainthood. Saint Vitus had a reputation for healing illnesses, particularly ones with trembling limbs. So you could see why the city of Strasbourg prayed to this guy for an assist.

Running out of ideas for how to stop this dancing plague, the city gave an unconventional method a shot. Taking a big swing, they piled all of those inflicted with dancing fever onto wagons and carted them up a mountain to Saint Vitus, a shrine to the saint. Dancers continued to fall on the altar. So the priest gave a mass over them and handed out little crosses and red shoes, which had been blessed with holy oil on both the tops and the soles. The red holy-soaked shoes apparently worked like a charm. Hallelujah! The affliction seemed to break. And the dancing parties slowly came to an end.

Most of the dancers regain control of their bodies. The time of the dancing mania soon became known as Saint Vitus's dance, either because the saint had cured the dancers or caused the whole thing.

Modern experts don't all agree on what exactly caused the 1518 outbreak. It's been suggested by some that a possible grain poisoning, which is known to cause convulsions, could be the culprit. That wouldn't account for the tight choreography, which was described less as random convulsing and more like coordinated movement.

Others suggested a group case of epilepsy or other medical conditions, which wouldn't explain, of course, how the mania became contagious since epilepsy is not something you can catch.

If your mind was floating towards weird dance cult, you are not alone. One theory out there is this was all the work of the secret members of a heretical cult that emerged every decade to revel in public. This, of course, fails to connect how the dancing seemed to spread amongst the people since it was clear the dancers were in complete agony and many died. Also, at a time when Europe was in a heightened alertness for suspected heretic cult antics, it's unlikely this one simply slipped under the radar.

The likely cause of the dance party that couldn't stop, wouldn't stop, was a classic case of mass hysteria. To say things in Strasbourg in 1518 had been pretty bleak would be an understatement. The city suffered from not one, not two, but four serious famines between 1492 and 1511.

In 1516, food prices shot way up. And in 1517, a fifth famine killed countless people. One chronicler labeled it "the bad year."

In 1518, smallpox and leprosy were on the rise. And the orphanage was overpacked with at least 300 new orphans. Fear of being possessed drove people insane. And the city was ripe for an outbreak of mass hysteria.

Superstitious beliefs led people to believe their minds and bodies were being controlled by a force so powerful the bodies were no longer their own to control. They were convinced they were victims of an unseen power, which makes sense considering the ultimate cure that stopped the dancing was a visit to the shrine of Saint Vitus and a new pair of holy-bless shoes. It checks all the mass hysteria boxes and explains how it began, how it spread, and how it was ultimately defeated.

The most dangerous supper club

Until about 1902, legal food preservatives included chemicals like formaldehyde, borax and copper sulfate. That is until an hero forgotten by history organized the Poison Supper Club to stop it and became the founding father of the FDA.

At the beginning of the century, in order to keep produce and canned food looking fresh and pretty, the manufacturers used a boatload of chemicals.
For example, copper sulfate, a common pesticide, made canned peas sparkle bright green.
Meat was packed with borax and formaldehyde to make it appear fresher.
At this time in our history, there were no food regulations: producers didn't have to label their ingredients. The government did not have any safety testing nor monitoring in place.

Dr. Harvey W. Wiley was a chemist obsessed with the strange idea that these chemicals had no place in our food. He decided to start hygienic lab trials so that he could officially test the effects of these poisons on the body. It was easy enough to get the chemicals (you could just buy peas), but he needed the bodies i.e., participants willing to test poisonous food.

He organized a group and called it the Poison Squad; after all, with a cool name you can get people to do practically anything.
The first 12 members of the Poison Squad were volunteers from the Department of Agriculture who had volunteered to eat the poisoned food for six months so that Wiley could track the effects it had on them.

Each day the menus would be different and Wiley's volunteers never knew which poison they were eating.
A dinner at the Poison Supper Club might look like this: applesauce, soup, turkey, canned stringed beans, sweet potatoes, white potatoes, chipped beef, bread and butter, coffee, rice pudding and a little borax.

During the six-months trials, Wiley observed signs of acute poisoning: including nausea, upset stomachs, diarrhea, vomiting, kidney damage, you know all the nice things that happen to you when you ingest poison.

The brave endeavor didn't stay a secret for long: the press caught on and in 1906, thanks to the public outrage that followed the scandals, the first food regulations were passed.
This ultimately led to the creation of the FDA.
So, if you think your food tastes better without all that borax, you know who to thank.

The freaky sex lives of the homo sapiens

Contrary to popular perception, scientists are really into a good gossipy sex scandal.
In fact, they love to talk about kinky sex, more specifically about the sex lives of our prehistoric ancestors. So, scientists are currently gossiping up a storm about the fact that our early ancestors, the homo sapiens, may have interbred with other species.

It's long been accepted by the scientific community that homo sapiens, like me and probably you, originated in Africa around 200,000 years ago.
As far as we can tell, they stayed there for about 140,000 years, until they started to get frisky and struck out into the unknown.
One of the things that these brave humans discovered out there in the wide world was an older, more primitive, bigger-boned, species of great ape that we now call Neanderthals.

Neanderthals are, of course, related to humans, but their evolutionary lines had split about 350,000 years before they met again.
But just because Neanderthals and humans were not the same species, did that prevent them from getting it on? No. They liked big bones and could not lie.
Not only that, apparently we were similar enough species that we were able to create viable offspring.

Studies have shown that, that even if Neanderthals officially went extinct about 40,000 years ago, they live on in us. According to these researches, between one and 4 percent of human DNA is actually Neanderthal DNA.
So, you might as well unstitch your family crest from your smoking jacket.

But Neanderthals are not the only ancient hominids that humankind had intimate relations with: the recently discovered Denisovans' DNA, which probably shared more in common with Neanderthals than with the Homo Sapiens, are showing up in the genome of people all over southeast Asia.

So, it turns out that we had a lot more choices of people, or, you know, sort-of people to mate with back in the olden days.

I am not done messing with your conception of what humanity is yet, because even if you might be appalled at the thought, some of your ancestors may, in fact, have done the deed with gorillas!
The reason they think this is not to do with our genome (which means that at least we didn't breed with them), it has to do with the genome of lice.

Most species of mammals have one species of lice that's specific to them, it lives on them and only them, but all over them.
Humans are a little different, because we have isolated pockets of hair. We are blessed by two species of lice: we have head lice and pubic lice, which are separate species.
Our head lice are different from every other mammals' lice, but our pubic lice are very surprisingly and upsettingly similar to the species that lives on gorillas! I mean, if you have to have sex with gorillas, use protection at least!

However, even if our ancestors were making sweet love to the ancestors of gorillas, which, hopefully, they weren't (I'm still keeping that as a possibility in my mind) it probably happened over 3.3 million years ago.
So, you don't have to run straight to take a hot shower or scrub your skin off with a pumice stone.

The enemy within

In August of 1971, Professor Philip Zimbardo began an investigation into the power dynamics that exist between guards and inmates in a prison setting. The object of the Stanford prison experiment was to determine if it was the acquisition of power that made guards turn brutal or whether brutality was actually intrinsic to human nature itself. The notorious experiment that ensued would kick off decades of academic controversy and suggests some very dark things about the nature of humanity.

During the 1970s, both the US Navy and Marine Corps were interested in learning about the hierarchies of power in military prisons.
Accordingly, the US Office of Naval Research issued Philip Zimbardo a grant to study the relationships between prison guards and prisoners.
The objective would be to determine if those relationships were shaped more by the prison environment or the personalities of the guards.
The grant would be used to create a mock prison environment in which to conduct the experiment and to pay the participants.

The Stanford prison experiment started with an ad Zimbardo placed in the classifieds.
It read, "Male college students needed for psychological study of prison life. $15 per day for 1-2 weeks."
70 people applied.
The applicants were interviewed and asked to take personality tests. Anyone who had a criminal record or record of abusing narcotics was eliminated, as was anyone who displayed personality disorders, physical disabilities, or psychological problems.

Ultimately, 24 college students, all white and all male were selected to participate. And they had no idea what they were getting themselves into.
Zimbardo and his team randomly divided the students into two groups, prisoners and guards.
There were 12 of each category, 9 that were active participants and 3 that were alternates.

On August 17, 1971, the experiment began when the 9 prisoners were arrested by actual police officers from the Palo Alto Police Department.
Each person was taken into custody, then had their mug shots taken before being fingerprinted, blindfolded, and moved into a holding cell.
Finally, they were taken into a mock prison that had been set up in the basement of Stanford's Jordan Hall.

The fake prison felt very real.
The researchers who created it had consulted with prison officials and ex-convicts before designing it. The cells were built in a space that was normally used as a laboratory. Each cell had a bar door, a cell number, and room for three prisoners. Other touches included a solitary confinement cell that had been created in a closet and a rule that prisoners had to be blindfolded before being taken to the bathroom.

To avoid selection bias, participants were assigned to be either prisoners or guards based on the results of a coin toss. Very different fates awaited each respective group.

Guards were given real prison guard uniforms, complete with nightsticks and whistles. Many guards even donned mirrored sunglasses, which were meant to prevent eye contact with the prisoners, or maybe just to look like Boss Godfrey from Cool Hand Luke.

Prisoners, on the other hand, were stripped, deloused, and dressed in sandals and an ill-fitting numbered smock. They weren't issued any underwear. But they were given nylon stocking caps, which they were asked to wear in lieu of having their heads shaved. Once dressed, a chain was placed on each of the legs. Prisoners were only addressed by their number and had to refer to themselves and the other prisoners in the same way. It was a recipe for dehumanization and oppression.

Zimbardo himself served as superintendent of the prison and researcher David Jaffe played the warden. The two were responsible for instructing the guards and laying down the scope of their duties. First and foremost, the guards were told to maintain order.
To this end, they were allowed to use any means necessary, short of physical violence.

Things that were permitted included harassment, the withholding of food, and the deprivation of privileges at the guards' discretion.
The guards, unlike the prisoners, were also allowed to work in shifts. The shifts, which each required three guards lasted eight hours. Off duty guards didn't have to be at the prison but were asked to remain on call in case of an emergency.

On the first night, the guards decided to use a whistle to rouse the prisoners from their sleep for a headcount at 2:30 AM. Some of the prisoners didn't take the headcount seriously and the guards punish them by making them do push-ups.
After headcount, the prisoners had already had enough and decided to rebel.

On what was only the second morning of the experiment, they removed the numbers from their uniforms, pulled off their stocking caps, and barricaded themselves inside their cells using their beds.

When the next shift of guards arrived in the morning, they were alarmed to find the prisoners yelling curses at them from their cells. They requested reinforcements and made plans to quell the uprising. They brought in the on-call guards, and the night shift volunteered to do extra duty. It was only day two and things were already getting ugly.

In order to get the cell doors open, the guards used fire extinguishers to force the prisoners away from the barricades. Once that was accomplished, they rushed into the cell, grabbed the prisoner, and stripped them naked, naked as a jaybird.
The birthday suit prisoner was then placed into solitary confinement. While they were there, the guards would remove the bed from their cell, meaning the prisoner would have to sleep on the floor when they returned.

Once the rebellion was controlled, the guards had to figure out how to prevent another from happening without having to have all nine guards perpetually on duty. The solution was to divide and conquer. The guards deemed one of the cells, the privilege cell.
Well-behaved prisoners were placed in the privilege cell, where they would get their uniforms and beds back and even get special meals. The other prisoners were not only denied of all these things, but were deprived of their normal food rations.
After a few hours, the guards would randomly move the prisoners around. The idea was to create confusion and sow the seeds of distrust among the inmates. And it worked.

In the wake of the uprising conditions deteriorated fast. The guards started making a point of dehumanizing the prisoners by making them call out their identification numbers.
Prisoners were also forbidden from using the bathroom at night and were forced to use bucket in their cell instead. Soon, the guards stopped emptying the buckets, reasoning that the bad smell was simply another punishment for misbehavior.

Despite what Zimbardo described as frequent reminders from the staff, the guards grew increasingly aggressive. The most egregious behavior occurred when the staff wasn't paying attention, which became stressful and frustrating for the prisoners.

The prisoners, as a result, became increasingly submissive. And the experiment was about to claim its first victim. After only 36 hours prisoner Doug Korpi began suffering from what was described as acute emotional disturbance, disorganized thinking, uncontrollable crying, and rage.
The guards used this opportunity to try and coax him into becoming a snitch. But when his erratic behavior continued, the staff realized Doug was in genuine distress and needed to be released from the experiment.

On the sixth day Zimbardo convened a mock parole board, which was headed by one of the experiments prison consultants. Inmates who believe they deserved parole would be allowed to present their case to the board. It was during these presentations that Zimbardo along with the other researchers began to theorize that the prisoners no longer saw themselves as participants in an experiment but as real prisoners.
According to Zimbardo, the prisoners had internalized the crimes as well as their roles as inmates.

As for the guards, he came to identify three different types: tough but fair guards who followed prison rules, good guys who did little favors for the prisoners and never punished them, and finally, guards who appeared to thoroughly enjoy the power they wielded.

Zimbardo felt this last group was hostile, arbitrary, and inventive in their forms of prisoner humiliation. Zimbardo concluded that most people were ultimately willing to fulfill whatever role they were given in a respective social setting. He even admitted that he had internalized his role as superintendent over his role as a psychologist.

At one point, Zimbardo brought in a real priest to talk with the prisoners. It was during this conversation that Prisoner 819 down sobbing. He was so hysterical that the staff agreed to take him to a doctor. The other inmates, for their part, turned on 819. Researchers offered to send him home, but 819 surprisingly refused, saying that he couldn't leave, because the other inmates had labeled him a bad prisoner. Zimbardo was forced to intervene.

Pulling the student aside, he forcefully reminded him that he was not really an inmate and that the experiment was not really a prison. The prisoner is alleged to have stopped crying and looked at Zimbardo like a small child awakened from a nightmare. After that, 819 agreed to leave.

On the sixth day, a recent Ph.D. recipient named Christina Maslack was brought in to interview the prisoners. Horrified by what she saw, she confronted Zimbardo, asking him how he could see what she had seen and not care about the students who were suffering? According to Zimbardo, he quickly realized she was right.

It was at that moment that he decided to prematurely end the study.

Later, he would reflect on his own behavior and claim that it wasn't until his discussion with Maslack that he realized how deeply he had internalized his role at the prison. Ultimately, he concluded he was thinking like a prison superintendent rather than a research psychologist.

Both the ethics and conclusions of the Stanford prison experiment remain highly controversial. Its scientific rigor has been repeatedly questioned by scientists who have been unable to duplicate its results.

And even Zimbardo himself has admitted the whole thing was more of a demonstration than a scientific experiment.

A 2018 book by French academic Thibault Le Texier dismissed the entire thing as nonsense. He argued that the guards had been told what results they were supposed to produce and were advised and guided by Zimbardo and his staff the whole way through.

A joyful bear goes to war

In 1942, a band of polish soldiers recently released from prisons and work camps stumbled upon an unlikely mascot, a brown bear cub. Enamored with his antics and friendly personality, the troops took on the cub as one of their own. The bear grew, and the war progressed. As the men ventured into combat, Wojtek the military bear served right by their sides, distinguishing himself enough to become an official part of the Polish military forces.

On September 1st of 1939, Poland was invaded by German military forces from the north and from the west. On September 17, Poland was invaded by Soviet forces from the east. As a result of the invasions, more than 400,000 Polish prisoners were sent to work camps in Siberia.

This double whammy on Poland was made possible by the German Soviet non-aggression pact, a pact which fell apart when Hitler directed German forces to invade the Soviet Union in 1941. Not one to take a double cross very well, Stalin ordered Soviet troops to release those same Polish soldiers taken prisoner a few years earlier to join the fight against Germany.

As these Polish troops made their way out of Siberia and into Iran, they met a young shepherd. The shepherd carried with him a sack. And in that sack, he kept a Syrian brown bear cub.
The bear was an orphan, his mother had been killed by hunters. The playful spirit of the cub won the troops over, and they made a trade with the shepherd.

The newly adopted bear left his old life to go on an adventure with Polish troopers in World War II.
The fighting men gave their new friend, the name, Wojtek, which means joyful soldier.

A brown bear in the ranks of soldiers tends to stick out, even if a Syrian brown bear is a rather small bear, at least as far as bears go.
As an adult they can measure up to 4 and 1/2 feet long from nose to tail and weigh up to 550 pounds. Their fur is light brown, closer to the color of straw. The hair between the shoulder blades is often a different shade from the rest of the body, sometimes appearing as a dark stripe. And it is the only bear species known to have white claws. Very stylish, but boy do they show dirt.

The bulk of the responsibilities to care for the brown bear cub fell on two men, essentially his adoptive parents. Dymitr Szawlugo and Henryk Zacharewicz. Henryk, in particular, formed a close bond with the bear. In most of the films and pictures that exist of Wojtek, Henryk can always be seen close by. Apparently, Wojtek had a helicopter parent.

In the wild a Syrian brown bear eats fruits, berries, seeds, plants, grasses, nuts, grubs, and small mammals. If particularly peckish, he will eat cultivated grains and livestock.

The military was ill equipped to care for a bear cub, so the troops made do with what they had. Wojtek was initially fed condensed milk from a bottle. But as he grew, his tastes expanded to include well, basically anything that was available. Not a real foodie. The larger Wojtek got, the more bold he became to roam around the camp's kitchen scrounging up a snack.

In the rare moments when his military family wasn't doing military things like packing, moving, working, or fighting, Wojtek was always up for mixing it up with his human friends. Whether Wojtek was entertaining the troops or the troops were entertaining Wojtek is hard to say. In any event, he threw back beers like one of the boys. But big talk over beers was not Wojtek style. He was a bear of action.

The larger he grew, the more he enjoyed wrestling. The brown bear loved to roughhouse with men, though it was a rare soldier who was brave enough to earnestly tussle with Wojtek. No troops ever got seriously injured, but it was common for a wrestling match to end with someone's body getting scratched or someone's clothes getting shredded. And that someone was never Wojtek. Perhaps that's why most of the men prefer to watch from the sidelines. As a side note, a friend who urges you to wrestle with a bear may not be your friend.

Wojtek behavior was influenced by his peer group, who happen to be war-hardened men with advanced skills in carousing. It's a tough environment for an impressionable young bear. Wojtek adopted their habits and fit right in. He had his own mug that he used to drink beer and wine from, and when it was empty, Wojtek would look mournfully at the cup until it was refilled. He also begged for cigarettes, though he insisted someone lit them before he would accept. Typically, after one puff, Wojtek would swallow it whole.

When the troops arrived in Palestine, they were organized into the 22nd Transport Company, Artillery Division Polish 2nd Corps. The men, however, would not abandon Wojtek, who was immediately adopted as the company mascot. But it wasn't just a symbolic gesture. Wojtek was part of the team.

One evening, while the camp was asleep, a thief crept into the compound looking for something to steal. Unfortunately for him, he awoke Wojtek, who rose to investigate. With a massive brown bear lumbering towards him, the frightened thief, understandably, forgot he was a thief. He made such a clatter that he woke the troops, and he was quickly apprehended. As a reward for his vigilance, Wojtek was given a bottle of beer.

When he was a cub Wojtek traveled with a company from site to site in whatever cab of whatever truck had room. But as Wojtek tipped the scale at 500 pounds, and it was harder to find any vehicle that had room for him to ride shotgun, he was upgraded to one of the company's recovery trucks.
A recovery truck is like a tow truck, but military sized and used to move tanks.
For Wojtek, it was a traveling home, like an RV built for a bear. He spent his trips lounging on the recovery trucks bed, and alleviating his boredom by climbing the crane to get a view of the surroundings.

Wojtek wasn't the only animal who accompanied soldiers in the Second World War, although he likely was the only bear on the battlefield. Some animals, like anti-tank dogs, served grim but useful purposes, while others were brought to battle as a mascot. Whenever he encountered other animals, Wojtek was always friendly.

The soldiers of the 22nd transport company love to talk about the encounters between Wojtek and Kasha the Monkey and Kirkuk the Dog, two of the war's most famous animal combatants. Consider them the A-list celebrity animals of the day.

Wojtek never suffered a bullet or shrapnel wound, but he did encounter a life threatening injury. Wojtek was once stung on the nose by a scorpion. Such an injury is often lethal. In fact, his friend Kirkuk the dog succumbed to a scorpion sting.

Wojtek's friend, Henryk, was beside himself. He refused to leave the bear side, doing all in his power to help nurse Wojtek back to health. For the first day and a half, the situation was critical, and it looked as if Wojtek might not make it. The soldiers feared the worst. But Wojtek fought back, and against all odds overcame, the scorpions venom. Within days, he was back to his carousing ways.

As the 22nd Second Transport Company received their assignment and was sent to the Italian battlefront in 1943, Wojtek had to be left behind in Palestine due to regulations that prohibited animals in combat. An active war front is typically not an ideal place for a bear, but Wojtek was not a typical bear.

To get around the regulation, Wojtek was officially enlisted in the Polish army. He was even given his own paycheck, rank, and serial number. This helped ensure his participation was recorded, and the world knew under which flag Wojtek served.

Though there was confusion, and likely a bit of aggravation about transporting a bear to the Italian battlefront, the Polish troops eventually got their way.

In Italy, there were a series of fortifications known as the Winter Line. In 1944 the Germans held the Western portion of that line. And the Allies determined that breaking through that line near a rocky hill known as Monte Casino would give them access to the Italian capital of Rome. Atop the hill was an abbey that had been converted into a fearsome stronghold. The abbey ultimately withstood three assaults before the Allies drove its inhabitants backwards into Rome.

During one of these assaults, Wojtek pal, Henryk, serving as an artillery spotter, pulled forward into battle, and had to leave his bear friend behind. Left among the men who armed and manned the guns, Wojtek refused to sit idly by. Mimicking the behavior of the soldiers around him, Wojtek to lift massive crates of ammunition and carry them towards the cannons, disregarding the gunfire and making himself useful throughout the assault.

By the time Monte Casino was in the hands of the Allies, more than 70,000 men on both sides had lost their lives. When the chaos of battle settled, the troops were able to rest and word of Wojtek exploits spread. His fearless actions and loyalty in battle made him a hero among the 22nd Transport Company. In honor of Wojtek deeds, the official seal of the 22nd Transport Company was changed to feature Wojtek marching towards cannon fire, a shell in each hand. The logo was then featured prominently on vehicles uniforms and the like.

After the war, the 22nd Transport Company moved to rural Scotland, where they were stationed at an airfield near the village of Hutton. The soldiers Wojtek had spent the previous three years following into battle were re-stationed or sent home. One by one, they came to say goodbye to their furry friend. Wojtek's battle adventures were ending, but his time in the spotlight was just beginning. Word spread that there was a Syrian brown bear nearby, and Wojtek became a local celebrity among the Scottish people. He was profiled in stories, visited by locals, and inducted into local organizations, such as the Polish-Scottish Association.

In 1947, Wojtek left the military. Rising from his initial rank as private, he was discharged as a corporal. He retired to the Edinburgh Zoo. There he enjoyed a good life as beloved celebrity, doing an occasional interview and appearing on a local children's show from time to time. As the years wore on, Wojtek was never forgotten by his army pals and was visited by Polish soldiers he had served with. As 82-year-old Polish veteran Augustyn Karolowski described his reunion with Wojtek, "As soon as I mentioned his name, he would sit on his backside, and shake his head wanting a cigarette. Still one of the boys."

In the wild, Syrian brown bears live between 20 and 25 years. Wojtek, for all his adventures lived to a ripe age of 21 and passed away in 1963

Smoky, the war dog

World War II saw lots of heroes, Winston Churchill, Charles de Gaulle, Commander Eisenhower, but one you probably don't know is Smoky, a Yorkshire Terrier: the smallest war hero the world ever saw.

Bill Wynne, a corporal who served during World War II, bought Smoky for $6.44 while he was serving in the Pacific theater.
Smoky was Bill's brother in arms through 150 air raids, 12 combat missions, and once even saved Bill from a Japanese bombing.
Later, Smoky also accompanied nurses on their rounds at a US Army hospital in New Guinea.

So, Smoky gets credit for being the first therapy dog on record.

Back in Bill's hometown of Cleveland, Smoky became famous doing tricks on TV shows. She could walk on a drum and she could ride a scooter.
Smoky died a celebrity in 1957, but she wasn't forgotten. She has memorials in Ohio, Pennsylvania, Australia, Hawaii, Tennessee.
But what is her biggest legacy? Popular belief is that Smokey's the reason that Yorkies are such a popular pet. So, thanks to Smokey the World War II dog we have all those cute little Yorkies yapping about.

The baboon that ran a railway

Monkey see, monkey do. Baboon see, baboon control a railway used by multi-ton trains and thousands of passengers.
What, you think the baboon can't do it? Well, joke's on you, because Jack worked at a station in Cape Town for 9 years and never made a single mistake!

That's how it worked in the late 1800's in South Africa. Radios didn't exist and since trains were loud, you couldn't just shout at the driver to tell them what to do. Therefore, in the 1800s, signals were developed as a way to tell incoming trains to stations what to do.

At first, lanterns and hand signals were used by signalmen to convey the information needed but as technology advanced signals that could be controlled by switches and levers were installed to ease the process.
These signals were similar to weathervanes in that they consisted of fixed posts with movable discs or signage that could be controlled via a switch.
Various colors meant to stop or go or proceed with caution, and there were other vanes on different axes to indicate which tracks to pull into once arriving at the stations and various other signs meaning to take it to the left, right, to criss-cross, to cha cha now, to cha cha again, and for everybody to clap their hands.

With the world going loco for locomotives at the time tons and tons of signalmen were needed to ensure that the trains stuck to schedules, were in working condition, and stuck to the proper tracks.

Signalmen, as their names imply, were also responsible for operating the levers that would set off the signals for the trains out of the signal house.

In the 1870s, one of the signalmen for the Cape Town to Port Elizabeth Mainline Railroad in South Africa was a man named James Wilde.
Wilde went by the nickname "Jumper" because he had a habit of jumping between the cars that would pass on the tracks and in a totally unforeseen and completely unpreventable twist of fate, Jumper once jumped a moving railcar and fell under it losing both of his legs in the process.

After this, Jumper continued working hobbling around on a pair of peg legs although he found himself limited in his ability to signal trains proficiently.

One day at the market, though, Jumper came upon a chacma baboon who'd been trained to lead an ox-drawn wagon. Though impressive, its intelligence isn't particularly surprising by today's standards.
We now know that baboons aren't so different from humans in their brain capacity.
Baboons can keep schedules, communicate with their own language, differentiate between scribbles and the written word, and the University of Rochester recently concluded that baboons are actually capable of counting.

Jumper begged and begged and finally convinced the owner to let him take the baboon and thus the prodigious primate pair was born.

The original owner warned Jumper, however, that the baboon would refuse to work unless he had been given plenty of brandy to drink. They're really just like us!

The baboon, named Jack, was first taught to observe and then respond to certain commands. When Jumper would hold up a certain number of fingers, Jack was to pull the corresponding lever.
From there, Jack learned that the trains were giving similar orders by the number of blats from their whistle.
Over time, Jack realized on his known which tracks needed which signals and would double-check his own work as he was doing it.
He also realized that conductors needed access to the coal sheds and would retrieve the key from Jumper unbidden to give to the incoming engineers.

Now, if your job is replaceable by a monkey you really shouldn't be expecting much job security and in fact Jack and Jumper's jobs eventually came under threat.

Jack was a beloved fixture of the railroad until some snobby high-society aristocrat noticed that he was, in fact, a monkey and narc'd on the pair. The bosses at the railway were aware that Jumper had found an assistant but were totally in the dark about his baboon-ness.
After the Cape Town executives launched an investigation, they found out the truth about the monkey business. So, naturally, they tried to fire both Jumper and Jack.

Jumper begged to demonstrate Jack's cleverness and so the rail managers agreed to put him to the test. Jack perfectly performed his signaling abilities, even checking both directions to make sure the incoming trains were heading to separate tracks at the station.

The managers were so impressed that they made Jack an official employee paying him 20 cents per day and half a bottle of beer every week.

It's been said that in the nine years Jack worked as a signalman he never made a single mistake, despite being constantly drunk and a monkey.

Jack became known as "Jack the Signalman" and worked and lived with Jumper in a small cottage not far from the signal house. He stayed there and worked for the railroad up until his death from tuberculosis in 1890 and his skull is now displayed at a museum in Grahamstown, South Africa not far from where he worked.

The craziest drunken bet

In 1956, the notoriously fearless (which is the polite way of saying "batshit crazy") American pilot, Thomas Fitzpatrick, made a bet that he could land a plane right in the middle of the streets of New York.

Thomas Fitzpatrick, or Tommy Fitz for his friends, was born and raised in Washington Heights, Manhattan. But even after he had moved to New Jersey (New York was expensive even then), he still hung out with his old friends from the neighborhood.
Tommy's crew were adventurous and enjoyed frequenting area bars, they were a "wild bunch."

Late in the night (or more accurately early in the morning) of September 30, 1956, as Tommy Fitz was leaving a tavern on St. Nicholas Avenue in Manhattan to return home, he bet one of his buddies he could make it back to the bar from New Jersey in just 15 minutes. This, of course, was an impossible to achieve by driving a car.

So, after he left the bar, Tommy went to the Teterboro School of Aeronautics in New Jersey where he stole a single-engine plane.
Hoping to evade authorities until he had won his bet was completed, he took off without lights at around 3:00 a.m.

According to the reports, his original plan was to land the plane on the field of George Washington High School, a few blocks down from the tavern, but the lights on the field weren't on that morning. So, the drunken Tommy chose to land the plane in front of the tavern itself on St. Nicholas Avenue near its intersection with 191st street. A great pilot, even drunk, he managed to thread the needle, successfully avoiding lamp posts and parked cars in his landing.

Of course, landing a plane in the middle of a street in Manhattan gets noticed and the cops were called in. Tommy was charged with grand larceny, but never convicted since the plane's owner, presumably amused by the whole endeavor and because no harm was done to his plane, refused to press charges.
However, since there was a city ordinance prohibiting landing planes on its streets, Tommy was fined a mere $100 (approximately $800 today) and had his pilot's license suspended for six months.

Just over two years later, again after spending a drunken night in a Washington Heights bar, Tommy repeated the feat. That time, he had been drunkenly boasting about his first flight when another drunkard questioned the authenticity of the story i.e., called him a liar to his face.

With his honor on the line, at about 1:00 a.m. on October 4, 1958, the shitfaced Tommy went to the Teterboro School of Aeronautics in New Jersey again and "borrowed" one more time a plane to fly back to New York City. This time he ended up landing the plane at the nearby intersection of Amsterdam and 187th Street.

After the landing, he initially fled the scene. However, when police were called in and found themselves with a plane sitting in the middle of a Manhattan street once again, they obviously remembered the unique incident happened two years before just a few blocks away. They decided to go investigate and see if Tommy Fitz had something to do with the new one too.

At first, he tired to deny it, but witnesses who saw him exit the plane and run off claimed it was him, ultimately inspiring Fitz to confess.

He succinctly summed up his decision-making paradigm in choosing to perform the amazingly stupid feat again, stating, "It's the lousy drink."

Taking into consideration that it was the second incident; the judge showed no mercy. Ruben Levy, the magistrate judge, went after him with all he had stating, "Had you been properly jolted then, it's possible this would not have occurred a second time."

The 28-year-old Tommy Fitz was sentenced to six months in prison for transporting stolen property.

Beyond his flying escapades and little stint in prison, Tommy Fitz had a full life, serving as a Marine in the Korean War and earning a Purple Heart, enjoying a 51-year marriage to his clearly very understanding wife, Helen, having three sons, working as a steamfitter.

Despite his juvenile antics, he lived to the ripe old age 79, dying in 2009.

The woman who gave birth to rabbits

Back in 1726 England had one of the biggest controversies of its long history. A young woman named Mary Toft started delivering rabbits and she was attended by more than six different doctors, including members of the Royal College of Physicians, but no one declared the pregnancies as hoaxes until Toft herself confessed on 7 December 1726.

It was on September 27, 1726, when a 23-year-old peasant by the name Mary Toft went into labour at Godalming, Surrey which is about 40 miles from London, England's capital.

This was odd to Toft's neighbors as she had just had a miscarriage in August a month earlier, even though rumors flew around of her still being pregnant.

However, Toft who was born Mary Denyer in 1703 in the same Godalming, gave birth on that fateful day in September with the help of her neighbor and her mother-in-law. The "baby" was monstrous.

With fright, the women withdrew a dead creature with four limbs from Toft and quickly summoned John Howard, a professional obstetrician.

When Howard arrived, the situation got worse and over the next month Taft had given births to nine dead rabbits.

Alarmed, the obstetrician sent a deluge of letters to the most skilled scientists and doctors all over England and of course to King George I through his secretary.

As the news kept flying all over England, Toft was still giving birth to more and more rabbits.

Quickly, the king sent one of the most famous anatomists of the time, Nathaniel St. Andre, who arrived when Mary Toft was giving birth to her 15th dead rabbit.

St. Andre had seen everything he needed to see. To his knowledge, this weird, miraculous birth would give him fame and stop his name in medical history.

In haste, the anatomist published a paper, "A Short Narrative of an Extraordinary Delivery of Rabbits". In the manuscript, Saint Andre explained what he termed "maternal impression", that a child could be influenced by the thoughts and experiences of the mother which could cause a human to give birth to an animal.

Mary Toft also claimed that while she was pregnant, she had failed to capture two rabbits when she went hunting. As a result, she felt a hunger for rabbit's meat and it would explain why she was giving birth to dead rabbits instead of a human child.

Saint Andre was ecstatic as he wrote these words even medieval medicine would have been skeptical of this occurrence.

Not satisfied, King George sent a German surgeon, Cyriacus Ahlers to verify the claims of Saint Andre, Howard, and Toft. But the surgeon found some new disturbing facts. Ahlers discovered that dung from inside one of the rabbits contained hay, stray and corn, none of which was eaten by Toft. Saint Andre stood his ground and remained committed to his theory.

However, Ahlers had Toft brought to London where a gathering of physicians, including the respected Dr. James Douglas, watched over her as she went to labor many times. Interestingly, Toft never gave birth to a single rabbit in the presence of these people.

This continued for some days, until a porter was caught trying to smuggle a small dead rabbit into the room.

He confessed to the doctors that Margret Toft, Mary's sister-in-law, had asked him to look for any rabbit he could find.

On December 7, 1726, a week after she arrived at London, Toft finally confessed that she, her mother-in-law and Howard had been conniving together to perpetrate the prank since that fateful day in September.

Only a few were surprised with the confession. But St. Andre's career suffered as he had already published his thrilling discovery on December 3rd, 1726, just four days before Toft's confession. It was the end of a medical career for him and the newspapers of the time had a field day.

So, how did Toft give birth to these dead rabbits?

In 18th century England, rabbits were widely available symbolizing the negligence of the upper class who built dens to sell their meat and fur as elite goods. These rabbits then escaped to the lower-class' gardens who saw them as pests.

Although the rabbits' births were ticklish, the pains Mary Toft suffered were real. With an alibi, she placed the dead rabbit inside her body; difficult, dangerous, and painful.

It was a miracle Toft did not die of a bacterial infection; instead, she ended up in prison for only a few months as a longer sentence would have drawn even more attention to the embarrassing events.

The darkest year in history

The term "worst year ever" gets tossed around a lot these days, mostly on the internet, and for reasons like "I was disappointed in the latest Star Wars movie".
But scientists and historians have actually argued that no year in the long history of this planet was worse than the year 536. In 536 AD a mysterious fog rolled over Europe, the Middle East and parts of Asia. The fog blocked the sun during the day, temperatures dropped, crops failed, and people died. The countries affected went without light for over 18 months: it was the literal Dark Age. While, sure, there have been plenty of worthy contenders for the worst year ever over the course of history, no single year has had more of a measurably bad impact for the decades that followed.

While serving as a military advisor to Belisaurius, one of the Byzantine Empire's most distinguished generals, Byzantine historian Procopius noticed some trouble was brewing in the air while traveling with his boss in Sicily in the year 536.
He reported of a "sun that gave forth light without brightness, like the moon, during this whole year. And it seemed exceedingly like the sun in eclipse for the beams it shed were not clear nor such as it is accustomed to shed". Translated, it was all dark outside, like, all the time.

He, of course, wasn't the only one to notice the sun appeared to be in a mood during 536.
A Byzantine scribe, Michael the Syrian, would later write about this period, "The sun became dark and its darkness lasted for 18 months. Each day it shone for about four hours, and still this light was only a feeble shadow. Everyone declared that the sun would never recover its full light. The fruits did not ripen and the wine tasted like sour grapes."

This wishy-washy sun situation cast a non-metaphorical dark cloud over the globe that darkened the sky for at least a full year in 536.
Researchers later discovered evidence of a massive volcanic eruption whose ash was likely a major contributor to the Seattle-like weather, minus all the rain, spreading ash and destruction on a global scale. Not to mention, it made the grapes sour and the wine bad. So that's an easy strike for the year 536.

Basic biology teaches us that plants need the sun to aid in their growth and survival. So not having direct sunlight for the duration of at least a year did a real number on the crop output around the world and sparked a widespread famine around the globe. And it's not just that the plants wanted to catch their rays, it was just too darn chilly for crops to grow. With the sun cloaked in an endless cloud, the temperature of the Earth dropped between 1.6 and 2.5 degrees Celsius, or 34.88 to 36.5 degrees Fahrenheit for all the Americans thinking that doesn't sound so bad. But it also cooled temperatures for decades to come.
Crop scarcities were reported far and wide around this time period, including Ireland, who suffered through their own horrible sounding food depletion they called "Bread Failure."

A dusty veil covering the sun wasn't the only bad thing in the air for these poor people just trying to live their lives in 536. There was also a plague or two waiting in the wings to strike on these vitamin D-deprived immune systems. Nobody was immune to this infestation. It swept through the lower classes all the way to the Imperial Palace. "Symptoms," as it was lovingly described, began with a sore that formed on the palm of the hand and progressed until the afflicted one could not take a step. The leg swelled. Then the buboes burst and pus came out.

With the plague beginning to make the rounds in Constantinople, the city began to stink, what with the piles of dead sick bodies just sort of being tossed around into the sea, only to resurface later. There wasn't a lot of burial planning going around back then. There was more of a "wing it" vibe around the Justinian Plague.

Emperor Justinian ordered the bodies to be removed from the city.

But all that did was expose more people to the disease, as healthy people were responsible for moving deceased, sickly bodies out of the cities. Things weren't all bad for Emperor Justinian since the plague that took all of these lives and made the city a smelly nightmare would later be named the "Plague of Justinian." So that was probably nice for him. Less so, for the estimated 50 million people that died from it, however.

Around 536, the climate in China started its journey into madness, doing perfectly normal things like raining dust you could scoop into your hands. Not only should it not rain dust, it certainly shouldn't be measurable by the scoopful. The Nan Shi, a sixth century chronicle, reported a yellow ash-like substance falling from the sky. They named their freak weather hui, or dust, and said it was yellow in color. Whether this was volcanic ash or just some random unexplained climate reaction is not known.

However, this was just the beginning of China's climate disruption.

The chronicles of the southern dynasties reported on a rare summer-winter weather event with frost in the mid-summer and snow in August. Like a Southern California girl in Chicago in January, the crops were not here for this cold snap. Summer crops were destroyed. And the city of Xinzhou, along with others, were thrown into a deadly famine that lasted for two years and resulted in the deaths of around 70% to 80% of the population.

Researchers discovered evidence deep in the ice sheets of Iceland and Greenland that indicated a major volcanic event occurred around 536.

Volcanic eruptions in Iceland in 540 and 547 thrust people into the literal Dark Ages, with ash lining the skies and blocking out the shiny, hot sun thing in the sky that the people of the 6th century were starting to get used to having around.

Based on a tropical volcanic ash later discovered, some scholars have suggested a volcano in El Salvador went blasting off around the year 535 or 536.

Others pointed to a volcanic eruption in North America as a contributor to the dark skies around the world. When combined with the two Icelandic volcano eruptions, it kicked off what was adorably called the "Late Antique Little Ice Age".

This cute little ice age cooled off the planet for at least a decade and resulted in the death of crops and, subsequently, people. Both directly through starvation and indirectly, a malnourished population was more susceptible to diseases, of which there were plenty running around.

By the time the 6th century rolled around, the Roman had migrated east to Constantinople and under the guiding hand of Emperor Justinian, the Romans sought to get back to the glory days of the empire, much like a high school graduate who still hangs around campus and wears their letterman jacket.

Though some of Justinian's generals saw success in this cool goal - most notable, Belisaurius, who fought against several different armies, including Goths, Vandals, and others - Justinian himself couldn't mirror the success due to constant uprisings and imperial instability.

To add sickness to war defeats, the Byzantine Empire would never fully recover from the disease and famine sparked by the events of 536. The Byzantine Empire lost between 35% to 55% of their population in the year 541.

Once the bubonic plague moved in, it did what the plague did best: kill depressingly high percentages of entire populations. Historians believe the plague could have been transported by plague-infested rats hitching a ride on military trains during this attempt to bring the Roman Empire back to its peak, which clearly backfired.

The horribleness of 536 didn't discriminate. The Moche civilization of Peru wouldn't count 536 as their banner year either. The Moche civilization, a once dominant force in the region, were known to be avid fishermen and developers of an advanced irrigation system that allowed a variety of crops to grow. Their agricultural talents were the backbone of their economy.

But the weather conditions in the 6th century caused their pocketbooks to take a deep hit. It was around this time that an unusually strong El Niño weather system caused waters to warm, which decimated the fish supply. The freak weather system also caused heavy flooding, which ruined their irrigation systems and devastated their ability to grow enough food to feed their people.

People, probably tired of reading Twitter users claim one or another year was the worst year ever, so a group of scholars set out to set the record straight once and for all.

Harvard historian Michael McCormick and a group of scholars decided to science their way out of the age-old question, what was the worst year to be alive? Initially, however, this was not the ultimate goal of McCormick and his group of 12 interdisciplinary scholars.

The group came together to study metal usage, coinage, and changes to the 7th century monetary systems. Somewhere in this thrilling subject matter, one probably began to ponder if they were living in the worst year to be alive.

Their findings included an analysis of volcanic fragments from an Icelandic volcano in ice core samples from Swiss glaciers that, yes, dated back to 536, confirming the volcanic event that thrusted a good portion of the northern hemisphere into unprecedented darkness, setting off a global catastrophe.

The popcorn ban

Popcorn, movies, a match made in theater heaven. But there was a time when it was banned.

Popcorn has been invented over 8,000 years before, but when it arrived on the American streets in the mid-1800s, it started selling like hot cakes…or popcorns. After all, it was cheap, it could be mass produced on the go, and it smelled amazing.

It was the go-to snack for circuses, sporting events, and fairs. In fact, the only place you couldn't find popcorn was in movie theaters.

Going to the movies used to be a major event. The only people that went were rich, fancy people. The reason for this class divide was that to watch silent movies, you had to be educated enough to read.

It was very fancy indeed, like coat check and heavy red drapes sort of fancy.

But they definitely did not have a concession stand.

However, there were savvy popcorn street vendors who set up shop outside theaters. They made a killing selling to waiting theater goers. Who in turn then started smuggling their popped treats inside the cinemas.

Not cool.

Early movie theaters kindly asked patrons check their popcorn at the fancy coat checks before entering.

Then, in 1927, films started adding sound, meaning everyone went to the movies. The Great Depression followed making movies a cheap escape. Popcorn were even cheaper, just 5 to 10 cents per bag! So, people started smuggling them in and the sound would cover the munching anyway.

Huge crowds plus crunch muffling sound equaled another revenue opportunity for theater owners.

By 1945, more than half the popcorn consumed in America was eaten in movie theaters. It's an unbreakable bond that has stood the test of time since then.

Now, 80% of the revenues of movie theaters come from the concession stands; it doesn't cost 5 cents anymore but even if the prices are marked up, we keep buying them because it wouldn't really be a movie experience without them.

Death by syrup

Ancient Rome was the greatest power of its era and one of the most spectacularly impressive empires in history. But then one day, it all collapsed.
While no one knows exactly why the empire disappeared into history, at least one researcher has proposed that the culprit might be something as simple as lead exposure.
And while recent studies have uncovered high levels of lead in Imperial Rome's drinking water, the real danger might have been an artificial sweetener.

The Roman Empire had an incredible amount of wealth. And like pretty much all rich people, wealthy Romans loved to throw a good feast.
Showing off one's bankroll by hosting elaborate dinner parties was basically standard operating procedure for the Romans.

Another was to sweeten the food with a thick grape syrup called *sapa*. The flavoring was made by boiling and skinning grapes, then mashing them through a sieve, and mixing the paste with sugar. It sounds pretty yummy and you can actually still taste it as *saba* in Italy, where is used in sweets in Sardinia and Calabria, and in Greece as *petimezi*, a sort of sweet molasses.
However, while this regional delicacies are made with modern cookware, Romans would cook the sapa in lead pots. The lead would then mix into the syrup, making it toxic.

So, while the *sapa* made the wealthy Romans' food tastes better, it was also slowly poisoning them. Bittersweet, indeed.
Sapa may have been toxic, but the Romans loved it and used it for more than just sweetening foods. It was also used extensively in winemaking.

Sapa was used to preserve wine, which had the unfortunate side effect of infusing the wine with poisonous lead. The Romans, much like a Real Housewife of Beverly Hills, had a large appetite for wine. The average Roman drank a liter of this stuff each day, which adds up to around 100 gallons of wine a year. That is a lot of lead. And we're just talking about the average Roman.
Elite Romans drank even more heavily.
For example, the Emperor Elagabalus was rumored to literally drink from a swimming pool full of wine.

Romans used *sapa* as a sweetener because it worked. The flavor does make wine and food taste better. But today, we know that the syrup was toxic. Modern science has determined that due to being made in lead pots, the mixture contained a compound called lead acetate, also known as Sugar of Lead.
We probably shouldn't take something so deadly and name it something that sounds so sweet. Downing as much lead acetate as the Romans did is not healthy.

The side effects of the poisoning include dementia, infertility, and eventually complete organ shutdown, which is pretty bad because your organs are important.

In the 1980s, research scientist Jerome Nriagu recreated *sapa* using ancient recipes that detailed the methods the Romans used to make the artificial sweetener. His results confirmed what he had long suspected, that the *sapa* turned out to contain a dangerous concentration of lead. Quantities ranged from 240 to 1,000 milligrams of lead per liter. That's way more lead than I like in my liter.
Nriagu explained that even one teaspoon of such a syrup would have been more than enough to give a person chronic lead poisoning. The Romans, of course, were ingesting far more.

How dangerous was ancient Romans *sapa*? Well, it was so bad that if it existed today, it would be outlawed in the United States. And we're talking about a country that loves Big Macs and Four Loko.
In fact, the modern threshold for lead is far, far lower. The Environmental Protection Agency will take action when drinking water reaches lead levels of 15 parts per billion.
By comparison, ancient Roman *sapa* was practically exploding with lead, at a terrifying count of 2,900 parts per billion. That's nearly 200 times the enforceable amount regulated by the EPA today.

So, if lead pots were so dangerous, why did the Romans use them? Well, for one, they were completely oblivious of the danger. But more importantly, Roman winemakers specifically used lead vessels to make the *sapa* because the end product would turn out noticeably sweeter.
This, ironically, was an effect of the lead acetate, which despite being a noxious compound, actually has a sweet taste. There were also problems with some of the alternatives.
One ancient winemaker wrote that lead pots were better than brass because in the boiling, brass vessels throw off copper rust, which has a disagreeable flavor.

For Jerome Nriagu, researching lead exposure in ancient Rome didn't stop at recreating the *sapa*.
He also researched the diets of over two dozen Roman emperors from 30 BCE to 220 CE. Based on his examinations, the scientist found evidence that as many as 19 emperors had a predilection to the lead-tainted wine and frequently enjoyed foods sweetened with *sapa*.
The inescapable conclusion was that multiple Roman emperors almost certainly suffered from lead poisoning. That being the case, it's not a far jump to wonder whether the effects of the exposure on the emperor might have weakened the empire itself.

As noted previously, exposure to lead can have many serious side effects. For example, long-term contamination can actually impair decision making. But there were other risks too.
Roman emperors, wealthy aristocrats, and others who consumed large amounts of lead were also more likely to have conditions like gout.
In fact, multiple emperors showed signs of having the affliction during their reign. These included Claudius, Nero, Caligula, and Tiberius.
These particular emperors were also known for their odd behavior, which is another thing you would expect of an individual who contracted lead poisoning.

Speaking of odd behavior, the Roman Emperor Claudius took power after his nephew Caligula died at the hands of Rome's enemies in 37 CE. According to the ancients, Claudius, who evidently wasn't the hero type, hid behind a curtain while his nephew was getting killed.
After he became emperor, Claudius's rule was marked by numerous uprisings.
According to Jerome Nriagu, Claudius had disturbed speech, weak limbs, an ungainly gait, tremor, fits of excessive and inappropriate laughter, and unseemly anger. Oh, and he often slobbered.

These are classic signs of lead exposure, which dovetails nicely with ancient descriptions of Claudius being dull-witted and absentminded. Or that last part might just mean that ancient historians weren't too fond of Claudius.

So how often did the Romans use *sapa* to sweeten their foods? Well, one fourth century Roman recipe book known as the Apicius, included no less than 100 different recipes that all, in one way or another, incorporated lead acetate. They might have used so much *sapa* in their cooking because they just loved the stuff. But there might have been another, more scientific reason as well.

Not too ironically, one side effect of lead exposure is a metallic taste in the mouth. If the Romans were experiencing that taste, it likely would have encouraged them to use even more *sapa* to cover it up, which would lead to a more metallic taste in the mouth, which would lead to a need for more *sapa*, which would lead to… well, you get it.

Despite the repeated warnings about lead poisoning, it's likely some of you are wondering if there's a way you can make your own sapa. Well, don't worry. Pliny the Elder has you covered.
Pliny detailed the recipe and process for making sapa way back in the first century.
Sounding like a hipster owner of a microbrewery, Pliny wrote, "Sapa is a product of art, not nature."
He then explained that his "art" began by boiling down the unfermented grape juice to a third of its original quantity. He was careful to distinguish this from defrutum, a different recipe that called for the grape juice to be boiled to one half of its volume. *Sapa*, Pliny stressed, was more concentrated.
This reduction would have made the *sapa* much sweeter than grape juice. And the Romans then further sweetened it by boiling it in lead pots.

While I would strongly recommend to not use lead pots, the rest of Pliny's recipe still works today. Moreover, *sapa* itself, to be perfectly clear, is completely safe to consume, as they still do it in Italy and Greece. Its only toxic if it's been heated in a lead vessel.

So what if they hadn't used lead pots to cook the *sapa*? Would history be different? Would the Roman Empire have lasted another thousand years? It's always hard to answer hypotheticals, but it's at least possible nothing would be different because even without the *sapa*, Romans still had a lot of lead in their diets.

The water many Romans drank was spring water that had been transported across the empire in aqueducts and lead pipes. Those pipes transferred lead right into the water, exposing the population to the heavy metal. *Sapa* or no *sapa*, the Romans were swimming in lead.

After traveling through the lead pipes, Rome's water supply would have become contaminated with lead.
How contaminated? Well, researchers recently estimated that the Roman water supply probably contained 100 times the levels of lead that would have been found in local spring water. And this wasn't just guesswork. It's science. The researchers actually compared sediments from local ports with traces of water found in ancient Roman pipes. The scientists ultimately concluded that the levels were probably too low to cause significant harm. But they acknowledged that drinking water contaminated with any amount of lead can be dangerous and problematic.

Given how widely *sapa* was used and enjoyed in the ancient Roman Empire, it's easy to assume that lead contamination was a major problem. But not all scholars agree.
In fact, when Jerome Nriagu first introduced the lead poisoning theory for Rome's decline in the 1980s, he immediately received a ton of pushback. He argued with other historians who called his theory a myth. And they claimed the Romans knew that lead was harmful.
Moreover, it was pointed out that *sapa* was used for centuries before Rome's fall, even during its Golden Age, which makes it difficult to pin the decline on its use. And indeed, modern researchers who have examined lead levels in ancient Roman drinking water have dismissed the idea that lead could have been the primary cause of Rome's downfall.

Nevertheless, many find it hard to completely reject the notion that centuries of consuming lead-tainted artificial sweeteners certainly couldn't have been good for Rome either.

CONTEMPORARY NUGGETS

Who says that life isn't as interesting as it used to be? Here are some contemporary nuggets to prove all jaded people wrong!

Up, up, and away in a flying lawn chair

Have you ever seen the movie Up? Well, long before it came out, one man actually went on a daring balloon adventure! Sort of. Larry Walters always wanted to be a pilot. But his dream would never come true because of his poor eyesight. One day he decided to do a flight of his own – he bought 45 eight-foot (2.4 m) weather balloons, filled them with helium, and strapped himself into this lawn chair.

In school, we learn about a lot of American icons, but many of our nation's greatest heroes get left out. We learn about Paul Revere's midnight ride, but not about Sybil Ludington, a 16-year-old girl who rode 40 rain-soaked miles to rally Continental army troops; we learn about Rosa Parks' courageous bus protest, but not about Elizabeth Jennings Graham, who refused to leave a whites only horse carriage in 1854; and, we learn about the Wright Brothers flying the first plane, but not about Larry Walters, a truck driver who in 1982 tied a bunch of weather balloons to a lawn chair and floated 16,000 feet up into the sky like some sort of redneck Icarus trying to escape from Los Angeles.
Let's correct this grave omission in the ink of the American story and learn the tale of Lawnchair Larry.

When Larry Walters was born in Los Angeles in 1949, there was no way to know that he would go on to become one of the most hard-core individuals in the history of the world, joining the likes of Genghis Khan, Winston Churchill, Betty White, and the turtle from Finding Nemo.

The first years of Larry's life were relatively inauspicious; he had hoped one day to become an Air Force pilot, but soon discovered he couldn't due to poor eyesight, because it turns out seeing is important for pilots.
Despite his poor vision, at the age 13, he saw something that would forever change his life, and—dare I say—the entire course of aviation history. It was a couple of weather balloons, hanging from the ceiling of a military surplus store—Larry looked at them and had the idea of using them to fly.

It was the type of seemingly impossible plan many of us had when we were young, like digging a hole so deep it went to China, or attaining social mobility in America, or getting through life without making the "I guess it's free" joke when a cashier has trouble scanning something.

But, at the age of 32, Larry made a decision that is somehow simultaneously the dumbest and the most brilliant choice of all time: he purchased 45 eight-foot weather balloons and a bunch of helium tanks and turned his childhood dream into a reality.

Because that quantity of weather balloons isn't commercially available for normal people, Larry had to do what all great explorers must do: overcome his foes with the spirit of adventure. In this case, his foes were federal regulations, and the spirit of adventure was a fake form saying the balloons were for a TV commercial.

Larry then gathered the rest of the high-tech gear necessary for his journey: a lawn chair, a sandwich, a pellet gun, a CB radio, a parachute, and, of course, an ice-cold beer, and once he was ready, in blatant violation of FAA regulations but firmly within the spirit of American greatness, he took off.

Quickly, Larry began to ascend—both into the sky and into the pantheon of legendary explorers like Amerigo Vespucci and Dora.
Soon, he reached 16,000 feet—about half the altitude that planes fly at where the temperature is about 2 degrees Fahrenheit, or -17 degrees Celsius. In other words, it's the type of situation where you'd probably want more than a lawn chair and a sandwich for protection.

After being seen by two commercial airliners—and presumably making the pilots seriously reconsider their sanity—Larry decided it was time to come down, and so, he began shooting his pellet guns at the balloons until enough popped that he started to descend—a method so beautifully hilarious that it's far better than any joke I could write about it.

He then accidentally dropped the pellet gun, but still slowly came back down to earth, where finally, in an ending that feels written by either Wes Anderson or a drunk toddler, his balloon strings got tangled in a power line in Long Beach and caused a 20-minute power blackout.

When Larry finally made it to the ground, something strange happened: instead of being immediately being given the key to the city or awarded the Presidential Medal of Freedom, as he should have been, he was arrested by the Long Beach Police Department. After Larry's arrest, they explained to local reporters, "we know he broke some part of the Federal Aviation Act, and as soon as we decide which part it is, some type of charge will be filed. If he had a pilot's license, we'd suspend that, but he doesn't."

Eventually, Larry was fined $1,500 for various violations of the US Federal Aviation Regulations, which isn't so bad, considering he got to be on Late Night with David Letterman, in an ad for Timex, and he was awarded the "At-Risk Survivor" title in the famous Darwin awards; he also sparked a new kind of sport called cluster ballooning.

The 639-years-long song

> ### Have you ever been to a concert that seemed like it lasted for ages?
>
> **Well, German musicians and philosophers decided to play a musical piece for ages (literally) and chose John Cage's Organ²/ASLSP for the job. They followed the composer's instructions to play it "as slow as possible" and thought that 639 years would be just enough.**

John Cage was an avant-garde composer, how avant-garde you may ask?

He wrote "4'33", which consists entirely of a musician or musicians "resting" for four minutes and thirty three seconds; he had a whole slew of even weirder songs (or at least ones you can actually listen to) —some of which involve toasters, blenders, bathtubs, Geiger counters, and sometimes, rarely, when he wanted to really get crazy, even musical instruments.

This is all to say that when the Maryland Summer Institute for the Creative and Performing Arts was having a piano competition in 1985 and they reached out to John Cage to compose a new piece to serve as the contemporary requirement, knowing full well who John Cage was, they got exactly what they had coming.

What was coming was the possibly brilliant, possibly insane, definitely weird ASLSP.

ASLSP is an abbreviation of As Slow as Possible, because that's totally how abbreviations work, and it's a simple, fun, easy-to-listen-to piece of music—if by simple, fun, and easy-to-listen-to you mean complicated, boring, and largely unpleasant. Don't take my word for it, take the word of Thomas Moore, the coordinator of the competition that commissioned it, who said that the audience and jury, "begrudgingly put up with" the piece.

ASLSP consists of eight sections, which should be played in order, but the player is instructed to choose one to skip and one to repeat, which they may do at any point regardless of order. Make sense? No? Perfect.

Most importantly, though, ASLSP does not specify a tempo. It simply says it is to be played "As Slow as Possible."

Now, because of the limits of how long a piano can hold a note, the piece would traditionally last anywhere from 20-70 minutes, which is a long time, but 70 minutes of boredom can be handled—just ask the first third of The Irishman.

But in 1987, Cage released a version of the piece that adapted it for the organ, called Organ2/ASLSP, which made things much, much worse—and not just because Organ2 sounds like an evil organ transplant harvesting program from a dystopian sci-fi novel.

Unlike a piano, an organ can theoretically hold a note forever. Pianos are percussion instruments, whose sound is produced by a hammer that hits a string, causing it to vibrate, and eventually that vibration will stop.

Organs, on the other hand, produce sound by having air pushed through them, and so as long as air is pushed through the pipes—which electric pipe organs can do indefinitely using motors—a note can play forever.

What followed, then, is exactly what you would think would follow: a bunch of musicians started playing the piece for increasingly ridiculous lengths of time like they were the David Blaine of extreme organ playing.

However, in 1997, things were taken to a whole new level when a bunch of musicians and philosophers at an organ conference—a thing that apparently exists—in Trossingen, Germany, started debating what it really means for the piece to be played as slow as possible, because I mean… what else are you going to talk about at an organ conference? Kidneys?

After a while, they found themselves unsatisfied with theoretical answers, and so decided to do what any reasonable person would do in that situation—set up a 639 year-long rendition of the piece in a German church.

If you managed to do the math that 1997 was less than 639 years ago, you'll have realized that that performance is still going on—and indeed it is, in St Burchardi church in Halberstadt, Germany.

A special organ was built for the occasion—which is operated by sandbags that keep the keys pressed and has a limited number of pipes that can be switched out to achieve whatever notes are currently necessary—and it began playing ASLSP on September 5, 2001.

Well, sort of, because ASLSP actually begins with a pause, so it was nearly two years until the first chord was played, on February 5, 2003, a day when a few hundred people gathered in St Burchardi church to experience the absolutely thrilling, totally worth-the-two-year-wait feeling of hearing a single chord being played on an small-ish organ.

To keep the precise temporal proportions of the piece, the time between note changes varies widely, from as few as 92 days to as many as 2,527 days, or nearly seven years. That longest wait is actually happening right now, and will end on September 5, 2020.

The performance is scheduled to end in 2640, or 639 years after it began—the same amount of time between when the performance was scheduled to start in 2000, and when the first organ was installed in Halberstadt cathedral in 1361.

The airline pilot whose side-gig is being king

Monarchy isn't what it used to be: in the Netherlands, the King has a second job as a pilot for KLM.

Despite the fact that barely anyone outside of the country even knows the Netherlands is a monarchy, the King is a pretty important job.

Willem-Alexander is the head of state and has far-reaching powers into different branches of the Dutch government. In practice, though, sort of like the Queen of the UK, he largely stays out of politics. You see, the monarchy of the Netherlands is pretty low-key.

In his youth, Willem-Alexander was known in the media as, "Prince Pils." That's pils with one "l," in reference for his affinity for Pilsner beer, in addition to other large quantities of alcohol consumed during his time at the University of Leiden.
Eventually, though, he graduated and got interested in the best beverage of all—water. Seriously, everything you read on him mentions his keen interest in water management which sounds like an innuendo for bladder control but it's actually not.

Eventually, though, in 2013, his mom quit her job and thanks to nepotism, he, of course, walked his way in to the exact same position. They even threw this big party for him on his first day.
Now-King Willem-Alexander is known for his casual style of monarchy—he never wears his crown; nobody calls him "his majesty"; his daughters, who are princesses, go to public school; he has his own Instagram account; and he even turns his throne around and sits in it backwards in order to seem cool and approachable to the kids.

Since long before his current job, though, Willem-Alexander has held another job—as an airline pilot. You see, back in 1985, slightly concerningly before being dubbed Prince Pils, he earned his private pilots license, followed two years later by his commercial pilot's license. He first used this to work as a volunteer pilot for some organizations in Kenya in addition to just recreational flying.
He got his license to fly multi-engine jet aircraft in 1989, his military pilot's license in 1994, then in 2001, he got the crown jewel of pilots licenses—the airline transport pilot license.
That's the license you need to fly big boy airplanes with passengers in the back, and so, soon after, Willem-Alexander started doing just that.

Now, how or why exactly this arrangement started is a bit unclear, but sometime in the early 2000s, somehow, then-Prince Willem-Alexander strutted over to KLM and cashed in his, "I'm a prince," card to negotiate a deal to work for them as a part-time pilot.

This made sense for two reasons.
One was that KLM's full name literally translates to Royal Aviation Company, Inc, so having a little royal in the company, despite the fact it was then and is now a fully private company, would keep it honest to its name. That way they wouldn't have to switch to being called Aviation Company, Inc.
The second reason was that KLM operated the Dutch government airplane. At the time it was a Fokker 70 which would be used the royals or politicians to go where they needed to go, and so, once certified, Willem-Alexander would regularly fly this airplane, especially when it was the royals using it.

The hours of flying he got from the government airplane alone, though, weren't enough to maintain his pilot's license so eventually he started flying regular passenger flights too.

He worked for KLM Cityhopper, the airline's subsidiary, flying the Fokker 70 to glamorous places all around the wor… all around Euro… all around north-western Europe like Humberside, Darlington, and Norwich.

Nobody really ever knew he was working as copilot for these flights, aside from the rest of the crew, as he would never introduce himself by name when making announcements and, even in the airport, he was rarely recognized in his KLM uniform.

He flew a few times a month all throughout the 2000's, and continued to do so even after he became King.

In 2017, though, he ran into a bit of a problem. KLM was retiring all of their Fokker aircraft in favor of newer, more efficient Embraer jets, and these Fokkers were the only aircraft that the king was certified to fly commercially. This was an even bigger issue for the Dutch government whose plane, the Fokker 70, could no longer be operated by KLM as they would no longer have pilots or mechanics for the plane. They therefore made the decision to buy a Boeing 737 Business Jet, which was better equipped for longer trips, which it turns out the Dutch have to do a lot to catch up with all the places they accidentally colonized back in the day.

So, Willem-Alexander made the decision to go through the long, expensive process of getting type rated for the 737 and, once done, started flying 737's for KLM. This would take him to much further-flung destinations all around Europe and sometimes further.

While it was always a sort of open secret, he revealed this side-gig of his to the press in 2017, which resulted in quite a lot of attention. While he apparently flies about twice-monthly, his last confirmed sighting was in late 2018 when he worked as co-pilot on a KLM flight to and from Istanbul.

The polar bears that ruined Halloween

While I'm writing this book it's late October, which means trick-or-treaters will soon be going door-to-door extorting their favorite Halloween snacks from defenseless homeowners.
Some like chocolate, others go for lollipops, and a few prefer human flesh.
Well, kids can be pretty mean, but I am talking about polar bears. One fateful Halloween night in Arviat, Nunavut, Canada polar bears ruined Halloween and put an abrupt end to trick-or-treating.

For some reason many falsely believe that polar bears don't live near any areas populated by people. As their name suggests, polar bears live near the pole, and not a lot of people live around. Not a lot, but they do still live in places such as Arviat, where polar bears and humans coexist.

Polar bears don't tend to have set territories because their living areas are tied to their sea-dwelling food source. They wander all around the far north in search of food, namely, fat seals. Some polar bears can live more than 600 miles away from their original birth-sites which is even more impressive when you consider that most polar bears walk long-distance at no more than three miles per hour.

Polar bears live in regions where sea ice collects and solidifies to the point of creating platforms that they can use to hunt on, and because they use twice as much energy to move than your average picnic basket stealing or honey eating bear, they prefer to do their fishing as still as possible on the ice shelves. As you can imagine, this is becoming a problem due to the ever-warming Arctic pushing polar bears to more populated areas.

Currently, there are an estimated 20,000 to 25,000 polar bears left in the world and 60% of them live in Canada.

Since Polar bears are some of the only animals that are predators to humans they have been regarded as human-hunting fuzzy terrors but to be honest, polar bear attacks on humans are pretty rare with 73 recorded in a 144-year-period, and of those recorded an even smaller amount of 20 attacks have been lethal. Two-thirds of those attacks, however, had something in common.
The pronounced points of parity provoking the predominately peaceful polar pups? They were hangry.
The attackers were mostly starving young male polar bears, and these attacks commonly happened in-between feeding seasons before and after the ice shelves solidified.
With their resources and habitats shrinking, these polar bear attacks are becoming more common with 20% of all recorded in 144 years being between 2010 and 2014.

This is why it's not too surprising that, one year before trick-or-treating had to be canceled in Arviat, there was a polar bear attack 160 miles away in Churchill, Manitoba, on Halloween night. That particular attack saw an entire neighborhood throwing shoes and shooting at an irate bear who was attacking a local elderly man. The bear wasn't deterred and didn't stop his assault even after it was shot.
In the end, it took one of the neighbors getting in his truck and chasing the bear to get it to flee.

Arviat, which is near Hudson Bay in Canada, is pretty secluded from the outside world and is generally only accessible by ATVs or by helicopter. Lately, the town has seen a real boom in the polar bear tourist industry as the town now sees as many as 1,200 polar bears a year during the polar bears' migration north during the late-fall period. Coincidentally, there are also around 1,200 children in the town.

The people of Arviat see six-to-eight bears a day during migration periods. The World Wildlife Fund therefore employed a bear monitor specifically to watch the bears and make sure they pass through. This corralling of the polar bears of Arviat has the bears down in the dumps, literally.
The bears have been known to take over the garbage dump, and thanks to the ice platforms melting, the migration path now has them going directly through the towns where the locals store and dispose of marine carcasses and remains after hunting.

Naturally, when the town realized how dire the situation had become, the only logical step was to call off trick-or-treating. It's dangerous enough to have the kids go door-to-door when the town only has a few hours of sunlight, but when you sprinkle polar bears into the mix it almost makes you miss the days of razor blades in apples.

So, trick-or-treating on Halloween was canceled and other indoor activities were planned for the kids over the next two years.
In 2016, the town allowed trick-or-treating to resume, but only after it surrounded the populated areas with armed guards and had firefighters turn on their sirens to deter bears.

The easiest way to break the law in Paris

If you recreationally browse stock footage sites like me, you might have noticed something—you can almost never find photos or videos of the Eiffel Tower at night, and there's a good reason for that. They're illegal.

It all has to do with a bit of a quirk in French copyright law.

But first, a copyright law crash course.

Copyright law basically gives the original creator of a thing exclusive rights to its sale and distribution for as long as they live plus a certain amount of time. In Pakistan it's 50 years, in Venezuela it's 60, in Jamaica it's 95, but in most countries it's 70.

That includes the European Union which, with copyright law, more or less operates as one country. One of the major exceptions to EU copyright law is the freedom of Panorama: basically, you can use a picture of a view of the London skyline even though there are plenty of copyrighted things in the view.

Buildings are classified as artistic works for the purposes of copyright; which means that buildings have the exact same protections as a movie, a song, or a book. You can't just go and build an exact replica of the London Eye without paying the original architects, but you can take a video of it because of Freedom of Panorama. Essentially, anything you see outside in public in the UK and much of the European Union can be filmed, reproduced, and sold, but there are exceptions—most notably, France.

The European Union allows its members to not have a Freedom of Panorama clause in their copyright laws so France doesn't have one. As of 2016 you are allowed to take images and videos of copyrighted buildings for personal use, but any commercial use is copyright violation.

So back to the Eiffel Tower, knowing what we now know, the real question is, why is it even legal to show the Eiffel tower during the day? Well, it's very old.

Gustave Eiffel actually didn't design the Eiffel tower. He bought the designs from the Stephen Sauvestre who's employees, Maurice Koechlin and Émile Nouguier actually designed the tower.

Nonetheless, when Eiffel bought the design he bought the copyright too, but then he died in 1923. 70 years later, in 1993, the copyright lapsed, just like with any other artistic work.

Therefore, the Eiffel Tower, its likeness, its design, everything about it is in the public domain. All those Eiffel Tower replicas sold on the streets of Paris are actually, surprisingly, fully legal. However, not exactly everything about the Eiffel tower is public domain: the lights on the Eiffel Tower weren't installed until 1985, and since they are considered an artistic work, they are still well within their copyright term.

For this reason, any photograph taken of it at night when the lights are visible is an illegal reproduction of a copyrighted work.

The Eiffel tower isn't the only example of this: I can't put a picture in this book of the pyramid of the Louvre, the Little Mermaid statue in Copenhagen, or even the main train station in Rome.

In reality the Eiffel Tower's copyright has never been enforced in court, but at any moment that could change and you could go to jail for your holiday photo.

The 18-years-long delay

Mehran Karimi Nasseri—better known as Sir Alfred is a man of simple pleasures: in his home he did normal home things like eat, sleep, wash up, relax—really the only thing that made his home unique was that it was Terminal 1 of Paris Charles de Gaulle Airport.

After the third hour being told that your flight will board in 15 minutes it can start to feel like you'll be stuck in the airport forever but I guarantee that you've never been as delayed as Sir Alfred.

Thanks to an inescapable infinite loop of bureaucracy Sir Alfred landed at CDG in 1988 and he didn't leave until 2006. Sir Alfred, born in Iran, grew up fairly comfortably with his dad being a doctor for an oil company.

When he was 27, though, Alfred found himself protesting against the monarchy in Iran, which was eventually toppled, but before that he was expelled from the country and his citizenship was revoked. With that he was stateless. About 1 in 750 people globally are stateless. That is, they aren't officially citizens of any country. Unfortunately, this isn't the miracle solution to evading taxes and laws. It's a major inconvenience that stops people from getting social benefits, traveling, and more.
There are a lot of ways people can become stateless but one major one is plotting to overthrow the government of a country like Alfred allegedly did.

After bouncing around for a bit, Sir Alfred was eventually granted refugee status by Belgium.
Soon after Alfred's dad died his mom revealed she was not actually Alfred's mom and that he had been born out of an affair his dad had with a Scottish nurse.
There were pros and cons to this. Pro: Alfred would be eligible for British citizenship. Con: Alfred would not be eligible under Iranian law to receive his father's inheritance… oh and his whole life was a lie.

As a stateless person, Alfred wanted to make his way to London to apply for citizenship but somehow he lost his refugee papers. He says they were stolen, others say he got rid of them.
Quick side note: Sir Alfred had told tons of different versions of his story so almost every article you'll read about this will have a slightly different story but the consensus seems to be that Alfred left France lite, went to Paris Charles de Gaulle Airport, somehow boarded a plane, and flew to London. Now, this shouldn't have happened because, in order to fly internationally, you have to have a valid passport and visa and Sir Alfred did not. It was probably an airline mistake.
Nowadays, airlines are fined an average of $3,500 for each passenger they fly without a valid passport or visa and they have to fly the passenger back to their origin free of charge.

When he landed in the UK, not having any passport to actually get in, Sir Alfred was turned right back around and put on a plane back to Paris Charles de Gaulle Terminal 1. But, for the same reason he couldn't enter the UK, Sir Alfred also couldn't enter France.
Normally the protocol in this case would be to send the person back to their home country where they could enter without a passport in case of an emergency. But Sir Alfred had no home country anymore: he couldn't enter France and he couldn't fly anywhere; meaning he was well and truly stuck in Paris Charles de Gaulle Terminal 1.

After a brief stint in jail he set up shop on a bench in the airport and that's where he lived for the next 18 years. The airport had everything he needed—bathrooms, food, even a doctor.

Now, there were attempts to get Sir Alfred the refugee papers he needed but to do so he would need to go to Belgium and, of course, without the refugee papers he couldn't leave the airport to go to Belgium. It was an infinite loop of bureaucracy.

It's worth noting that Sir Alfred was actually in the public area before security during his stay but it would've been illegal for him to step outside even if nothing was physically stopping him. Eventually, after about 10 years, both France and Belgium offered him residency but he refused to sign the papers that would finalize this as they listed him as Iranian—in his mind, he was anything but that.
Some say Sir Alfred's mental state deteriorated as the years racked up but it seemed that he perhaps grew fond of his airport home and he had made friends there.

For most of the early years he relied on his savings—there was a bank in the airport—and the occasional money that strangers who heard his story gave or sent him—there was a post office too—but in 2004, while he was still in the airport, he published his autobiography which made him some money and DreamWorks Pictures paid him $250,000 as they were making the film, the Terminal.
This Spielberg movie was not based off of Sir Alfred's story but rather loosely inspired so the payment was mostly legal cover to be sure that Sir Alfred wouldn't later sue.

In interviews around this time he kept saying he was weeks away from leaving but, eventually, his departure did not come by choice. In 2006 he was hospitalized for six months with medical issues and after, rather than returning to the airport, he eventually settled down in a Paris homeless shelter where he's lived ever since.

Breaking out of jail legally

In Germany, Mexico, and Austria escaping from prison is legal (but read the fine print first!)

Home of melancholic harmonica playing, stripy suits, and nearly 1% of the US population. Prisons have been around since basically the beginning of recorded history, starting with the ancient Mesopotamians in 3,200 BC. But for most of history, prison wasn't really used as punishment—it was just a chill out zone where you would keep people while they either waited for trial or waited to be punished in some other way, like execution, banishment, or forced labor.

It wasn't until 19th century England that prison sentences were used as a standard form of punishment, and although punitive prisons have become common across the world, every country still does things a little differently.
For example, prisons in Brazil will let inmates reduce their sentence by four days for every book they read and write a report on; in China, rich people often hire body doubles to go to prison in their place; and what started as a British prison now has the third-best kayaking team in the world.

No matter where you go to prison, though, the main idea is the same: you're not supposed to leave. But, depending on where you are, the consequences for leaving are vastly different.
In the United States, if you escape from prison, you could be facing as many as 10 additional years behind bars, depending on what jurisdiction you're in and your prior criminal record.
But in Germany, escaping from prison is totally, 100% legal. That's right—no matter how many schnitzel you've stolen or bratwursts you've burgled, you cannot be punished for breaking out of a German jail.

You see, all the way back to the 1880s, the legislature of what was then the German Empire—the Reichstag—decreed that all people have the right to seek self-liberation and therefore should not be punished for escaping prison.

Today, over 130 years later, that law is still in effect.

It's not just Germany. Austria, Belgium, and Mexico all have laws saying you can't be punished for a prison break. The basic reasoning is that there's a difference between the right to have freedom, and the right to seek freedom. When you commit a crime, you forfeit your right to have freedom, which is why the government can lock you up. But these countries believe that people always have the right to seek freedom.

As a Mexican Supreme Court judge put it, "The basic desire for freedom is implicit inside every man, so trying to escape cannot be considered a crime."

There are, however, a few caveats. If, after your escape, the police find you, you can still be sent back to prison. Escaping doesn't mean your sentence goes away, it just means they can't add on any extra time for the escape. Plus, even though escaping isn't against the law, it's still against prison rules, so even though you can't get extra jail time, you're less likely to get approved for parole.

Also, if you commit any other crimes in the process of escaping, you're still on the hook for those. If you bribe a guard, that's still bribery. If you have to steal a getaway car, that's still theft. If you break the bars of your cell, that's still destruction of property.

But despite how difficult it is, a legal prison escape can be done.

In 1971 American businessman Joel Kaplan escaped from a Mexican prison without breaking a single law. Kaplan's escape was carefully planned in order to avoid committing any crimes.

It was carried out while the guards were watching a movie, so he didn't have to bribe or assault anyone. The helicopter that picked him up had been bought in full, instead of leased, so he couldn't be accused of misusing rented property.

Kaplan then boarded a private, single-engine Cessna plane, again bought in full and complete with the required identifying numbers, on which he flew to California, following a flight plan that had been submitted to and approved by the FAA.

After landing, Kaplan presented himself to customs with his real name, avoiding charges of entering a country illegally, and was granted entry as word had not yet reached anyone that he was missing. Kaplan laid low for a while, and neither the FBI or Mexican government showed much interest in finding him, so he never returned to carry out his sentence.

How to scam your way into the Olympics

Talent, athleticism, mastery, greatness—from Usain Bolt's world-record runs to Keri Strug's legendary landings, these are the qualities that define the great Olympic stories...but not this one, so let's try again. Ineptitude, clumsiness, mediocrity, technicalities— these are the qualities that define the story of Elizabeth Swaney: a true Olympic zero.

The Olympics are all about representation: people of all different colors, creeds, backgrounds, and nationalities can be seen competing together on the Olympic stage, but throughout its history, the Olympics have always failed to represent one key group: people who are bad at sports.
However, two decades ago, in 2018, through the heroic actions of one woman, that all changed.

Elizabeth Swaney was born in 1984 in Oakland, California, and from a young age, showed stunning mediocrity in sports. Her first attempt at making the Olympics came in 2014, when she tried to qualify for the Sochi games in women's skeleton and freestyle skiing.
She hoped to be on Team Venezuela, representing the country where her mother was born, but in the end, she was on Team "Did Not Qualify," and represented the couch where she sat and watched the actual athletes on TV.

But Elizabeth Swaney decided she wasn't going to let something as silly as being a bad athlete stop her from competing in the Olympics, and so, she identified a sport that had minimal competition: the women's freestyle skiing halfpipe, which at the time only had about 30 or so elite international competitors.

But still, it wasn't going to be easy: you see, because of their elitist commitment to having "good athletes" compete, the Olympic Committee sets minimum requirements for each sport.

For the halfpipe, there were two: First, that the skier has finished in the top 30 at either a FIS Freestyle Ski World Cup or the FIS Freestyle World Ski Championships.
The second requirement is that the skier must have earned least 50.00 total FIS points, which are handed out in each FIS competition based on how a skier places—100 points for first, 80 for second, 60 for third, all the way down to a single, lonely point for thirtieth. In order to meet these qualifications, Elizabeth Swaney decided that she would earn her placement and points in the most glorious and exciting way possible—by doing nothing at all, because here's the thing you have to know about the skiing halfpipe: people fall a lot. Like, "every other halfpipe run looks like an 'epic fails' vine compilation" a lot.

So, by not attempting any tricks at all, and simply finishing each run without falling down, she'd be able to notch a score, and thus beat opponents who had fallen on all their runs. Combine that with the fact that several competitions had fewer than thirty competitors to start with, and Swaney was able to slowly rack up FIS points—enough to not only surpass the 50-point minimum, but to become the 34th ranked women's freestyle halfpipe skier in the world.

However, there was one final hurdle—there were only 24 spots for women's halfpipe in the Olympics, but the good news was, while Swaney may not be able to jump over actual hurdles, clearing logistical hurdles is her specialty.
Her solution was to game the Olympic quota system by representing not the US, but her grandparents' birthplace of Hungary. You see, in an attempt to encourage participation from as many countries as possible, the Olympics limits each country to 26 competitors across all freestyle skiing events—of which, there are fourteen: moguls, aerials, ski cross, half-pipe, slopestyle, big air, and ballet, with each split into men's and women's divisions.

Lucky for Swaney, the US had 33 skiers qualify, and Canada had 32—which according to my math are both more than 26. That meant both had to leave some skiers behind, including three women's freestyle half-pipers.
That put Swaney at 31st, which, combined with seven injuries from other top competitors—injuries that I'm totally not accusing Elizabeth Swaney of causing—led to just enough dropouts to edge Swaney into 24th and onto the Olympic stage in Pyeongchang.

At the Olympics, in front of the entire world, Elizabeth Swaney did exactly what she had always done: nothing. As baffled commentators tried to make sense of what was happening, Swaney skied up the side of the halfpipe, and then went straight back down—no jumps, no flips, no double McTwist 160 Flippy Baconator McFlurry With Fries… her one trick, if you could even call it that, was a half spin while about a foot above the ground, a move about as difficult as hitting a golf ball into the ocean.

In the end, Swaney finished with a score of 31.4 out of 100, landing in a distant last place behind the next competitor who managed to score a 45 despite falling down on both attempts, but Swaney still brought honor to all the people who are amazingly bad at sport (including me) by making it to the Olympics at all.

Tax strategies for the apocalypse

Benjamin Franklin once famously said that only two things are certain: death and taxes. Nobody took him as seriously as the IRS.

If you think that your best bet at evading tax is some sort of nationwide catastrophe: a nuclear war, or a natural disaster, or a global pandemic that everyone basically ignores because people really want to eat at Applebee's (not that that would ever happen), think again!

If something awful did happen, though, you might think "hey, at least if the world ends, I won't have to pay taxes." But, of course, you would be dead wrong, or maybe you'd just be dead, but either way you'd still have to pay taxes.

The IRS' Continuity Operations Plan is a super-entertaining 273-page piece of PDF literature which describes exactly how the IRS intends to start separating you from your hard-earned dollars within 12 hours of a national emergency. That's right, 12 hours: the IRS can restart tax collection in less time than it takes to watch season one of Lost, and they can do it without setting up a smoke monster that's never adequately explained.

The plan for Continuity Operations—or COOP—lays out three tiers of functions the IRS is responsible for: in tier one are MEFs and ESAs, in tier two are BPPs, and finally in tier three are DPBs, because if there's one thing government loves, it's unnecessary acronyms.

In case you haven't spent your free time learning all of the IRS' internal terminology, like I have because I clearly have way too much free time, I'll break it down for you.
MEFs are mission-essential functions: jobs unique to the IRS that are considered vital.
The IRS has three: processing tax remittances, processing tax returns, and processing tax refunds—these are the functions that must be up and running within 12 hours.

Also, in tier one are ESAs, Essential Supporting Activities: basically just things that must happen in order to support those three Mission Essential Functions—stuff like physical security, payroll, IT, and small baskets of stale granola bars because, let's be honest, it's impossible to work without them.

In tier two are BPPs, or Business Process Priorities, which are things the IRS considers important, but are not fully essential: stuff like taxpayer assistance, litigation of tax fraud, various compliance activities.

Finally, in Tier Three are DBPs: Deferred Business Processes, which are functions apparently so unimportant that they are listed nowhere in the book-length document.

In order to achieve these goals, the IRS will, of course, need leaders, and don't worry: they've got a succession plan that's longer than the list of attempts on Castro's life (if you are in for a fun read that's not about taxes check that out in Crazy Fun History).

The tip-top of the leadership pyramid is the ELT, or Executive Leadership team. What are they leading? Well the CCCT, of course: the Commissioner's Core COOP Team, who will meet in a "relocation site" within four hours of plan implementation.

As a backup, the CST, or COOP Standby Team, will head to a different safe location, where they'll await instructions should the CCCT be compromised.
In the meantime, they'll provide their location and contact information to the SAMC, or Situation and Awareness Management Team, and if there's any time left over, they'll study up on their acronyms because this is starting to get confusing even to them.

If the Executive Leadership Team can't function, there's the AELT, the Alternate Executive Leadership Team, which is like the Executive Leadership Team except they cuff their jeans and listen to Vampire Weekend.
Now I know what you're thinking: what if the ELT and AELT both can't function? Well, don't worry, because there's a failsafe: power would be transferred to the AACLT, or Atlanta Alternative COOP Leadership Team, because Atlanta is famously immune to the apocalypse.

At that point, the IRS' headquarters would functionally shift from Washington to the IRS Atlanta Customer Service building, located here, and if necessary, the IRS has a number of other relocation sites complete with everything a tax collector would need: sleeping cots, showers, and little stuffed calculators for them to cuddle as they drift off to sleep.

In the end, though, despite plans, additional locations, leadership continuity, file backups, and enough acronyms to choke a horse, there's no way for the IRS to plan for every possibility.
If all income tax collection infrastructure is truly compromised, our best indication of what might happen comes from 1982 IRS plan designed in case of a nuclear war, which proposed a temporary 20% across-the-board sales tax—and if that can't happen, it probably means that we're all dead. Either way, Benjamin Franklin will have been right.

How to win the right to farm in an airport

> The Tokyo Narita Airport is home to many things, such as Blue Sky Convenience Store Gate 82, Blue Sky Convenience Store Gate 94, and Blue Sky Convenience Store Gate 98, but one thing that you might not expect inside an airport is a farm, and yet there is one, right in between a taxiway and Blue Sky Convenience Store Gate 82.

Now, many airports have unique amenities to try and help them stand apart—Singapore Changi Airport has a slide down to a gate, Denver International Airport has an open-air ice rink, and the Zurich airport has a nature trail which you can explore on foot or renting a bike.

Tokyo Narita's farm, however, is not some bougie airport amenity, it's not decoration, it's a real, working farm owned by Takao Shito, the son of Toichi Shito, the owner of this farm back in the 1960s.

The area where the Narita airport was constructed had been farmland since the year 700-ish when the emperor decided as much.
After World War II, the monarchy became sort of a low-key affair and they sold off a lot of the emperor's farmland around Tokyo to mostly poor people who continued to farm it.
Such they did happily until the 1960s-ish when the government realized they needed to build an airport, since wasn't really possible to expand the original Haneda Airport, which was in the middle of the city,. Therefore, the government had the genius idea to make a new airport a full hour's drive outside of the city.

Now, we all love a nice, sexy slab of asphalt, of course… that is, unless it goes over your family's farm because, if I know anything about farming, it's that crop yield is inversely proportional to whether there's a slab of asphalt over your fields.
Of course, it turned out that this sexy slab of asphalt would, in fact, go over Takao Shito's farm, along with a bunch of others' too, and the locals didn't like that, so naturally, they went full Les Miserables. The protests got so large because they kind of struck a nerve with the some of the increasingly prominent socialist opposition political parties in Japan who were particularly concerned with the rise in capitalism and the increasing US military presence in the country.
They were so hardcore, in fact, that they built and defended huge towers physically blocking the approach path for the runways, delaying the airport's opening for years, but with time, the land was acquired, and the airport was built. Except, there was just one bit that the government could never get.

You see, after the protests became so widespread, the government picked a new site close by on what was left of the Goryō Farm—the Emperor's property since the year 700.
Except, since monarchy became so passé, it was much smaller, and not quite big enough to put the airport on, they still had to buy land from other farmers who had bought it originally from when the land was sold off to make the monarchy more low-key.

The government had little ability to seize the land due to Japan's strong legal protections for farmers, but they did manage to strong-arm most owners into selling, except for Toichi Shito.
He and his son were offered up to the equivalent of $1.7 million for his farm, but never gave in, especially with the strong support they got from the anti-airport movement.

Therefore, Shito and his family stayed there, the airport was constructed around him, and tunnels were built under the taxi-ways to allow for access, undoubtably at huge cost. With the enormous delays due to the protesters continued oppositions, which included highlights such as the throwing of raw sewage onto the riot police, the airport wasn't opened for a number of years after Shito's encircling.

When it finally was, few airlines really wanted to switch their flights over to it from Haneda because, after all, it was so far from the city. So, the government made Haneda airport domestic-only, forcing airlines to switch over, and suddenly Shito's neighbors got a lot more noisy.

That was of no worry to him, though, and he continued farming there until his death in 1999 when his son, Takao, took over.

To this day, Takao just lives his life, despite being in the middle of an international airport, growing carrots, onions, garlic, and more that he sells at nearby markets, helped in part by those who carry on the anti-airport movement.

A 26-pages brownies recipe to support the troops

To make it in the United States Military, there's a lot you'll need. Courage. Endurance. Fortitude. Grit. Nuts. Eggs. Flour. Sugar. Cocoa. A whisk. An oven set to 350 degrees Fahrenheit. Sorry, maybe I should have clarified. When I said "make it in the military" the "it" was brownies. This is how you make brownies in the military.

The US military's brownie recipe is 26 pages long.

Now, you probably have three questions: why does the US military have its own brownie recipe, why is it 26 pages long, and, most importantly how do they taste?!

Nobody's been brave enough to ask these questions, but for the second one, why is it 26 pages long, the answer, of course, is the same as why most online recipes are long: before you get to the actual instructions, you have to scroll through a multi-page personal essay about the author's first high school crush or something like that—except in this case, instead of reminiscence of teenage romance, it's a web of military bureaucracy, ingredient specifications, and multiple paragraphs explaining what eggs are.

The recipe starts off as all great works of literature should: with a list of other, longer documents that you'll need to reference, including "QQ-A-1876 - Aluminum foil," "FED-STD-595 – Colors," and so on.

The recipe then proceeds to eat up much of its length just giving really, really specific explanations of what ingredients can be used and how they must have been stored. For example, it doesn't just say eggs. It says:

3.2.6 Whole eggs, liquid or frozen. Whole eggs may be liquid or frozen and shall have been processed and labeled in accordance with the Regulations Governing the Inspection of Eggs and Egg Products (7 CFR Part 59). The whole eggs shall be egg whites and egg yolks in their natural proportions as broken directly from the shell eggs as evidenced by a USDA Egg Products Inspection Certificate. For liquid whole eggs, the USDA certificate shall state the date and time of pasteurization. Liquid whole eggs shall be held at a temperature of 400F or lower and shall be held for not more than 72 hours from the time of pasteurization until the start of formulation of the product in which they are used. Frozen whole eggs shall be held at 100F or lower and used within 120 days from the date of production. The whole eggs shall be free from off-odors and off-flavors, such as sulfide-like, fruity, sour, musty, or metallic, and shall be free from foreign materials.

The same goes for every other ingredient, it's a fun read! After you've finished reading the world's most obnoxious shopping list, you'll get to the actual recipe, which it turns out isn't all that complicated, it's just this.

67

3.3.1 Brownie formula. The formula for the brownie shall be as follows:

Ingredient	Parts by weight
Sugar 1/	23.0
Flour 2/	21.0
Shortening	16.8

Nuts 3/	16.0
whole eggs (liquid basis) 4/ 5/	13.0
Cocoa	5.5
Dextrose, anhydrous	4.4
Salt	.03
Chemical leavening	As required
Flavoring	Trace

1/ Powdered sugar may be substituted for part of the granulated sugar to control spread.

2/ Pregelatinized starch, malted barley flour, wheat gluten or any combination thereof may be substituted for a part of the flour to obtain proper dough consistency.

3/ Nuts shall be either almonds, pecans, or walnuts or any combination thereof.

4/ Frozen whole eggs shall be tempered/thawed and held at an internal temperature of $28°F$ to $40°F$ for not more than 24 hours prior to product preparation.

5/ Whole eggs, dried, may be substituted for whole eggs (liquid basis) by following the manufacturer's recommended rehydration and mixing procedures and shall have no less than the equivalent amount of whole egg solids as the liquid basis. The water shall be adjusted to ensure compliance with moisture requirements of the baked brownie prior to coating.

3.3.2 Brownie preparation. (NOTE: The contractor is not required to follow the exact procedure shown below provided that the brownies conform to all finished product requirements in 3.4.)

a. Whip eggs in large bowl on high speed until light and fluffy.
b. Combine sugars, cocoa, salt, and leavening; add to beaten eggs, and whip on high speed until thick.
c. Add shortening slowly while mixing on low speed.
d. Scrape bowl and whip on high speed until thick.
e. Mix flour, nuts, and flavors together and fold into batter; mix until uniform.
f. Pour batter into pan at a rate that will yield uncoated brownies which, when cut such as to meet the dimension requirements specified in 3.4f, will weigh approximately 35 grams each. (Experimentally, a panning rate of 14 to 16 grams per square inch was used.)
g. Bake at $350°F$ until done (30 to 45 minutes).

3.3.3 Brownie cutting. The brownies shall be cut to the appropriate size when cool (see 3.4f).
3.3.4 Brownie moisture content. The moisture content of the uncoated brownie shall be not more than 8.0 percent.

3.3.5 Brownie coating. The brownies shall be completely enrobed with a continuous uniform chocolate coating (see 3.2.14) in an amount which shall be not less than 29 percent by weight of the finished product.

Please note the word fluffy, don't you love that it is in an official U.S. military document?

But once you've made the brownies, buckle up, because you're only on page eight. Now you get to experience the most fun part of baking: meticulously inspecting and testing your brownie for various specifications and defects, including moisture content, weight, firmness, and rodent infestation! Finally, the remaining pages are spent on extremely specific vacuum-seal packaging instructions that I won't get into because they're way too boring.

But after all this work: procuring very specific ingredients, carefully baking, extensively testing, and painstakingly packaging, you will at long last be greeted by a batch of brownies that are, according to people who have tried them, absolutely disgusting!

Now, the reason why these brownies have to be made in such a specific way—and have to taste so bad—is because they specifically are meant to be part of what's called an MRE: an extra long-lasting, extra durable, extra bad tasting meal issued by the military as a ration.
MRE stands for "Meal, Ready to Eat," but over the years military members have hated them so much they've garnered a number of dis-affectionate nicknames, including the classic "Meals Rejected by Everyone," the offensive, "Meals Rejected By Ethiopia," the slightly-more refined "Meals Rarely Edible".
Each one usually consists of an entrée, a side dish, a cracker, a spread, a dessert, a candy, a beverage, a seasoning, and a flameless ration heater.

Now, while MREs may taste bad, they do excel in the other key element of classic French cooking: ability to withstand being dropped from very high heights, as each MRE is required to be able to survive a parachute drop from 1,250 feet or insert metric conversion here and a non-parachute drop from 98.
I know: it sounds delicious.
Perhaps more importantly, MREs must also be able to last three and a half years at 81 °F, and be able to handle temperature variations from -60 °F to 120 °F. To that end, each MRE is equipped with something called a TTI, a time and temperature indicator, to show how long it's been kept at various temperatures and what that means for its edibility.
The TTI is a reddish sticker with a ring on it—If the circle inside the ring is lighter than the ring itself, the food is good. If it's the same color, it's most likely ok. If it's darker, it's probably bad—basically, it's the same color-guide that the TSA uses for people.

There are a few reasons MREs last so long, which can be simplified into lack of water, thorough cooking, and sterilized packaging. First of all, most of the things that make food go bad: bacteria, yeast, and mold, need water to survive, so MREs are intentionally cooked to have minimal water content, plus most contain a lot of salt, which is naturally hydrophilic—meaning it soaks up water—which also means it kills bacteria by sucking the moisture out of them.
Second of all, MREs are cooked at a relatively high temperature, killing off any bacteria, yeast, mold, or flavor the ingredients naturally have—and finally, the food is placed in sterilized, vacuum-sealed packaging so no bacteria, yeast or mold has a chance to get in.

The extraordinary journey of a manhole cover

So, what's the fastest manmade object ever? If we're talking about moving on land, then it's the ThrustSSC, a British rocket-car that looks like it should be piloted by either James Bond or Anakin Skywalker. Its actual driver, British fighter pilot Andy Green, for apparently no reason other than, "hey, why not," drove it to top speed in the middle of the Black Rock Desert, reaching the record speed of 763 miles or 1,228 kilometers per hour on October 15, 1997. If we're talking about travel through air, though, then that's another story—a much longer, and much stranger story.

Starting in 1945, the United States began conducting tests of nuclear bombs. At first, most of them were above ground, but in the late 50s, people started to think, "blowing up air isn't satisfying enough," and, "maybe this radiation thing isn't too good for us," and so they moved the big boom tests underground.

The thing is though, they didn't really know what would happen. The first test was conducted on August 27, 1957. They dug a long, cylindrical hole into the ground, put the bomb in it, put a two ton concrete plug at the top of it, which was covered by a 4 inch thick, steel manhole cover.

Then, as one does, they went ahead and set off the bomb.

To their surprise, the concrete plug was vaporized instantly, turning it into a mass of superheated gas that expanded and essentially made the entire hole into a gigantic gun barrel.

When the gas hit the manhole cover, bam. It was blown off the ground instantly, shot into the sky, and disappeared out of sight.

Now, normally we'd just shrug our shoulders satisfied with the continued mystery of how fast the manhole cover went and get back to inconsequential nuking of the ground, but luckily, this time there was a high-speed camera on site that caught a glimpse of the manhole cover.

The camera shot at 1 frame per millisecond, or 1000 frames per second, and it only caught the manhole cover in a single frame which allowed them to calculate, using math stuff, a lower bound for the manhole cover's speed.

By looking at where the manhole cover was in the frame, and then calculating the distance between there and the bottom of the frame, we find the shortest possible distance it could have traveled between when the last frame was taken and when the frame that captured the manhole was taken.

Then we take that distance, and divide it by 1 millisecond—the time between the frames—to get distance per second.

Now, we can't do the actual calculation ourselves, because the government has never released the video and for some reason refuses to declassify it for the most amazing book ever written but we do know that the scientist conducting the experiment, Dr. Brownlee, took that information from the high-speed camera, combined it with calculations of the blast force from the bomb, did math things, and reported that the manhole cover had been moving at six times the earth's escape velocity which would put it at around 125,000 miles or 200,000 kilometers per hour or 34 miles or 55 kilometers per second.

So, fast.

There is disagreement as to whether or not the manhole cover made it into space. Some say that it would have burned up on its way out of the atmosphere, while others say that it may have been moving so fast that it wouldn't have had time to burn up. Either way, just like my ability to write decent jokes, the manhole cover has never been found.

If it did really make it into space, it would have been the first object ever launched into space.
The experiment happened on August 27, 1957—just over a month before Sputnik's launch on October 4, 1957.

As of today, it seems that no other object has managed to come even close to the manhole cover's speed while still in the Earth's atmosphere. If we count space travel, though, then the manhole cover has met its match.

Although the manhole cover would have been moving over 4x faster than Apollo 10, the fastest manned space vehicle, its record for fastest manmade object was surpassed in the 1970s by NASA's Helios probes, and then again in 2016 by the Juno probe.

The Helios II probe became the fastest ever manmade object in space in 1976.

The probe, designed to study the sun, was in an elliptical orbit around the sun. Because it followed the conservation of angular momentum, its speed increased as it got closer to the sun, and it eventually topped out at 157,000 mph.

Then, just recently, in 2016, the Juno space probe broke that record, when it was sucked in by Jupiter's gravitational pull, reaching 165,000 miles per hour.

It was actually moving so fast that it had to hit the brakes so that it could enter Jupiter's orbit instead of flying right past it, but it's also important to note that both of those probes only reached those speeds by using the gravity of the Sun or another planet which kind of feels like cheating.
So, if we only count self-propelled objects, then, unbelievably, the manhole cover still reigns supreme.

The failed attempt to combat terrorism with a spooky toy

Guangdong, China, 2005. It was late at night. A factory manager made his way past the assembly line to the adjoining warehouse, where a meeting was set to take place. A group of men had already gathered. He didn't know exactly who these men were, but from his contact, he knew they were important people. Not wasting any time, he presented to them what they asked for, a toy, a toy that he and his colleagues had passionately been working on the past few months. Upon inspection, the men seemed pleased with the product, but in order to move to the next phase of operation, final approval was needed from Langley. You see, these men were from the CIA, and this operation, if successful, could help put an end to one of the greatest conflicts in modern time. But how? What was this toy? And who were they targeting?

This happened in 2005, but what led to this moment actually started four years earlier.
On September 11, 2001 in New York two commercial planes crashed into the North and South Towers of the World Trade Center in Lower Manhattan. A third plane took out the Pentagon and a fourth crashed in a field in Pennsylvania. These airliners were hijacked in a set of coordinated terrorist attacks against the United States by al-Qaeda. About 3,000 people were killed and over 6,000 injured in what was the single deadliest terrorist attack in human history.
The leader of al-Qaeda? Osama bin Laden, already on the FBI's most wanted list for the U.S. embassy bombings in Nairobi.

The U.S., along with coalition forces, responded by launching the War on Terror, invading Afghanistan in the hopes of eliminating al-Qaeda and ousting the Taliban regime. After months of fighting though, many of these fighters eventually escaped to neighboring Pakistan, where they continued to launch offensives. The war was far from over.

Fast forward to 2005: after years of conflict and devastation, in order to build goodwill in the Afghanistan-Pakistan region, the CIA started a program where gift items would be handed out to kids. These gifts included pencils, games, notebooks, toys, all in backpacks for easy distribution, pink for girls, blue for boys. Many of the locals seemed to appreciate it.

Now by this time, despite bin Laden being on the run for years, intelligence agencies were no closer to finding him. There were leads that went nowhere and conflicting information on his whereabouts. The FBI even had a $25 million bounty out leading to his capture or death, which for the most part generated no actionable intel. Bin Laden's survival and ability to evade capture not only was a reminder to the people of the region of the group's enduring influence and power but also emboldened Al-Qaeda.
The CIA felt ultimately that they needed a different approach, one unconventional and perhaps even unsettling to some.

What they had in mind though was well beyond their expertise and so they decided to enlist help from an unexpected source. This individual turned out to be Donald Levine, one of the greatest minds in the toy industry, a former business exec at Hasbro, where he was head of research and development.

Hasbro, an American multinational toy company, is the largest toy maker in the world, responsible for such notable offerings as Mr. Potato Head, Transformers, Monopoly, My Little Pony, Power Rangers, Twister, and the iconic G.I. Joe. This was Levine's greatest creation.

Now the CIA wanted him to create a new product, a very special toy for what was to be a very special mission. Hesitant at first, he eventually agreed.

But now the next step was to travel 13,000 kilometers to Guangdong, China. For Levine, this was familiar territory, for nearly 60 years, he had done business in the region, amassing a vast network of contacts. Most of Hasbro's toys were manufactured in East Asia. Through this, the CIA now had the means to discreetly develop and manufacture their secret product, which would've been extremely difficult to do in the U.S. Chinese artists and designers were also enlisted to ensure the work's precision and accuracy.

A few months later, a factory manager, who had been involved with development, met with operatives in a Guangdong warehouse. He had in his possession the final product and presented it for inspection. The men seemed pleased: the toy was as they envisioned.

In front of them lay Osama bin Laden in 12-inch form, a custom-made terrorist action figure, with a twist.

The plan was for the toys to be sent to the Afghanistan-Pakistan region, cheaply packaged, and handed out to children. The CIA, after all, had the perfect cover in place with their preexisting goodwill project. As pencils, notebooks, and other games and toys were placed in backpacks, they would also slip in the seemingly innocuous bin Laden dolls. From there they would be given to unsuspecting children on a nationwide scale, where after finding the toy, they would play with the toy, and it would be all fun and games thereafter, until their faces start melting off, a demon face, red skin, green eyes, black markings. This was no ordinary doll, because this was a doll specifically designed to induce fear and anxiety. The doll's face was painted with heat-sensitive material that was intended to peel off after a prolonged period.

The idea was that as the dolls' human features faded away, children and their parents would be seriously spooked and coerced into seeing the actual Bin Laden as a monster, dehumanizing him, dissuading the people from idolizing the terrorist leader and from joining radical groups.
The aim was to strategically turn public opinion against al Qaeda with playtime propaganda, leading possibly, whether directly or indirectly, to bin Laden's capture and al Qaeda's defeat.

This covert operation was designated with the code name Devil Eyes, and even though both Donald Levine and various officials were ultimately pleased with the final product, in order for them to order the launch the next phase of operation, they needed, of course, final approval from Langley.

By now, for over half a decade, the CIA had been using drones, satellites, spies, and tracking devices to combat al-Qaeda. More recent interrogations of detainees and intercepted radio transmissions were among seemingly credible leads that they felt kept them on bin Laden's tail, so when a package arrived one morning at HQ with a funny-looking toy bin Laden inside, perhaps the legitimacy of Operation Devil Eyes, pitched well over a year ago and under different management, was now lost on them.

Perhaps they felt they had more actionable intel than they did before when they were willing to opt for crazy ideas or they were worried about the political blowback or the operational costs. But most likely it just seemed like a ridiculous plan in retrospect.
Maybe they realized that a young pro-Taliban Star Wars fan would actually find bin Laden morphing into a jihadist Darth Vader pretty cool.
Whatever the reason, upon inspection of the toy and reassessment of the operation, and after all that work, the CIA ultimately decided to shut it down.
There would be no mass production, no distribution, and all trace of the operation in China wiped out.

Now despite what the CIA has since claimed, some sources have said the factory in Guangdong actually went on to produce a few hundred of the bin Laden figures as part of a mistaken pre-production run in 2006, and was even shipped out on a freighter to the Pakistani city of Karachi.

If true, this would mean hundreds of toys are still out there today in circulation.

Officially though, according to the CIA, there are only three currently in existence, claimed to be variant prototypes. Two of them were discovered in a basement years later by Neil Levine, son of Donald Levine who had then since passed. He subsequently auctioned them off to anonymous buyers for hefty sums.
The third and final bin Laden doll though, well, it remains fittingly in the possession of the CIA, at the agency's headquarters at Langley.

The origin of the rat tribe

There are a few things you need to keep in mind if you want to survive a nuclear blast. Firstly, depending on where you are and where the missile is being launched from, you'll have anywhere from 10-45 minutes to prepare—in the case of Hawaii's missile scare in 2018, officials estimate that Hawaiians would've had about 12 minutes between the accidental push notification warning of Hawaii's fiery demise and Hawaii's actual fiery demise. Now, with that 10-45 minutes, the rest is easy: don't look directly at the explosion, stay inside a reinforced concrete building, ingratiate yourself into the tribe of mutant squirrel people that rule the fallout-ravaged hell-scape. But the only thing that will guarantee your survival really is to dig a massive underground city built to house millions of people in the event of a nuclear war. Coincidentally, that's exactly what China did under Beijing in 1969.

Now, it's easy to forget that there are parts of world history that don't include the United States, but believe it or not, the Cold War wasn't just an audition for "America's Next Top Nuclear Warhead Target"—there were lots of other countries with their own missiles and their own post-war tensions. Even China and the Soviet Union had their differences—some ideological spats, a few border disputes, and a teeny tiny 7 month military conflict where a few hundred troops were killed.

Knowing that things can get kind of sticky when you've started gunning down Soviet soldiers, Mao got to work digging one of the largest bunker systems ever designed. And by "Mao got to work," I really mean "300,000 Beijingers, including maybe, possibly a few schoolchildren, got to work digging 33 square miles worth of tunnels by hand while Mao was chilling in his imperial palace."

The resulting shelter was equipped not only with living spaces, but with restaurants, schools, medical facilities, factories, grain warehouses, movie theaters, roller skating rinks, and a mushroom cultivation farm.

Now, in the event of an impending nuclear strike on Beijing, any resident could pop into one of 90 entrances strategically placed around the city to access the shelter—theoretically, Beijing's underground city would be able to house all six million inhabitants for about four months, at which point they could be safely released into the apocalypse, fresh and rejuvenated.

Of course, digging an underground city isn't exactly a weekend project, and Sino-Soviet relations were in a much better place when the project was completed 10 years later in 1979.

There was no longer any worry of bombs, or gas, or bombs filled with gas so that when they explode they release gas everywhere, so the completed underground city was, fortunately, never used… well, at least for its intended purpose.

You see, when Mao stepped down in 1976, and by stepped down I mean "died," he was replaced by Deng Xiaoping. Deng was much less interested in ideology than Mao, and much more focused on expanding China's economy, so like any good capitalist, when he realized that there were tens of thousands of unused living spaces under China's second most populous city, he did what Google did to our browser histories and ordered them to be commercialized.

Slowly, Beijing's underground city was transformed into a collection of underground markets, office spaces, hostels, and ultra-affordable housing. In fact, over a million people currently live under Beijing in these renovated bomb shelters that are often cramped, windowless, and poorly-maintained—they're sort of like college dorm rooms, if college dorm rooms were bigger and affordable.

This underground society, which some locals refer to as "The Rat Tribe," is mostly composed of young Chinese immigrants from other provinces looking to start new lives in the city without worrying too much about housing costs.

Most of these rooms can be rented for around 400 yuan a month—that's the equivalent of 57 US dollars, which, in New York, can get you one night in a haunted AirBnB or about 45 minutes in a nice one-bedroom apartment. Now, although nearly 5% of Beijing's population lives underground, they need to do so in relative secrecy—while most local officials usually turn a blind eye, these dwellings are all actually technically illegal, since the Chinese government forbids anyone from living full-time in the underground city.

I mean, after all, what's more dangerous than living in the most elaborate bomb shelter ever built?

How to rent a country on Airbnb

> Lichtenstein is located between Austria and Switzerland and it is one of the smallest countries in the world, with an area of only 60 square miles or 160 square kilometers, which is home to 38,557 people. There are a lot of things that make Liechtenstein weird: it's the world's number one manufacturer of false teeth, it only started letting women vote in 1984, it was once accidentally invaded by Switzerland, and its national anthem is just a lazy rip-off of God Save The Queen.
> And in 2011, for the low, low price of $70,000 a night, Liechtenstein began offering people the opportunity to rent out the entire country… on Airbnb.

Now I want to be clear: even though it may sound like the type of weird made-up kingdom that would be featured in a hastily-written Netflix Christmas rom-com, Liechtenstein is a very real country.
It's a member of the United Nations, it has a written constitution, and it even has a rather impressive economy given its small population, with $5.3 billion in annual GDP, which breaks down to $98,432 per capita, which is among the highest per-capita GDPs of any nation in the world. For context, that's nearly $98,433 per person.
So, you may be wondering, why is an actual, honest-to-goodness country, you know, rent-able?

Normally renting is for cars, tuxedos, and bowling shoes—not sovereign nations. Well, it isn't completely clear what the impetus was behind the idea, but it seems as though the inspiration may have come in 2010, when rapper, actor, and weed connoisseur Snoop Dogg attempted to rent out Liechtenstein to shoot a music video.
Surprisingly, Liechtenstein said they were open to it, but in the end, Snoop's request was denied because he didn't give them enough notice.

A year after Snoop's failure, though, the internet was graced something that soon joined the likes of History of Japan, the launch of Windows 95, and Eel Slap as one of the most bizarrely magnificent things ever to be posted on the World Wide Web: the very real Airbnb listing that reads simply, "Rent the country of Liechtenstein!"
The rental program was a collaboration between Airbnb and a Liechtenstein-based marketing company called Xnet which runs a program called Rent-a-Village that lets rich people rent towns—because why spend your money to help the poor when you could use it to temporarily take over entire municipalities, like some sort of bizarre sharing-economy version of Alexander the Great.

Now, the Liechtenstein rental did come with a few caveats. First of all, the 38,557 people who actually live there would get to stay in their homes, and as the renter, you'd still have to, like, follow laws and stuff—you don't get to run a small-scale, European version of the Purge.

Plus, the minimum stay would be three days, and you'd be subject to a very strict cancellation policy—if you cancel 30 days or more before your stay, you can get half your money back, but any later and you get nothing: all your hard-earned cash gets fed straight into Liechtenstein's creepy fake-teeth-based economy.

So, what would you get if you rented Liechtenstein?

Well, first off, there's the obvious: accommodations. 500+ bedrooms and bathrooms, which the listing says can hold between 450 and 900 people.
For check in, your point of contact would be the actual Prince of Liechtenstein, Hans-Adam II, who the listing recommends meeting in his personal vineyard, where you have the option of joining him for a wine tasting.
But, if old grapes aren't your style, you can also meet him in the capital city of Vaduz, at a medieval market near the Gutenberg Fortress, or in a, "Wild-West style town" on the banks of the Rhine.

Afterwards, you'd be led to a kick-off celebration, and presented with a "symbolic key to the state," just in case you ever need to open the symbolic door to the state.
After that, you'll be transported to your various Liechtensteinian activities—which you can do in either vintage American cars or traditional horse-drawn carriages, in case you prefer forms of transportation that stop in the road for bathroom breaks.

After that, the options are pretty wide open, seeing as you literally rented the entire country, but to help get the ball rolling, the official listing mentions some ideas, which include personalized fireworks displays, a range of museums and trails for hiking, tobogganing, skiing, a "custom medieval festival" to be held in your honor, and even options to print your own temporary currency, and rename city streets.

For check-out, it suggests a "regional jazz-brunch," which it doesn't define any further, but which I imagine involves eating bacon egg and cheese saxophones, after which you would finally return to your regular, miserable, non-country-owning life.

Now, sadly, nobody ever took Liechtenstein up on their offer. One couple was reportedly going to book it for their wedding, but their marriage was called off for non-Liechtenstein related reasons, and, now, it is with a heavy heart that I must inform you that Liechtenstein is no longer listed on Airbnb—but the good news is, if you're still in the market to for a trip that screams, "I have far too much money," you can rent out a medieval castle in Burgundy, a 16th century villa in Tuscany or a six-stories tall wooden elephant on the Jersey Shore, named Lucy.

The highway where horseless carriages are banned

Highways are traditionally used by cars, but it's also important to remember that life is a highway, and that life is unpredictable—which means that by the transitive property, highways are unpredictable, which may explain how we ended up with the strange, confusing, charmingly bizarre Michigan road that is M-185: the only highway in America where cars are completely banned.

Now, you may be wondering, why would a highway ban cars? Aren't cars the whole reason highways exist—for cars to drive on them?

While most highways go to scary places, like hell or the danger zone, M-185 goes around beautiful Mackinac Island, a 4.4 square mile, or 11.3 square kilometer island in Lake Huron that looks like the kind of charming, picturesque small-town community that would be rocked to its core by a grisly murder in a Stephen King novel.

Mackinac Island has many attractions for tourists of all kinds: if you're into sports, you can check out their famed golf course, if you like culture, you can visit their renowned art exhibits, and if you're afraid of the inevitable takeover of mankind by machines, you can enjoy the island's total ban on cars, which has been in place for over 100 years.

Back in 1898, the good people of Mackinac became terrified of a strange new-fangled invention called the automobile: so scared, in fact, that they passed a city ordinance declaring, " that the running of horseless carriages be prohibited within the limits of the village of Mackinac."

It's the kind of law that's funny because it was clearly written in a different, less enlightened era, like the laws that prohibit buying booze on Sundays, or the Second Amendment.

Anyways, after Mackinac Village outlawed those dastardly horseless carriages, they probably thought that would be that—but then in 1900, a law-defying rapscallion named Earl C. Anthony brought his Locomobile onto the island, and while driving in Mackinac State Park, he ended up scaring several horses, which was particularly a problem because those horses were attached to carriages, and those carriages had people in them, and people in carriages don't like crashing into things, which is what tends to happen when the horses they're attached to get scared.

So, in 1901, the Mackinac Islands State Park Commission passed a separate law, which banned all cars from Mackinac Park—which takes up over 80% of the island. Seeing as the other 20% is taken up by the village, which had banned automobiles three years prior, 100% of the island had banned cars.

Yet, despite this ban, from 1900 to 1910, the state of Michigan began building a road on the island, with the intention of helping people get around using other modes of transportation that were popular at the time—carriage, horseback, foot, even those stupid bicycles with one giant wheel.

In fact, the road was intentionally built more narrow than traditional highways, because the state didn't intend for cars to drive on it, but how did it become a highway? After all that is what qualifies it as an interesting story.

Well, simply put, it's a highway because the state of Michigan says so.

Highways don't actually have to meet any sort of technical requirements in order to be highways; they just have to be designated as such by the state government, and in 1933, the state of Michigan designated that road as a state highway, which means that it is.

Despite the ban, though, there have been a few instances of cars on the island. In 1979, Mackinac Island was the filming location for a movie called Somewhere in Time, in which Christopher Reeves—the first actor to portray Superman—plays a man who falls in love with a woman based solely on an old photograph of her—so basically, it was a movie about Tinder.

In the film, Reeves travels back in time to court the woman, and at one point his character drives an old-timey car, and so a car was allowed on the island for him to drive it, because you know, it's hard to say no to Superman. Just ask Batman.

The next automobile allowed on the island came in 1998, when a car was allowed onto Mackinac in order to commemorate the 100-year anniversary of the automobile ban—which, you have to admit, is a bit ironic. That's like commemorating the anniversary of the drug war by planting weed in the Rose Garden.

Most recently, in 2019, Vice President Mike Pence brought a motorcade onto the island for security reasons, and finally, emergency vehicles have always been allowed on the island—in fact, they were the source of the only ever car crash in the history of Mackinac Island, which came when the fire truck nicked the door of the ambulance when they were both responding to an injured ferryboat passenger. Don't worry, though—when the crash happened, everyone was alright; there just so happened to be an ambulance right there.

The day drugs were legal in Ireland

The Republic of Ireland has many claims to fame: great musicians like U2, great actors like Colin Farrell, great beers like Guinness, and great food like… you know what? Never mind about the food.
But Ireland has another claim to fame that fewer people know about—the shortest period of drug legalization ever.

Relaxation of drug policy is a growing worldwide political movement. In the US, cannabis is legal in at least some form in 33 states.

Some countries, like Portugal, have decriminalized all drugs and have started treating drug use and possession as a public health issue instead of a criminal one and while Ireland has started to move towards decriminalization and relaxation of medical marijuana laws, no politician or cabinet member in Ireland meant to move towards legalization quite as quickly as they did on March 10, 2015, also known as the day Ireland accidentally legalized all drugs.

So, you might be wondering, how can you accidentally legalize drugs?
I mean sure, people make mistakes, but usually it's something like spelling cologne like colon (which, in my personal opinion, unlike weed, should be outlawed).
Yet, legalizing crystal meth seems like a pretty big and avoidable mistake. Did the whole Irish Parliament get a little too into Breaking Bad and take their Walter White cosplay too far? Well, not exactly.

To understand how it happened, you have to first understand the structure of the Irish Government. Ireland is a parliamentary democracy, and like many modern democracies consists of three branches, each of which holds different powers.
Legislative power, which is the power to make laws, is held by the Parliament, also called the Oireachtas. The Oireachtas consists of two houses—the upper house, the Seanad Eireann, is appointed, while the lower house, the Dail Eireann, is elected. The Dail is the one that actually matters; even those the Seanad is the "upper house," they have very little power.

Executive power, which is the power to enforce laws, is not held by the President like in the US. Rather, the presidency is a largely ceremonial role currently served by Irish Bernie Sanders, also known as Michael D. Higgins. The executive power is held by a cabinet of 7-15 ministers—a body that is somewhat confusingly called The Government. It includes the prime minister, or Taioseach, and other government ministers—like the Minister for Finance, who handles monetary and financial policy, or the Minister for Health, who handles healthcare, or the Minister for Magic, who doesn't listen to Dumbledore and puts the entire wizarding world at risk because he's so damn stubborn. That last one also might not be true but you get the point.

Judicial power, which is the power to hear cases and interpret laws, is held by The Courts of Ireland, whose highest court is the Supreme Court. The Supreme Court has the power to declare laws unconstitutional and strike them down.

So, what does all of this have to do with drug legalization?
Well, in 1977, the Parliament used its legislative powers to pass the 1977 Misuse of Drugs Act. The act basically said that that it was illegal to use or possess certain drugs, and then it listed every drug you couldn't do. I know what you're thinking: total buzzkill.

But the thing is, drugs are like Spider-Man reboots: there's a new one pretty much every week. So, the Parliament included a section in the law that said, "The Government may by order declare any substance, product or preparation to be a controlled drug for the purposes of this act."
Basically, that meant that The Government—that cabinet of ministers—could add stuff to list of illegal drugs whenever they wanted.

Therefore, for years, from 1977 until 2015, the Government kept adding news drugs to the list. Drugs like crystal meth, ecstasy, and ketamine—all of them got put on the list.
And everything went fine until March of 2015, when a guy named Stanislav Bederev, was caught possessing the drug 4-Methylcathinone, or Kat for friends, which had recently been added to the list of controlled substances and he decided to go with an interesting legal defense.

Instead of arguing that he didn't do it, Bederev said, "Actually, I did have 4-Methylcathinone, but it doesn't matter, because the law that says this drug is unconstitutional," which sounds like the type of defense you would give if you were high on 4-Methylcathinone, but it turns out, he was right.

So why was he right?
Well, the Government—that group of 15 ministers who had added 4-Methylcathinone, along with a bunch of other drugs, to that list—only has executive power, not legislative power.
They have the power to enforce laws, but not to make them.
What the Irish Court of Appeals said was that every time a drug got added to that list, it was basically The Government making a new law—which they aren't allowed to do—because only Parliament can make laws.
So, the Court said that every single time a drug had been added by The Government to the original 1977 list, it had been unconstitutional which meant that every drug that had ever been added to the list was now legal.

This is how, for a single day in March of 2015, crystal meth, mushrooms, ketamine, ecstasy, and over a hundred other drugs became totally, 100% legal to possess and use.
The Irish Parliament tried to fix it, but they could only act so fast.

The decision was made on a Tuesday, and even though the Parliament immediately passed a new law making all the drugs illegal again, the law didn't go into effect until Thursday which meant that meant that for Wednesday, March 11, 2015, if you were in Ireland, you could go full Scarface and there wouldn't be a thing anyone could do to stop you.

A ban on death

In Longyearbyen, Norway it's illegal to die.

Longyearbyen is so far north that by going over the North Pole, it's closer to Barrow, Alaska than Barcelona, Spain. It is so insanely far north that the sun does not even bother to rise for four months in the winter, but to compensate it stays up for four months in the summer. It's so insanely far north that the average winter temperature has warmed six degrees in the past 30 years, oh wait, that's not a very fun fact. That's not a very fun fact at all!

For how far north it is, Longyearbyen is a surprisingly large town—over 2000 people live there.
In fact, there is no larger town further north than Longyearbyen. That is the reason why Longyearbyen shatter a lot of "northernmost records": it has the northernmost university, circus, art gallery, bowling alley, cell tower, swimming pool, bus station, gas station, commercial airport, bank, department store, fire station, ATM, Toyota dealership, bar, and kebab shop in the world.

It's a legitimate town, but it's still 1,200 miles north of Oslo so there are some quirks.
For example, polar bears live there too and they occasionally they like to snack on people, which is bad, so it's actually illegal to leave the Longyearbyen city area without a gun.

Possibly for related reasons, there's also a monthly limit to how much alcohol one can buy at 24 cans of beer, 2 bottles of liquor, and half a bottle of fortified wine.
The local residents must carry an "alcohol card" to track their quota, while the visitors have to present their airline boarding pass from their arriving flight at the liquor store.

Longyearbyen has also a ban on cats in order to save the local population of arctic birds.
They just love banning things there, so why not a ban on death?

From what you have read, as you might imagine Longyearbyen is not exactly a beach resort. The average temperature in February is one-degree Fahrenheit, which means that things tend to freeze and to stay frozen.
Places as cold as Longyearbyen are neatly covered in what is called permafrost, which means that the ground stays below freezing permanently, not just in February.
While it may rise above freezing above ground, places with permafrost, such as Longyearbyen, will always be below freezing below ground, which happens to be where you put dead bodies.

The same principle that keeps your chicken nuggets edible for years on end in the freezer does the same to bodies (just to be clear, I am not in any way suggesting cannibalism).
While it may seem pretty great for bodies to not rot away, it's not.

You see, in 1918 a few people got the flu—about half a billion to be exact—in what came to be known as the Spanish Flu Pandemic.

Of the up to 100 million individuals who died, 11 were in Longyearbyen so they built a graveyard.

Small caveat though, when you put a corpse into a giant underground freezer it turns out that you don't just preserve the body, you also preserve the viruses inside the body and so lurking below Longyearbyen are some of the only active samples of a flu strain that killed 5% of the world's population, which is actually quite useful.

Researchers still don't fully understand why the 1918 flu was so deadly and they don't just have samples lying around, so these bodies buried in the arctic permafrost potentially hold some of the clues that could stop a future global pandemic (although apparently it wasn't that helpful, as I am proofreading this in 2020).

In the meantime, you really wouldn't want other diseases that could obliterate future civilizations lying in wait a few feet underground preserved for eternity, and Longyearbyen agrees, so that's why death is now illegal in this small, freezing cold, bear-ridden, ban-loving, but otherwise lovely Norwegian town.

If you're near death, you're flown down to the mainland to live out your final days and if you die unexpectedly, well, there's no space for you in Longyearbyen.

The town on fire

> The world's largest wetlands, Lithuanian pop songs, me when I play darts drunk—these are all things that are on fire (I know the first one isn't so funny, but in an 80000-words-long book on mostly useless information, you might want to forgive a bit of climate change proselytism). Also, on fire is the town of Centralia, Pennsylvania, or at least the ground under it.

The story of Centralia begins pretty identically to that of any other mid-Atlantic coal town.

Some rich guy buys land, finds coal, mines coal, town starts to exist, town starts to get cool with saloons and hotels and general stores, there's a heyday, and then town's cool factor diminishes as coal demand decreases.

Basically, by the 1960's, all the mines had closed and the population had decreased from its peak of 2,800 in 1890 to 1,400.

Because they hadn't yet invented the environment, when it came to doing the annual landfill cleanup in May 1962, the good people of Centralia decided to just burn the trash.

So, they hired five firemen to set fire to the fill then fight the firemen-set fire until it became not a fire.

It turns out, though, that astonishingly, in the coal mining town there was a coal mine under the landfill and it also turned out that there was an open mineshaft under the vast pile of trash and it also turns out that coal burns. Surprise, surprise, the fire spread underground into the mine.

While this theory is the predominant one, there are other competing theories for how the fire started such as via a non-fireman induced fill fire or that it wasn't even started in 1962, that it was just the continuation of a coal fire from decades earlier.

There are three main factors leading to the longevity of coal fires: coal burns slowly, coal is underground, and where there's coal there's a lot of coal.

Coal fires are therefore relatively speaking, common: some can last for a few months, others can last a few centuries, like the aptly named *Stinksteinwand* (stinking stone wall) in Germany, and the longest coal-seam fire has been burning for millennia: the more banally named Burning Mountain (for the ever-growing lists of Australian things that can kill you, this particular coal fire under Mount Wingen in New South Wales, Australia has actively burned underground for about 6,000 years).

Coal-seam fires advance at a steady pace of three feet or one meter per year as it destroys the land above it which would be a bigger issue if anyone lived here.
People did live in Centralia, Pennsylvania and so this coal fire was a massive issue!
Obviously, as soon as it ignited Centralia and Pennsylvania began a massive operation to extinguish the fire before its spread threatened human life or property, but coal-seam fire are pretty hard to extinguish.
In response, the town of Centralia sent a letter to the Lehigh Valley Coal Company, who owned the mine, informing them of the fire. Over the next few years, they tried a few different methods at stopping the fire including digging trenches and pumping water underground but nothing worked.

By 1972, as the fire inched closer and closer to the populated part of town, the effects grew and the land became inhospitable.
The fire would make the land unstable, open up holes to the underworld, and emit carbon monoxide which has the effect of making humans, well, not alive.

By 1984, 22 years after it started, the underground fire grew to a size where it could no longer be ignored.
The federal government allocated $42 million to buy all the houses in the town so the residents could move away and so they did.

While 1,017 people lived in the town in 1980, only 63 remained by 1990.
These 63 that remained refused to leave with the government's offer to buy their homes so the government invoked eminent domain to take ownership of their homes by force.
While the government now owned the houses, the residents still refused to leave and the government eventually gave up on trying to evict them since it was bad for PR.

The only upside of this was that, since the government now technically owned their houses, the residents didn't have to pay property tax or mortgages. Now you know the one easy step for living for free.

Eventually the government got back into the eviction mission and, by 2013, only seven of the town's most stubborn residents remained.
The government agreed to let them live the rest of their lives in Centralia and, in exchange, the houses would be turned over to the government upon their deaths.
 This town that was once home to thousands now only has five houses, two churches, a cemetery, and a municipal building.

The only real sign of the fire is the gasses rising from the barren ground but soon, the fire will likely start to threaten the nearby towns of Girardville, Ashland, and Aristes as it continues advancing slowly year by year

Ballots from space

Given that the United States has famously always treated everyone equally and fairly, you might be surprised to learn that to this day politicians engage in blatant voter suppression tactics, which range from closing polling places, purging voters rolls, and putting big signs on voting booths that say "DO NOT ENTER; BACHELORETTE SPOILERS INSIDE." But this isn't a book about the ways America systematically oppresses its most vulnerable people and attempts to take away their most precious civic right, that would be boring. This is a book about entertaining stories to whip out when the conversation dies down at dinner, so this is a story about space voting.

The process for Americans voting in space is simple: a secret government lizard sends a ballot to Studio 7 in Burbank, California, where the actors playing astronauts film their space videos, the actor fills it out, and finally… OK, that was the wrong source: 4chan instead of Wikipedia. I hate when that happens. Let's try again.

Back in 1996, astronaut John Blaha was about to be sent to the Russian Space Station Mir when he realized, "I sure would love to be able to vote on which guy is deciding to shoot me up into the sky in defiance of both god and man."
So he took the issue up with NASA, who then took it up with Texas, because nearly all astronauts live in Houston near Johnson Space Center, and it turned out that while Texas doesn't like voting by poor people or people whose last names end with "o" or "z", they're all for astronaut voting, and so they passed a state law in 1997, which set up a process for voting from space.

The process begins with a Federal Postcard Application, a standard form for all US military members, on which the astronaut indicates, among other things, which elections they want to vote in—local, state, intergalactic, multidimensional, or federal.
But because Uncle Sam keeps forgetting his Wi-Fi password, that form must be physically mailed in, so the astronaut must fill it out while they're still on Earth, sometimes a year in advance of the election.

As election day nears, the county clerk in the astronaut's home county, which is usually Harris county, will send a test ballot to Johnson Space Center, where someone (we don't know who) will use a space station training computer to make sure that the test ballot can successfully be filled out and sent back to the clerk.
Once The Clerk receives the "space ballot is a go" message, they'll create a secure electronic ballot, which is sent to Johnson Space Center, who uplinks it to the ISS.
On the ISS, the astronaut will stop whatever magical floaty science they're up to, go into their email inbox, scroll past their space junk mail, and find a message with special credentials sent from the County Clerk, which lets them access their ballot.

Then, they'll simply fill it out, list their address as "low-earth orbit" (that is not a joke, I swear, and you know it's true because it is actually funny, unlike my jokes) and downlink it to Johnson, who sends it to the County Clerk, who has their own password which they must enter to access it.

Oh, and the astronaut must vote by 7 pm local time on Election Day, so it's best they give themselves plenty of space to do this important task: after all, the gravity of voting is astronomical.

Now, you probably have one, key question: "how on Earth (wink, wink) does the international space station have email or internet?" That one takes some explaining.

So, on Earth we built antennae on the ground which form the Space Network, and put satellites in high orbit called TDRS, which stands for Totally, Definitely Rockin' Satellites (or if you want to be a know-it-all, it stands for Tracking and Data Relay Satellite), which are grouped over the Indian, Pacific and Atlantic Oceans, and move in geosynchronous orbit—meaning their speed matches the Earth's rotation, so they are always above the same terrestrial spot.

The ISS sends data-carrying radio waves to whichever satellite is nearest, which zooms them to the ground antennae, which swooshes the data through a landline to various NASA centers. Data goes to the ISS in the exact reverse way: centers whoosh data to antennae, antennae zoom it to satellites, and satellites kabloosh it to the ISS.

Now, there are a lot of things exclusive to Americans: spray cheese, the electoral college, girl scout cookies, dressing dogs like people, and electing pro wrestlers as governors. But unlike those things, space voting is not an American-only phenomenon.

In 2020, Russian cosmonauts voted on proposed constitutional changes via both online ballots and proxy voters: people on Earth designated to cast a vote on their behalf.

The same process used by a French astronaut in their 2017 election.
The other ISS partners, Canada and Japan, haven't ever had astronauts vote from space—but to be fair, they don't have the same ongoing ISS presence as Russia and the US. This year, in the 2020 Presidential election, American astronaut Kate Rubins has already early voted from the ISS.

12 days of traffic

> **If something's crammed, communist, and a country it's probably China. The country's grown enormously in the past few decades both in population and wealth. As the wealth grew and socialist ideals dwindled, they abandoned the cute little bicycles of the propaganda posters, and more and more people bought cars. So many that in 2010 they had a traffic jam that lasted 12 days.**

There are now 217 million cars on Chinese roads which, considering there were only 59 million ten years ago, is a lot. That means that in ten years, China has essentially had to triple the capacity of its roads which is basically impossible. Hence, traffic. The National Highway 110 connects inner Mongolia, the part of Mongolia that's in China, to Beijing, the capital. G110 didn't used to be so busy, but when your country transforms from being mostly composed of poor rural farmers to relatively rich urban populations you need energy to power everything.

China didn't really go for that hippy wind or solar energy; they went for coal.
70% of their overall energy need is fulfilled by it. Of course, this isn't sustainable long term as coal isn't a renewable resource like wind or Batman reboots but for now, it's a cheap and easy source of energy.

That's helped by the fact that China has about 13% of the world's coal in its ground while Mongolia, China's neighbor, has about 10%. A good amount of China's coal is in inner Mongolia, the region, and they also import plenty of coal from Mongolia, the country.

What China doesn't have, though, is coal transportation infrastructure… or a free press, a market economy, freedom of movement, freedom of speech, a freely floated currency, or time zones, but the transportation infrastructure is the important thing it's missing in this case.

There are only seven roads that cross the border from Mongolia, the country, to China, the country. What's worse, there are barely any railways and trains are the primary means of transportation worldwide for coal as it's really not very dense and trucks can't carry that much.

This lack of railways means that there are huge amounts of trucks driving from inner Mongolia to Beijing carrying coal each and every day.

There are a few routes these trucks can take into Beijing but the most popular one is G110.

That's because much of the coal coming from inner Mongolia comes from illegal, unlicensed mines and, while the other routes from inner Mongolia have inspection stations to combat illegal mining, G110 does not.

All these factors compounded to create the beginnings of a traffic jam on August 14th, 2010.

It was the busy summer season and the highway just couldn't handle the amount of trucks but the real problem started five days later as maintenance work began on the highway to fix damage from overuse.

That shut down half the lanes at points and this traffic jam, which had already been going on continuously for five days to a lesser extent, just became a parking lot.

At its worst, the congestion lasted for 60 continuous miles and drivers were only able to move as little as 0.6 miles per day. It took some close to a week to make their way through a stretch of highway that would normally take an hour.

A whole temporary mini-economy sprung up as villagers from near the highway walked or biked up and down selling food and drinks. Water, which normally sells for 1 yuan, went for 15.

Drivers took naps under their trucks, played cards, took walks, there really was no reason to be behind the wheel as nothing was moving.

Throughout this all, authorities desperately tried to reduce the traffic by sending trucks on different routes and telling people not to drive.

As the jam entered its second week nothing seemed to be working although, with time, as it gained national and international media attention, people eventually stopped taking the highway and then, finally, after twelve whole days of bumper to bumper traffic, the congestion dissipated and National Highway 110 was back to normal.

China has since built railways, expanded highways, and cracked down on illegal mining which has prevented any more apocalyptic jams but August 1st 2010 on G110 is now believed to have been the worst traffic jam in world history.

Let them have wider trains

Since this book is full of surprises, here is a free French lesson for you. No, don't skip it, it's really very easy, because there are a lot of words that are almost identical to the English ones, for example they call trains les trains, they call rails le rails, and they call what happened to their trains and rails in 2014 stupide. See, it's all very easy to comprendre.

Our story begins in 2009, when les trains and les rails were getting a bit run down, and so, faster than you could say un, deux, trois, the French government decided to spend $20 billion dollars, or dix-huit milliards d'euros, to get a new fleet of sleeker, faster, roomier trains.
Fantastique, you might think, but in fact, things were far from fantastique.

The French rail operator, Réseau Ferré de France, is a separate operation from the train company, which is called Société Nationale des Chemins de Fer. I would abbreviate Réseau Ferré de France as RFF and Société Nationale des Chemins de Fer as SNCF, but this story is just an excuse to discover how much of my high-school French I remember.

Back in 1997, the rail operator, whose name, again, is Réseau Ferré de France and the train company—again, Société Nationale des Chemins de Fer—were all one company, which was also called Société Nationale des Chemins de Fer. In 1997, a new EU directive imposed that the government split them up into two different government-run entities: one for les rails and one for les trains. It was exactly this separation that created the opportunity for miscommunication.

But still, things should have been easy—it wasn't like they had to play La Vie En Rose on a croissant; all the rail company, Réseau Ferré de France, needed to do was tell the train company, Société Nationale des Chemins de Fer, how wide to make the trains.
The problem was, they took all their measurements from train platforms built within the last 30 years, forgetting that the older platforms in rural areas were built to a different standard, and ran about 8 inches, or vingt centimètres narrower than the newer ones.

They then gave those flawed measurements to the train company, Société Nationale des Chemins de Fer. Fast forward a few years and voila, 2,000 new trains had been completed, and the trains were beautiful—sleek, fast, roomy; everything looked like it would be magnifique—but that's when they discovered that getting the new trains into the older stations was like trying to stuff a baguette into a bottle of sauvignon blanc… they just wouldn't fit.

To be clear, this wasn't just a little mistake, it was a full-blown catastrophe.
1,300 of the 8,700 stations in France—about one in seven—were too narrow for the new trains to fit into.
At first the government tried to keep their mistake a secret—but soon, the news was broken by the magazine Le Canard Enchainé, prompting cries of, "sacrebleu," from the train makers, and cries of, "why is our government dumber than a bucket of escargot," from all the French people.

Seeing as, "fitting into stations," is one of the more important qualifications a train needs to check, alongside, "fitting on train tracks," and, "not being an airplane," the French government quickly got to work fixing the problem by shaving off the edges of the older, narrower platforms.
It wasn't a particularly difficult fix, just an expensive one.
According to the Société Nationale des Chemins de Fer, these repairs cost the French about $68.4 million dollars, or soixante millions d'euros.

To put it in context, that's enough euros to buy 7.1 million copies of Les Miserables on DVD, or 2.5 million plates of foie gras de canard at Le Comptoir de la Gastronomie in Paris.

But, if you're heading on vacation soon to Paris or Bordeaux or even Montpellier, don't worry: the platforms have been fixed and everything runs as smooth as a bowl of mousse au chocolate, and this French faux pas feels as distant as déjà vu.

How to sell ice to an Eskimo

Chances are that somewhere on the internet you've heard the "fact" that Iceland was named Iceland by its Viking settlers to stop their enemies from coming to the island. Well, that fact is about as wrong as pineapple on pizza. The truth is that the first Norse settler of the island was feeling a little bummed out upon arrival since his daughter and livestock died en route so he just stayed for the winter before returning to Norway and, since the particular area he stayed in happened to be icy he figured all of the island was icy and therefore called it Iceland. Of course, that'd be as absurd as, you know, seeing that the sidewalk was flat and deciding the whole earth must be flat. Iceland is cold and has plenty of snow and ice during the winter but as a whole, the country is fairly green. Still, for such a northern and wintery country the idea that it imports ice is pretty absurd. Nonetheless it's a reality and Iceland's ice importation has a surprisingly rational explanation.

Now, taking ice from one place and selling it in another is nothing new.
As it turns out, centuries ago people's refrigerators didn't have ice dispensers. For the majority of history people just dealt with having warm drinks like cave-people but when the 19th century rolled around that all changed.

An entrepreneur named Frederic Tudor started taking ice from cold places like Maine and selling it in hot places like Cuba. Genius, right? Only problem, ice melts.
Frederic understood this and insulated his cargo with sawdust and, with enough ice, at least some of it would make it through the 1,600-mile journey from Maine to Cuba.
At first Frederick received a frosty reception from the hot place people as they were doubtful that they needed ice so Frederic channeled his inner drug dealer and gave them their first bit of ice for free to get them addicted. Soon, business was booming.

Now, places like New York and DC get too cold in the winter for people to want ice but in the summer, they too get swelteringly hot so Frederic wanted to make a way to be able to sell ice in the mid-Atlantic summers.
Really the only solution was to take a whole lot of ice, put it in an insulated building, and hope some of it lasts until summer and, crazily enough, that worked.
Most of North America started to rely on ice so it was time for Frederick to take the ice trade intercontinental.

The rest of the world also had hot places like India so Frederic Tudor set up a regular shipment of ice to Calcutta, India which became hugely popular with the rich English colonialists who were used to cooler temperatures.
Amazingly, he had the process refined so well at that point that the ice from New England was selling in India for, adjusted for inflation, only $1 per pound.

Soon after, ice from New England was shipped and sold in London, in Rio de Janeiro, in Cape Town, in Hong Kong, the New England ice even reached as far as Sydney, Australia where it sold for only $2 per pound.

So, was it a coincidence that the climate starting rapidly warming only a century after the world's elite started using ice shipped from the other side of the world by steamship all so they could have a chilled beverage? I'm not saying the ice trade singlehandedly caused climate change, but it certainly didn't help.

Of course, with time artificial refrigeration became cheap and widespread but not before making Frederic Tudor a very rich man.

Iceland today, despite what some may think, is not some backwards heathen society that shuns the use of refrigerators. Its importation of ice has to do with something else—economics.

You see, Iceland is a very expensive place. Like many isolated, northern counties, Iceland relies on imports for many things like oil, wood, wheat, and other food.

It just doesn't have the ability to produce these items domestically due to its geography but shipping to Iceland is also relatively cheap since its economy is export-driven.

While fish is Iceland's biggest export this is mostly shipped by plane but the country also has an enormous aluminum industry thanks to its low electricity cost.

Aluminum, along with most everything else Iceland makes, is exported by ship which means that there's demand for shipping from Iceland.

That means that ships are already coming to Iceland to bring items elsewhere so its relatively inexpensive to fill those ships with other goods to bring to Iceland.

At the same time, the average Icelander makes about $57,000 per year, it's one of the highest income countries in the world, so that means making things in Iceland, in most cases, is expensive. If you go and check your handy dandy Icelandic schedule of tariffs, though, you see that water, ice, and snow have no import duty if imported from the European Economic Area.

Therefore, Iceland imports ice from other less expensive countries in the EEZ such as Scotland and the only additional cost is the cheap shipping. While there are plenty of other countries that don't charge import duties on ice, there are few that have the mix of high domestic labor costs and cheap inbound shipping that make it worth it for Iceland to import ice.

That's why Iceland's grocery stores are stocked with this imported ice from hundreds or thousands of miles away as it ends up being about 40% less than Icelandic ice.

EXTRAORDINARY (AND EXECRABLE) LIVES

History has heroes and history has foes; but every life is an exciting story. I have compiled a weird and wonderful collection of little-known heroes and little-know facts about true villains.

The swashbuckling tale of a pirate queen

Grace O'Malley was the fierce pirate queen of Ireland in the mid-1500s. The stories surrounding this badass, swashbuckling mother of four are legendary, from giving birth to a child and immediately fighting a battle at sea, to being a staunch defender of Ireland's independence. Grace O'Malley was a badass mother.

Grace, unlike most pirates, was born into a life of comfort in County Mayo, Western Ireland. She was from a family of pirates: not some gnarly group of ragtag pirates, but upper middle class pirates, if there is such a thing.
Her father, Owen Blackoak O'Malley, perhaps the most Irish name ever spoken, was the chieftain of her family's clan and had a reputation for being quite the seafarer.
Their family motto - a thing families had back in the days - was *terra marique putens*, which means valiant by sea and land.

Grace was technically carrying on the family business of pirating, since most of the family's coin came from pillaging and plundering.
Since Grace's family was really into sailing and taking things that weren't theirs, she learned how to navigate the seas at quite the young age and conquered an important position within her clan.

Long before Channing Tatum classic and Best Picture Oscar snub, She's the Man told us that women can sometimes cosplay as a man to accomplish a task, Grace O'Malley was pulling the same move as Amanda Bynes just wanting to play soccer with the guys.
In fact, it is rumored that Grace developed a taste for the sea so intense that she insisted that her father allow her on his voyages at sea. Her parents, who despite being pirates were good parents, refused to let her go on account of the fact that children traditionally do not belong on dangerous sea voyages. Grace, ever the rebellious spirit at heart, refused to take no for an answer.
According to the legend, she cut off her hair, disguised herself as a dude, and snuck onto the ship. Even pirates need to find some way to rebel against their parents' wishes.
This feat gave Grace a new pirate-y nickname, Grace the Bald.

Despite being born in a family who already had power and wealth, didn't stop her from marrying men who would prove to be beneficial to her legacy and coffers and increase her power. In fact, since Grace was the daughter of a chieftain, she was the one who brought money into the relationship. Grace was first married at the ripe old age of 15 to Donal O'Flaherty, a man with many ships, which she would acquire when O'Flaherty was killed at sea while fighting, the leading cause of death for most pirates.

At 23 years of age, Grace was a widow with a fleet of ships, a castle, and a cavalry of loyal followers that she brought back with her to her hometown of Mayo. She was living large. In their eight years of wedded bliss, Grace birthed three children with Donal, two girls and a boy, but she wasn't a regular mom.
She was a fierce fighter and a respected widow, one who picked up on the sea traits of her husband.

Grace married for a second and final time to Richard Burke in 1566, yet again a strategic move on Grace's part. In fact Iron Burke was a talented land fighter with another nice castle for Grace. Grace and Burke were only married for a year before, legend has it, Grace screamed out the window: "Richard Burke, I dismiss you," which was not a legal way to end a marriage, even in those days.
The two remained legally married according to English law. The two remained friendly exes and allies and co-parents to their son Tibbot na Long, or Toby of Ships. We get it, Grace. You really liked ships.

Speaking of Toby Ships, his legendary birth story is one for the books, and certainly one any good mother would bring up no less than four times a day if Toby were to give her any crap.

Grace was at sea with her fleet when Toby decided it was the time to make his grand entrance. The birth of her son was the second most eventful thing to happen to her that fateful day in 1566; in fact, soon after her ship was attacked by corsairs. But did Grace sit this one out due to the very credible medical excuse of I just pushed out a baby? She tucked the baby away safely, went full mama bear, and led her men to victory.

When Grace lost her father, Owen O'Malley in 1553, she became chieftain of the O'Malley clan, a rarity in that era to have a female leader. Grace also took over her father's ships, continuing the family business.
But it wasn't the only thing family passed on to her.
Her marriage to Donal O'Flaherty in 1546 was also the beginning of a crucial family alliance, and she was so respected by her husband's men, they continued to loyally fight for her after the death of Donal.
Sure, the daughter from a family of well-known seafarers inherited a little piracy when she took over for her father as chieftain, but once she took the helm, she went pirate heavy on England in response to them taxing the hell out of Ireland.

The English had raised taxes on the goods her company traded, so Grace decided two could play at that game, turned around and imposed her own sea tax on passing ships. Her castles were built in strategic locations where her eyes could rear window the seas and monitor for passing ships. If she saw one, she'd lead her ships to overtake the passing ships and explain that safe passage costs money now. If the ship was non-compliant, they'd raid the ship. That's textbook pirate stuff right there.
She didn't stop at English ships either. Any ship that passed through was susceptible to Grace's raids, whether Irish, Spanish, or Turkish.

Even if we don't know much about her formal education, we do know that Grace had a well-traveled youth and reportedly spoke several languages. Historians agree that Latin was her second language. It's also believed she spoke Scottish, Gaelic, Spanish, English, and French. But it is historically proved that she used Latin when she spoke with Queen Elizabeth.

In fact, in 1593, Grace sought the help of Elizabeth I about the issues she was having Richard Bingham. Sir Richard Bingham was the English governor of Western Ireland where Grace O'Malley lived rent free, since she refused to pay taxes. So, she traveled the Irish sea to London to go over Bingham's head and petition Queen Elizabeth directly. In all fairness, Richard was being a real Dick ever since he came to believe that Grace was attempting to resist Irish rule. After a rebellion in Western Ireland in the 1580s, the Dick confiscated some of Grace's property and threw her into a prison. None of this was great, and surely she was unhappy being a prisoner with confiscated land. However, when Richard took her sons as captives, he officially crossed the line.

During the meeting between two most badass women of the time, O'Malley chose to forgo the formal greeting of bowing before an English queen since she didn't recognize her authority.
Despite this petty slap in the face, Elizabeth I granted her request and intervened with the governor, so long as Grace swore not to rebel against her.

Grace was a loyal woman not to be messed with, so when somebody came for her man, she came back for them in full force. In the 1560s, she took on a lover: she had rescued a survivor from a shipwreck and the two started a passionate love affair, as one does in times of crisis. O'Malley's whole pirate thing began to alienate and anger a bunch of rival Irish clans, including the pesky MacMahons.
As soon as they learned that Grace had a new lover, the MacMahons saw an opportunity. They tracked him down while he was out on a hunting trip and killed him.

Grace was understandably pissed off, but writing a stern letter or sulking quietly in a corner really was not her style as you might imagine.
She tracked down the men who slaughtered her lover and slaughtered those jerks right then and there. After she was done, she seized the MacMahons' Donna Castle.

On the other hand, Sir Richard Bingham didn't stop being a thorn in Grace's side even after her meeting with Queen Elizabeth. If anything, things escalated, pretty brutally. He started targeting her explicitly, because in his mind, he saw her as someone fueling the rebellion in Ireland. He took things way too far, however, when his brother John somehow lured Grace's son Owen out of his castle to steal his cattle. The situation went way out of hand when John who had tied Owen up, eventually murdered him.
Despite Sir Richard Bingham's brother straight up murdering her son, she realized that she still had to work with the English for political reasons and Grace was nothing if not cunning.

England and Ireland have a complicated history, which by the 16th century had reached a bit of an apex. England was super into Ireland at that point for hundreds of years, and the Tudor administration only saw the clingy controlling ways grow exponentially.
Grace wasn't a fan of their interference especially after the whole "murdering her son" matter, and frequently sought out and spoke for independence from the English constraints.
However, O'Malley was also shrewd in her ways and even lent ships and men to England in 1577, when it was politically convenient.

In fact, despite her reluctance to bend to the English crown, she wasn't completely unreasonable when it came to offering some assistance to the English state if she believed it would benefit her.
In 1577, she offered three galleys and 200 men to Lord Deputy Sir Henry Sidney, who reflected on this later in a letter to the Queen's secretary in 1583, calling her a famous, feminine sea captain, which was probably meant as a compliment.

The prostitute turned pirate who ruled over the South China Sea

While female pirates weren't uncommon off the coast of Asia in the 18th and 19th centuries, one woman stood above them all.

Her birth name isn't known, but this Cantonese pirate went by the name Ching Shih (also, by Zhèng Yi Sao, "wife of Zhèng", and Zhèng Shì, "widow of Zhèng".)
Ching Shih was born sometime around 1775 (the exact date isn't known). At the age of 26, she found herself working as a prostitute in a floating brothel in Canton.

While there, she caught the eye of Zhèng Yi, already a successful pirate with a small fleet of ships at his command, known as the "Red Flag Fleet". Exactly how the two ended up together is disputed.

Some historians hold that Zhèng Yi sent a raid to plunder the brothel and asked his men to bring back his favorite prostitute, Ching Shih, for his portion of the loot, while others claim he simply went there himself and proposed that they wed, which she only agreed to after he consented to give her equal share of his plunder and to allow her to help run the organization. Whatever the case, once married, Ching Shih did indeed begin helping Zhèng Yi run the Red Flag Fleet.

In the course of the next six years, their fleet grew from about 200 ships to 600 ships thanks to some key alliances, including forming the Cantonese Pirate Coalition with pirate Wu Shi'er. The fleet expanded again to 1700-1800 ships by 1807, as more and more pirates united under their banner.
Unfortunately for Zhèng Yi, on November 16, 1807, he found himself caught in a typhoon and didn't manage to survive the ordeal. Rather than step aside, handing over the organization to someone else, Ching Shih convinced Zhèng Yi's second in command, 21-year-old Chang Pao, to support her in taking over the Red Flag Fleet.

Chang Pao was the son of a fisherman and had actually been captured by Zhèng Yi when Chang Pao was just 15. He was then forced into the life of a pirate. He quickly gained favor in the eyes of Zhèng Yi due to his intelligence, bravery, and skill in a fight and was adopted by the pirate captain and Ching Shih as a son and made second in command of the fleet.

Chang Pao focused on leading the troops in raids and other pirate-y endeavors, while Ching Shih used her considerable cunning on the "business" side of things, planning military strategy, governing their unruly pirate fleet, and growing the organization into something that went way beyond what the partnering pillaging pirates could have ever dreamed of.
At the Red Flag Fleet's peak in 1810, she was the commander of about 1800 ships, both big and small and 70,000-80,000 pirates (with 17,000 male pirates directly under her control. The rest were pirate groups who had sealed an alliance with her, then female pirates, spies, children, farmers enlisted to supply food, etc.) This huge organization had the power of a small state and, in fact, controlled almost the entirety of the Guangdong province directly, had infiltrated a vast spy network within the Qing Dynasty, and dominated unchallenged the South China Sea.

Ever the savvy business woman, she didn't rely solely on looting, blackmailing, and extortion to support her troops like normal pirates do. She setup an ad hoc government to support her pirates including establishing laws and taxes. Since she controlled pretty much the entire criminal element in the South Chinese Sea, she was also able to guarantee safe passage through it to any merchants who was wise enough to pay.
Should they be foolish enough not to pay, they were fair game for her blood-thirsty pirates.

In order to manage the unruly ruffians under her command and get them to do all she said without questioning her ever, she imposed a strict system of law within the Red Flag Fleet which could be easily summed up in: "you either follow the rules or you lose your head, without exception or mitigating factors."
To make the nature of these laws clearer, here are some examples.
The punishment for disobeying an order: getting your head cut off and your body thrown in the ocean (not sure what happens with your head).
The punishment for stealing something from the common plunder before it has been divvied up: getting your head cut off and your body thrown into the ocean.
The punishment for raping anyone without permission from the leader of your squadron: getting your head cut off and your body thrown into the ocean.
The punishment for having consensual sex with anyone while on duty: getting your head cut off and your body thrown into the ocean (the woman involved wouldn't end up much better as she gets something heavy strapped to her and then she is also tossed in the ocean.)
The punishment for looting a ship or a town, or otherwise harassing them even if they have paid tribute: getting your head cut off and your body thrown into the ocean.

The punishment for taking shore-leave without permission: getting your head cut off and your body thrown into the ocean.

The punishment for trying to leave the organization: getting your head cut off… just kidding, in this case you just get your ears chopped off and probably thrown in the ocean.

Ugly women who were captured in the raids were to be set free unharmed. On the other hand, captured pretty women were shared or purchased by members of the Red Flag Fleet. However, if a pirate was awarded or bought a woman, he was considered married to her and was expected to treat her with the according respect. If he didn't, guess what? He would get his head cut off and his body thrown in the ocean.

She didn't just restrict herself to sea raids, like so many near-sighted pirates do. She put to good use numerous shallow-bottomed boats and sailed on the rivers raiding towns along the way and defeated any armies that came against her.

For instance, once two towns united their forces and pooled their resources to raise an army and sent it against her forces pre-emptively. The Red Flag Fleet not only won the battle she also subsequently marched her army to the two towns and ransacked them and beheaded all male citizens for good measure.

Of course, the Emperor was quite displeased that a pirate, a female pirate no less, controlled and terrorized a large region of his land and ruled over his subjects. Therefore, he raised a fleet of ships to attack Ching Shih's Red Flag Fleet.

If you thought that something as an imperial fleet could stop her, you might have underestimated her, just as the Emperor unfortunately did. In fact, Ching Shih was a brilliant military strategist and rather than running from the Emperor's armada, she sailed out to meet it with her fleet, which defeated the puny fleet quite easily.

Moreover, to add insult to injury, she managed to steal 63 of the large ships the Emperor had sent against her and convinced most of the surviving crews to join her, guess how?

She let them choose between being nailed to the deck by their feet and then beaten to death or becoming pirates of the Red Flag Fleet and celebrating the victory with the rest of them. Needless to say, she found herself with more pirates than she started the battle with.

The Admiral of the fleet sent against her, Kwo Lang, committed suicide before he could be captured by Ching Shih.

Naturally, the Emperor kept on attacking her fleet; after all, she wasn't just pestering a few Guangdong farmers and villagers anymore, she had defied and defeated the Qing Dynasty directly. However, the Emperor didn't have a fleet large enough anymore to take her on, so the Qing Dynasty government enlisted the aid of the British and Portuguese navies, who were becoming super-powers in that stretch of sea and was equally displeased with Ching Shih's pirates, as well as many Dutch ships, paying them large sums for their help.

These combined forces rained down Sulphur and fire on Ching Shih's organization for two years, but yielded little success. She won battle after battle until finally the Emperor decided it was time to put matters of honor aside and take a different path.

Instead of trying to defeat her, he offered her and most of her pirates amnesty.

Ching Shih initially refused the terms of the amnesty treaty. But, in 1810, she unexpectedly showed up at the home of the Governor General for the region of Canton to work out a peace treaty that would benefit her.

The deal that she struck was that the Red Flag Fleet would disband and give up most of their ships.

In return, they would grant amnesty to most of the members of the organization and allow them to keep any loot they had acquired during their years as pirates; with the exception of 376 of her crew, of which 126 were executed and 250 received varying degrees of punishments for their crimes.

All the rest, meaning almost 60000 pirates, got off without so much as a parking ticket and if they should decide to do so they were to be allowed to join the Chinese military.

Her second in command and now husband, Chang Pao, was given 20 ships in the Qing Dynasty navy to command. Ching Shih was also given an hefty sum to distribute to her crew to help offset the cost of them switching from a life of piracy at sea, to one in the mainland.

Ching Shih negotiated for herself the rights to keep the fortune she had accumulated. She also acquired a noble title: Lady by Imperial Decree. The title guaranteed her various legal protections as a member of the aristocracy.

She retired at the age of 35 and opened a brothel and gambling house in Guangzhou, Canton, which she managed until her death at the age of 69.
After she brokered the peace, she also became a mother to at least one son and later a grandmother. One can only imagine the bedtime stories she told her son and grandchildren!

She was not only arguably the most successful pirate who ever sailed the Seven Seas, but unlike pretty much every other pirate who went down in history, she also managed to escape being executed or being punished in any way for her crimes, retired extremely wealthy, and became a member of the aristocracy having been born a poor prostitute.

The secret life of a Belgian cartoonist

Tintin is one of the most beloved comic book characters of all time. He's appeared in countless comics, films, TV shows, and radio plays. But did you know his creator held a dark secret? Tintin's creator, Hergé, had a propensity for creating racist imagery and he was arrested for being a Nazi collaborator.

George Prosper Remi was born on May 22, 1907 in Etterbeek, Belgium. He was born into a lower middle-class family. His father, Alexis Remi, worked in a bakery. His mother, Elizabeth Dufour, was a housewife. Growing up, Remi fell in love with the animation of famed cartoonist, Windsor McCay.
He was specifically taken with the Gertie the Dinosaur cartoons, which inspired him to take up drawing.

As a boy, Remi would draw simple cartoons and comics in the margins of his school notebooks. At 12, Remi joined the Boy Scouts. He was quickly promoted to troop leader of the Squirrel Patrol, gaining the nickname Curious Fox for his inquisitive nature. The Boy Scouts was a positive experience for the young Remi, who found that his scout leader was an encouraging influence toward his fledgling artistic efforts, even going so far as to publish a drawing Remi had made in their Never Enough newsletter.

It was during this time creating illustrations and woodcuts for Boy Scout magazines that Remi would land on his now iconic pseudonym. Initially trying out Jérémie and Jérémiades, Remi finally settled on Hergé, a name inspired by the French pronunciation of RG, his reversed initials.

Hergé's earliest successes came from the extraordinary Adventures of Totor, a proto-Tintin-style character who was, you guessed it, a Boy Scout. Hergé would eventually reboot this character for the Catholic newspaper called Le Petit Vingtieme, or The Little Twentieth, a children's offshoot of Le Vingtieme Siecle, AKA The Twentieth Century.

Saying that the The Twentieth Century was a conservative newspaper is a bit of an understatement, kind of like saying that when the Nazis invaded Poland, they were just going on an enthusiastic vacation. Some consider the paper to be a pro-fascist publication. It would often publish pieces that voiced anti-Semitic points of view and racist imagery, not really the ideal publication for your kids' comics. But art and commerce are built off of compromise. So basically, Hergé made a choice.

After working on a few strips with other writers, Hergé became dissatisfied in a collaborative aspect of the job and decided to create his own character. This character would be Tintin, a Belgian boy reporter who solves crimes and has adventures in far off lands.

While working at The Little Twentieth, Hergé became close to Norbert Wallez, one of the Catholic priests that worked at the paper. Wallez became something of a mentor to the young Hergé, filling the void that was never quite filled by Hergé's biological father. He taught Hergé about life, encouraged his faith, and stoked some of his darker impulses. Prior to this, Hergé was apolitical.
However, under Wallez' influence, he began to grow further and further to the right. At the same time, Tintin became something of an overnight success.

The antics of the boy adventurer captured the imaginations of young and old alike. The strip was serialized every Thursday in the newspaper. These were later compiled into oversized collections by the much famed publisher, Casterman. As an added tidbit, the French refer to comics as bandes dessinées, or bay day for short, which literally translates to drawn strips.

The initial two Tintin adventures were Tintin in the Land of the Soviets and Tintin in Africa. These comics are filled with offensive and racist imagery, so much so that the collections that are still circulating to this day don't include them. Tintin in Africa, or Tintin in the Congo, as it was originally released, features offensive caricatures, and stereotypes, and racial bias.

During this time, Hergé would meet his first wife, Germaini Keickens. Germaini was Wallez' secretary. Hergé would parlay these successes into creating a few other strips like Tintin in America and Tintin in the Orient, which would later be renamed Cigars of the Pharaoh. Tintin in America was very well received by the reader base.
Tintin Travels to America gets caught up in a plot and then has to fend off Native Americans and cowboys, survive a train heist, and mix it up with the mob.

By this point, Tintin was a money-making machine, so much so that when Hergé announced he was going to be doing a book set in China as his next project, it made international news. The world was smaller in 1935. However, everybody wasn't exactly thrilled by the idea of Hergé tackling China.
Father Gossett, a Catholic priest who was living and working as the chaplain of Chinese students at the University of Leuven, wrote to Hergé and encouraged him to, well, actually do research about China.

It was around this time that Norbert Wallez was removed from church and given a position overseeing the preservation of the ruins of Aulne Abbey. This news hit Hergé hard: he loved Wallez and the fact that he was being taken out of Hergé's day-to-day life seemed to be a direct affront.
Hergé was pissed and even tried to quit the paper in protest, but they paid him some more money and loosened his deadlines, so, he ended up staying.

Eventually, Hergé was open to the idea of taking on a bit more research for his next project. Father Gossett provided an introduction to Zhang Chongren, an art student at the Brussels Academie Royale des Beaux-Arts. This would set in motion a key and defining era for Hergé.

Zhang would prove to be a lifelong friend and positive influence. Zhang would go on to become a sculptor of much acclaim and later an art teacher. He and Hergé would become fast friends. Zhang's influence on the Tintin strips was immeasurable, catapulting Hergé's technical facilities.

Hergé learned three-point perspective from him, drawing from life and the practice of taking reference photos. Zhang also introduced Hergé to Taoist philosophy, many Chinese illustrators and artists, and the practice of calligraphy.

The two men's friendship blossomed, many historians arguing that this one relationship fundamentally altered Hergé's view for the rest of his life.

The book Hergé worked on with Zhang was titled The Blue Lotus. It dealt with the Japanese invasion of Manchuria, a highly taboo subject at the time. The lead-up to the Second World War created an environment where everything was extremely polarized. And as such, the fact that Japan had invaded China in 1931 and would eventually set up a puppet country named Manchukuo, was a hot-button issue. If you're wondering, Manchukuo doesn't exist today. It would exist until the Soviet Union and Mongolia overtook the province in 1945. The Blue Lotus was received with overwhelming positive reviews. It has since gone on to be viewed as Hergé's first masterpiece.

During the lead-up to World War II, Hergé worked on a few more volumes of Tintin, including The Broken Ear and The Black Island. However, these strips are largely ambition lists and wrote exercises in narrative. Zhang moved back to China after graduating. The tension surrounding politics were rising.

Without someone to push him artistically, Hergé rested on his laurels. And here's where the proverbial s**t hits the fan: Belgium got invaded by the Nazis.

Inorder to attempt to escape the conflict, Hergé and his wife fled to France. This was a common plan for Belgians at the time, as tens of thousands did the same. Hergé originally found refuge in Paris before moving to Puy de Dome. They lived there for six weeks.

However, on May 28, 1940, the Belgian King Leopold III surrendered in an attempt to stop the bloodshed. Hergé and many Belgians were in support of this development. So, when the king put out a call to all the refugees to return home, they did.

Upon returning home, Hergé discovered that his home was being used as an impromptu home for a Nazi officer. It's like a fascist version of the Three Bears.

To make things even worse, the Nazis shut down the paper that had been publishing Tintin comics. Hergé had his back against the wall.

He needed to make money in order to survive and also, because he owed tax money to the Belgian government.

He was offered a job at Le Pays Réel, another far right newspaper published by yet another Catholic-affiliated entity, the Rexist Party. The party's leader, Leon Degrell, was a longtime friend of Hergé's. The two knew each other, because Degrell was a former reporter. To make things even weirder, some people have suggested that Tintin was even based loosely on Degrell.

There are conflicting reports about if Hergé outright turned this offer down. Then along came Le Soir, the largest francophone newspaper of the day. Tintin was to be rebooted by Hergé for Le Soir in a brand new adventure story, Crab with the Golden Claws.

Roughly 600,000 people read the strip during this time, and then the inevitable happened. The Nazis, who were in control of Belgium and eventually, France, seized control of Le Soir. Here is where things get gray.

Hergé was attempting to be better and not work for these papers, but he was enticed by the financial rewards that came from the large readership. In the next Tintin adventure, which was entirely produced under Nazi supervision, Tintin would go up against a rich Jewish-American businessman.

Later in life, Hergé would say that no ill intention was behind the drawing. It was here that Hergé would begin overseeing colorized reprints of his previous works and collaborating with the artist Edgar P. Jacobs and Alice Devos to aid him in coloring and generating the art for the new volumes. This is often looked back on as the highest point that Tintin ever reached, which was under Nazi supervision.

Hergé would soon go on to create Secret of the Unicorn, Red Rackham's Treasure, and The Seven Crystal Balls. This trilogy of books is often referred to as the best work that Hergé ever produced and his second masterpiece. And, as is the case with most good things in life, as soon as it got great, it all came crashing down. The Allied forces liberated Brussels. And Le Soir was shut down on September 2, 1944. The next day, Hergé was arrested after being named in a document known as the "Gallery of Traitors."

The Allied forces seized control of Le Soir and fired all the journalists. They were legally barred from practicing the craft again. The criticism surrounding Hergé's decisions was such a part of the Belgian conversation, that a high-profile resistance newspaper named La Patrie made a parody comic called Adventures of Tintin in the Land of the Nazis. The ire and vitriol aimed at Nazi collaborators during this time was at a fever pitch.
Over 5,500 people were sentenced to life imprisonment for how they had acted during the occupation. Some military courts handed out as much as 30,000 charges in minor violations and 25,000 in serious violations. Raymond Leblanc, a former conservative Resistance member, approached Hergé in October of 1945 about consulting on a new magazine for children that would feature comics.
He was interested, but barred from working, due to his collaborator status. Leblanc approached Walter Jean Ganshof Van Der Meersch, the head of the military tribunal that was trying cases against Nazis and their supporters. He looked into Hergé's case file and decreed that "In regards to the particularly inoffensive character of the drawings published by Remi, bringing him before a war tribunal would be inappropriate and risky."
The leniency that was afforded to Hergé did not extend to his co-workers at Le Soir. Six of the journalists that worked there were sentenced to death. And others were convicted of lengthy prison sentences.

From here, Hergé was able to leave these aspects of his past behind him and successfully propelled himself to being a globally recognized cartoonist. He launched Tintin magazine, published 24 volumes of Tintin, and licensed the character to appear on merchandise in films and on TV shows.

The real-life King Midas

If someone asked you who the richest people in history were, who would you name? Perhaps a billionaire banker or corporate mogul, like Bill Gates or John D. Rockefeller.
The correct answer is actually the African King Musa Keita I. He ruled the Mali Empire in the 14th century CE. Mansa Musa, also known as the King of Kings, amassed a gigantic fortune that made him the wealthiest person who ever lived to this day. However, his vast wealth is only a part of his rich legacy.

Mansa Musa came to power in 1312. At that time, much of Europe was racked by famine and civil wars, while many African kingdoms and the Islamic world were flourishing.
Mansa Musa played a great role in reaping the fruits of this prosperity to his own realm.
He strategically annexed the city of Timbuktu and reestablished power over the city of Gao, so that he could gain power over the important trade routes between the Mediterranean and the West African Coast, starting a period of expansion for the kingdom of Mali, which dramatically increased its size.

The territory of the Mali Empire was already blessed by natural resources, such as gold and salt. But the world world first became aware of the extent of Mansa Musa's wealth in 1324, when he took his pilgrimage to Mecca. Now, the wealthiest person in history does not travel on a budget, so he brought with him a caravan stretching as far as the eye could see.

Accounts of this very expensive journey are largely based on oral testimonies and differing written records, so it's difficult to substantiate the exact details. But what most historiographers agree on is the extravagant scale of the caravan.

All the chroniclers describe an entourage of tens of thousands of civilians, soldiers, and slaves; at least 500 heralds proudly bearing gold staffs and elegantly dressed in fine silks; and many horses and camels carrying an undetermined amount of gold bars.

When he stopped in larger cities, such as Cairo, Mansa Musa reportedly spent a good portion of those substantial quantities of gold, buying souvenirs, giving to the poor, and building the occasional mosque along the way. In fact, it is said that his spending may have destabilized the regional economies, by causing mass inflation. This journey might have taken over a year, and by the time Mansa Musa had returned to his Empire, the stories of his amazing wealth had been spread to the ports of the Mediterranean. Mali and its kingdom were elevated to something akin a legendary status and his legacy was cemented by their inclusion on the 1375 Catalan Atlas.

The Catalan Atlas was one of the most important world maps of Medieval Europe, it depicted the King of Mali holding a scepter and a gleaming gold nugget. With one lavish journey, Mansa Musa had literally put himself and his empire on the map.

Material riches weren't Mansa Musa's only concern, especially since he had so much of it. He was a devout Muslim, which was why he took a particular interest in Timbuktu, that was already a center of religion and learning before he had annexed it. After he returned from his pilgrimage, he commenced the construction of the great Djinguereber Mosque, which was built in Timbuktu with the help of an Andalusian architect.

He also established a major university, to further elevate the city's reputation and attract scholars and students from all over the Islamic world.

Under Mansa Musa, the Empire of Mali became urbanized: he saw that mosques and schools were built in hundreds of highly populated towns all over his empire. The king's rich legacy and wisdom persisted for generations and to this day, there are mausoleums, libraries, and mosques survive as a testament to the golden age of Mali's history under his most prolific King.

The burning mystery of a virgin warrior

She may be the most famous person to ever get burned at the stake, but do you really know everything there is to know about Joan of Arc? Joan of Arc, or la Pucelle as she preferred to be called, was one of the most iconic and brilliant female soldiers of all time. And there's a whole lot more to her rags to riches to rags story than you'd probably ever realize.

You know you're an icon in the making when a world-famous wizard predicts your emergence onto the international stage. Merlin, the legendary wizard who counseled King Arthur, had predicted a maiden would come out of an ancient forest to rescue France. And Joan certainly delivered on that. And it wasn't just Merlin. Other prophecies were circulating at the time that a virgin from Lorraine, Joan's hometown in France, would come and save France from England.

The prophetess Marie of Avignon claimed a woman in armor would save France. Was it a coincidence or was Joan of Arc, a woman who loves armor, destined to live out the life she did?
Living out a prophecy from Merlin is a pretty cool way to carve out a path for yourself.

We all know Joan of Arc was burned at the stake by the English, but what if she wasn't? Some scholars theorize that it was at least possible that a substitute maiden could have been burned in Joan's place, with Joan assuming a new identity after the fact. After her death, it became a tradition for women to essentially cosplay as Joan and claim to be her. Scholars are pretty sure they were all fake, but one woman stood out, Claude des Armoises.
In one version of this history, Claude was a real-life wife and mother who was supported by Joan of Arc's real-life brothers. They supposedly recognized her at first sight as their sister and Claude assumed that identity in order to gain their support. The story goes she didn't last long in the role of Joan, and eventually confessed her guilt. However in the alternate version of this tale, Claude is the identity the real Joan took on after the bait and switch at the stake. What a baller move, Joan.

But unfortunately, Joan wasn't perfect. With all that warfare, she was bound to have a skeleton or two in her closet. While Joan was devoutly religious and pious during her entire life, she did accidentally associate with some shady characters. One of Joan's most trusted and important soldiers was Gilles de Rais.
Gilles, who was said to have been guilty of torture, rape, murdering hundreds of kids in a dungeon, and worshipping the devil, led Joan's troops and also aided Joan when she was injured at Orléans. Joan may have had a direct phone line to God, but the girl was a mess when it came to picking friends.
I mean, the guy was also probably one of the first ever recorded serial killers.

Was Joan's ascension from poor maiden to friend of the royals a case of nepotism? Probably not, but some have said she had really intense kingly connections, so much so that she was actually a secret royal lovechild. Scandalous!

One theory suggests Joan wasn't born a peasant girl, but she was really Charles the VII's illegitimate half-sister cousin, the child of his mother-- the famously licentious Queen Isabeau of Bavaria-- and her lover, his uncle, Louis, duke of Orléans. Talk about a tangled web of incest drama. It's like Game of Thrones with a better final season. Some say this was the reason Joan was able to recognize the dauphin among a bunch of his courtiers when he met him for the first time. Unfortunately for conspiracy theorists, these dramatic rumors are most likely untrue. But they did make for some seriously salacious 13th century tabloid fodder though. Can you imagine the headlines?

When she hit puberty, Joan began to hear saints speaking to her. They told her to be pious and eventually to save France from the English. At the time, she was considered a saint receiving the word of God. But by today's standards, Joan was afflicted with something a lot less heavenly. Modern psychiatrists have posthumously diagnosed Joan with a slew of conditions such as schizophrenia, bipolar disorder, or a specific kind of epilepsy that might explain her hearing voices.
Considering that no modern doctor ever got a chance to meet Joan, it's hard to say officially just what was going on in that head of hers. Aside from mental illness, some modern scholars have suggested that she suffered from bovine tuberculosis, postulating that the consumption of unpasteurized milk could have given Joan brain lesions. When all else fails, blame it on the bad milk.

Joan definitely had all the right friends in all the right places, and there's likely a reason for that. Some say the powerful royal Duchess Yolande of Aragon, later Anjou, used Joan as a political and propaganda tool to push the future King Charles the VII's agenda. You see, Yolande was Charles' mother-in-law and a big advocate for him to take power over the English and his rival, the Duke of Burgundy.
Perhaps, Yolande knew that the people would feel inspired by Joan's story of God telling her to save France from England. It's said that Yolande used Joan for propaganda to get her way or maybe the royals just liked Joan a whole lot.

Maybe it's because she found ways to win them over, like the time she caught onto one of Charles' cheeky little royal pranks. It must have been boring being a member of the French royal family in 1429 because Charles, the heir to the throne, was certainly up to some weird behavior when Joan met him in the March of that year. Obeying the voices in her head, Joan schlepped all the way to his court in Chinon. But when she got there, someone else was sitting on his throne. As a bit of a prank perhaps, Charles had chosen to blend in with the crowd and had a friend take up residence in the royal chair.

But there was no fooling Joan of Arc. Joan of smarts was able to pick Charles out of the crowd and address him directly, even as he was in his commoner disguise.

Her powers of intuition were so strong that their attempted prank on what they thought was a naive country girl fell completely flat on its face.

If reading this you've been thinking, "Joan of Arc sounds cool, she might be someone I'd like to be friends with", you might want to think again. Joan of Arc may have been a fierce warrior and vessel for heavenly messages, but she was kind of judge-y.

Truth be told, unless you were a devout Christian that fell directly in line with all of her beliefs, she probably wouldn't want to sit at the same lunch table as you.

In fact, despite her hard-won status as a young virginal female warrior prophetess, Joan wasn't too kind to marginalized Christians, or, as she called them, heretics.

In a letter she wrote, or rather dictated to a scribe, she harshly condemned the Hussites, a group that historians identify as one of the first movements of proto-Protestants.

She called them followers of an unlawful and disgraceful superstition. Joan rant on about them saying "you persecute and plan to overthrow and destroy this faith which God Almighty, the Son, and the Holy Spirit have raised, founded, exalted, and enlightened a thousand ways through a thousand miracles."

Joan went so far as to say that if she wasn't so busy fighting the English, she'd drop everything and fight them herself. In that same letter, Joan insulted Muslims and their faith. Joan, you need to calm down.

Puberty is a rough time for all of us, but Joan of Arc had an especially tumultuous go of it. At the same time her friends' and peers' bodies were changing, Joan started hearing voices of some saints and an archangel. She was only 12 or 13. And you thought your middle school experience was humiliating.

On top of dealing with normal puberty, Joan had to try and make sense of these new and strange feelings. Joan was literally receiving directives to lead an army to victory from the voices in her head. That's almost as confounding picking out your first deodorant. Did the rush of hormones cause her to hear voices?

Well, it's noteworthy that the first thing they ever told her was that she shouldn't pursue a man, but she remain a single virgin instead. Clearly, her preteen hormones were not ready for that first kiss anytime soon.

Most teens are moody, but Joan was, let's just say, a bit of a hurricane. Joan's teenage tendency toward anger revealed itself through her moral righteousness as she took it out on the adult male soldiers she was leading. If you've ever met a teenage hall monitor with a bone to pick, Joan would blow them out of the water.

Some say that while leading her troops, she'd forbid any and all swearing or failure to attend mass. What a narc. Joan drove mistresses and prostitutes out of the camp with her sword. Once when a Scottish dude confessed to eating stolen meat, she attempted to slap him in retribution.

Rather than just going by Joan, this warrior woman dubbed herself la Pucelle, best translated from French as the maid or the girl. In fact, she preferred being called by that nickname rather than with her regular name, probably because of its religious connotations. She loved being associated with purity, especially it highlighted her own virginity and her similarity with the Virgin Mary. Also, Joan probably liked the moniker because it distinguished her from many of the other women hanging around soldiers, a.k.a. prostitutes, or maybe she just didn't really like the name Joan.

Joan of Arc's mysterious path to martyrdom and sainthood is one filled with intrigue, conspiracies, and magical portents. From the voices in her head that may or may not have been the most prescient form of mental illness in history to Merlin's prediction of her coming, Joan of Arc is one of the most intriguing figures of the Middle Ages. So was it God? Was it magic? Was it mental illness or did the girl just want an excuse to boss a bunch of adult male soldiers around? Either way, it's clear that her place in history is cemented eternally for a reason. While the British may have burned her body at the stake when she refused to confess, her story is a candle that will burn on forever.

The tragic fate of the man who taught us to wash our hands

> Just over 200 years ago, a child was born here in the old city of Buda, in central Europe who would save thousands of lives and bring hope to people around the world. He became known as the saviour of mothers and the father of infection control.

Ignaz Semmelweis was born into a world of dying women. One in every six women were dying in child birth. In some areas, the mortality rate was as high as 30 percent. He became a doctor and decided to do something about it. He wanted to find out why all these women were dying.

As he began to study and investigate, he discovered something shocking, something appalling. The doctors were going from the morgue where they'd prepared dead bodies for burial directly to the maternity ward and deliver babies. They didn't know about germs at the time and didn't realise that they were transferring deadly infections from the morgue to the birthing rooms.

Semmelweis started to experiment. He found that if the doctors washed their hands after working in the morgue before going to the birthing rooms, the death rate dropped from one in six to one in fifty. He'd found the cure. All you have to do is wash your hands. It's just as simple as that.

But the response of the medical fraternal to his discovery was truly surprising.

The magnificent capital of Hungary was once two towns on either side of the beautiful Blue Danube River. The hilly town of Buda on one side and across the river on the plains was the town of Pest. In 1873 the two towns were united as Budapest. Budapest is considered one of the most romantic and beautiful cities in Europe and attracts over five million international tourists every year. It has something for everyone. From dramatic history and flamboyant architecture to healing thermal waters, mediaeval monuments and wonderful museums. During the 18th century, the towns were under the rule of Charles the Third. Buda and Pest were insignificant provincial towns that later fell under the control of Vienna and became part of the Austria-Hungarian empire. This empire became one of Europe's major powers in the late 19th century and lasted from 1867 to 1918. It became the second largest country in Europe after the Russian empire. But broke apart into several states at the end of World War One.

One hundred years earlier, on the first of July 1818, Ignaz Philipp Semmelweis was born in Taban, an area of Old Buda. He was the fifth child of ten born to the prosperous grocer family of Joseph Semmelweis.
Their son, Ignaz Semmelweis was known as a curious child. He would often get into trouble at school for asking too many questions that disrupted the class.
When Ignaz finished school, he left his home in Budapest and travelled to Vienna, the capital of Austria. There in the autumn of 1837, Semmelweis began studying law at the University of Vienna.
But the following year he switched to studying medicine.

He graduated in 1844 and was awarded his degree in medicine from the University of Vienna. He applied for an appointment in a clinic for internal medicine and was bitterly disappointed when he didn't get the position.

He decided to specialize in obstetrics, the branch of medicine and surgery concerned with childbirth and midwifery. In 1846, Semmelweis was appointed assistant to Professor Johann Klein in the first obstetrical clinic of the Vienna General Hospital and soon became an obstetrician in his own right at the Vienna Maternity and Labor and Delivery Hospital. Semmelweis loved his work but he became increasingly distressed by the number of women that died after childbirth.

At that time, in the first half of the 19th century, women giving birth in Europe were ravaged by puerperal fever, also known as childbed fever. Which was caused by bacterial infection following childbirth or a miscarriage.

The women would suffer from high fevers, severe abdominal pain, chills, pale skin and discharge, and many would eventually die from the infection. The standard procedure by medical staff at this time was to bleed the patient.

Now the process of bleeding involved cutting the patient's arm and letting at least half a litre of blood flow out. Few women recovered after the bloodletting.

This medical procedure worried Semmelweis and by 1847 he decided to investigate what was causing the childbed fever and find ways that it could be prevented.

Semmelweis was just 29 years old when he became the chief obstetrician of two maternity wards in two separate clinics in Vienna. One of the wards was part of the medical school in which pregnant women were treated by experienced doctors and medical students. The doctors in this first clinic had a regular daily schedule.

Their first task at the beginning of each day was to perform autopsies in the morgue on corpses of women who had died the previous day. Then the doctors would move on to treating other patients with infections or diseases. And finally, they went to the maternity ward to the women in labor and delivered the babies.

The second clinic was a gratis institution that offered free medical care to poor or underprivileged women, including prostitutes. In return for the free services, the women would be the patients of midwives and their students. So, at this charity clinic for pregnant women, all the babies were delivered by midwives. In fact, virtually all the work of this clinic was performed by midwives and midwifery students. What was interesting was that the mortality rate from childbed fever at this clinic was only two percent.

Whereas at the first clinic where the doctors performed the work, the average mortality rate from childbed fever was about 16 percent, which meant that the supposedly better clinic had a significantly higher death rate than the second clinic.

Now of course the big question was, what was causing the difference? Why did the doctor's clinic have a much higher death rate than the midwife clinic?

These mortality rates soon became widely known outside the hospital. Due to the bad reputation of the maternity ward of the medical school clinic, women who were admitted there desperately begged the doctors to be admitted to the second clinic that was run by the midwives. Semmelweis described desperate women begging on their knees not to be admitted to the first clinic. This worried Semmelweis. He desperately wanted to find out why the doctor's patients had so many more deaths than those of the midwives.

The dominant view at the time was that something in the air or putrid tendencies in Vienna caused childbed fever. But Semmelweis considered this nonsense as both clinics were in the same hospital and close to each other.

Another theory was overcrowding. But that was also ridiculous because the free charity clinic was far more crowded than the clinic for paid patients run by the doctors. Even the diets and general care in both clinics were the same. Moreover, even the way the babies were delivered was the same because both the doctors and the midwives were using the same methods and techniques.

So, Semmelweis decided it was time to begin a more thorough and painstaking investigation into the practices at the hospital. Without understanding how, he discovered that infection is spread from one patient to another by contact. And in particular, facilitated by frequent internal patient examinations by the doctors and medical students. These doctors and their medical students, as we've seen, went from the morgue where they examined corpses straight to the delivery rooms. Semmelweis began to realize that there must be a connection.

The doctors must have carried something on their hands from the dead body to the women giving birth. The doctor's hands were almost always dirty and had a foul odor after leaving the morgue and they didn't wash their hands before going on to see their patients. This gave Semmelweis an idea.
He thought he could develop and implement a strict protocol of hand washing with disinfectant by the doctors before they had contact with every new patient.

To his amazement, just the simple practice of the doctors washing their hands between patients reduced the hospital death rate down to practically zero. He'd found the cure. All you have to do is wash your hands. It's just as simple as that.

But the response of the medical fraternal to his discovery was truly surprising. They flatly rejected this simple cure. The hospital administration and general medical community refused to adopt Semmelweis' ideas of practice. Their open resistance and ridicule surprised, dismayed and angered him. Lives were at stake. This was a life and death matter. Semmelweis was so enraged at the medical establishment's failure to even consider a simple hand washing trial to save lives that he wrote letters to medical journals accusing the doctors of being murderers. Of course, this didn't endear him to the medical fraternal or make him popular with his peers.

It was only after a colleague accidentally punctured his finger with a scalpel during an autopsy in the morgue and subsequently died of septicemia a few days later that Semmelweis had proof of the connection between the morgue and the maternity rooms. His friend developed a high fever and all of the other symptoms that the women had when they died of childbed fever.
Semmelweis concluded that his doctor-colleague and the women with childbed fever died from the same cause. He now had proof that there was a connection between the soiled hands of the doctors and childbed fever in women who were examined by them.

Semmelweis then established a system of cleaning hands for all those working in the first clinic. He ordered that all doctors, medical students and midwives wash their hands in chlorinated lime before examining the women. The result was remarkable. In one year, the death rate from childbed fever dropped from around 16 percent to 1.2 percent in the doctor's clinic and from 2.8 percent to 1.3 percent in the midwife's section. He even recommended that all instruments used on patients also be cleansed with chlorinated-lime solutions.

Unfortunately, Semmelweis found continued skepticism and scorn among his colleagues wherever he went. His focus on clean hands and cleanliness was considered extreme and largely ignored. Rejected or ridiculed. In desperation, he began passing out hand bills in the street telling women to demand that their doctors wash their hands.

But this is where Semmelweis ran into more trouble. Unfortunately, his observations differed with the established medical opinion of the time. His perfectly reasonable hand washing suggestions were ridiculed and rejected by his contemporaries and even by Professor Johann Klein, the medical director and his first boss in Vienna.
It was none other than Professor Johann Klein who stripped Semmelweis of his university and hospital position and repeatedly blocked his career progress in Vienna after he went public with his opinion. His contract in Vienna was terminated and he was dismissed from the hospital for political reasons.

Even though hand washing had proved hugely successful and in spite of the various publications of proven results in 1861 that definitively showed that hand washing reduced mortality to below one percent, Semmelweis' ideas were rejected by the medical community and those in authority.

The problem was mainly that Semmelweis couldn't offer any acceptable scientific explanation for his findings, he "only" had empirical proofs on his side, but no convincing underlying theory. Moreover, some doctors took umbrage at the suggestion that they should wash their hands and lashed out at him, without considering his opinion. Some doctors refused to believe that their hands, a gentleman's hands, could transmit disease.
He was continually harassed by the medical community in Vienna and was eventually forced to move back to Budapest.

Semmelweis couldn't find a job so he worked as the unpaid head physician at the obstetric ward in Pest's Saint Rochus Hospital and virtually eliminated the epidemic of childbed fever there. Yet Ede Florian Birly, Professor of Obstetrics at the University of Pest, considered Semmelweis crazy and mentally unstable and continued to believe that childbed fever was caused by a dirty colon and treated it with enemas. Fortunately for the patients, Semmelweis replaced him in 1854.

He immediately implemented chlorine hand washing and instrument washing, and childbed fever almost disappeared in his clinic. In 1857 he married Maria Weidenhofer who was 19 years younger than him and they had five children. All this time Semmelweis was focused on his work. He was outraged by the continued indifference of the medical profession to the cure for childbed fever.

Desperate to have someone listen to his theory, he began writing increasingly angry open letters to prominent European obstetricians, going as far as denouncing them as irresponsible murderers. Not surprisingly, that didn't help much. Having lost all hopes, he became severely depressed.
Overawed by his frustration and inability to save the mothers of Europe. His contemporaries, including his wife, believed he was losing his mind and in 1865, nearly 20 years after his breakthrough, he was committed to an insane asylum in Vienna.
Ignaz Semmelweis died on August 13th, 1865, at 47 years of age, barely two weeks after he was committed. He most likely died due to a gangrenous wound on his right hand caused by a struggle with the guards. The autopsy reported the cause of death as septicemia, otherwise known as blood poisoning. Talk about the irony!

Semmelweis was buried in Vienna on August 15th, 1865 and very few people attended the service. Short announcements of his death were published in a few medical journals in Vienna and Budapest.
Even if the rules of the Hungarian Association of Physicians and Natural Scientists specifically stated that a commemorative address had to be delivered in honor of the members who had died in the preceding year, they didn't bother to enforce this rule for Semmelweis. After all, he was widely hated and despised, and had died in disgrace.
His death was never even mentioned. It went unnoticed. His remains were transferred to Budapest in 1891.

On the eleventh of October 1964 they were transferred once more to the house in which he was born. The house is now a historical museum and library honoring Ignaz Semmelweis. Janos Diescher was appointed Semmelweis' successor at the Pest University maternity clinic. Immediately, mortality rates jumped six-fold to six percent. But the physicians of Budapest said nothing. There were no inquiries, no protests. Almost no one, either in Vienna or in Budapest seemed to have been willing to acknowledge Semmelweis' life and work and implement his simple cure and recommendations.

Even if he never lived to see it, Semmelweis' advice on chlorine washings was more influential than he could have ever realized. Already a few years after his death, many doctors, particularly in Germany showed themselves quite willing to put aside their pride and experiment with the practical hand washing protocols that he had proposed in Budapest.

However, Semmelweis' practice earned widespread recognition only years after his demise, when Louis Pasteur developed the germ theory of disease, offering a theoretical and scientific explanation for Semmelweis' empirical findings. Today, Semmelweis is considered a pioneer of antiseptic procedures.

We recognize Semmelweis as one of the founders of modern antiseptic methods and a proud son of Hungary. He's honored by numerous institutions named after him, including hospitals, universities and clinics. Even stamps and coins have been issued bearing his name and image.

That's quite a legacy. Hospitals, universities, clinics, museums, stamps and coins carry the name Ignaz Semmelweis today

The most underrated wild man of the American Revolution

Despite there being over four scores of Founding Fathers to the United States, most of us can only name the most famous of the bunch. But considering how often Americans enjoy outrageous stories of womanizing and booze parties, it's a bit weird that the name Gouverneur Morris doesn't come up more often. Nicknamed the "Penman of the Constitution," not only did Morris substantially contribute to the founding of America, but did so while living a life of public sex, seedy affairs, and vengeful dismemberment.

Morris had grown up in the Bronx and he worked for the New York revolutionary government before becoming one of the youngest members to serve in the Continental Congress. He was a hard worker who spearheaded multiple committees and became close friend with George Washington, a man he would support for many years to come.

The nickname of Penman of the Constitution was not for nothing. Morris earned the title quite literally on account of him writing the United States Preamble, coining key phrases you might have heard such as "We the people of the United States." During the Constitutional Convention at Independence Hall of 1787, Morris held the distinct honor of addressing the crowd more than any of the other delegates, exactly 173 times.

In a time when the most influential men of our newly minted country owned thousands of slaves, you might be surprised to hear how adamantly Gouverneur Morris hated the practice. In one of his many speeches before the Constitutional Convention in 1787 he succinctly called "The Curse of Slavery," Morris denounced the practice as a nefarious institution that "in defiance of the most sacred laws of humanity tears away his fellow creatures from their dearest connections and damns them to the most cruel bondages."

Along with pointing out its unfathomable cruelty, Morris correctly foresaw the rift such an institution would create in the country, essentially predicting the inevitable civil war to follow.

To move on to a sillier subject, the most known proclivity of this Founding Father was getting it on in public. And while the more adventurous types amongst you could possibly relate, I am willing to bet that your tales of public display of affection don't involve getting it on in the Louvre.

Before it was the most famous and crowded art museum in the world, the house of Mona Lisa was the house of the French king.

One particular resident happened to be a married woman who was rather friendly with Gouverneur Morris. In one of his journal entries, Morris described a visit to this lady friend saying, "We take the chance of interruption and celebrate in the passage while Mademoiselle is at the harpsichord in the Drawing Room. The husband is below. Visitors are hourly expected. The doors are all open." While that might sound perfectly innocent, it takes a much different meaning if you note that Mr. Morris often used the word "celebrate" as a code word for "sex." Put it simply, Morris "celebrated" with this mysterious woman in an open hallway in the Louvre to the romantic sound of a harpsichord while her husband was just a few feet away.

And that's not the only record of this heroic and patriotic philanderer having a "celebration" with a married woman.

Unless you're doing it wrong, sex generally doesn't result in the loss of a limb. But he was nothing if not a brave pioneer, so he was definitely up to the challenge.
In 1780, according to the historian Dave Kimball, Morris was confronted by an angry husband who had caught his wife in the company of the Founding Father presumably "celebrating."
After a chase through the Philadelphia streets, we're hoping Morris was clothed at the time (even though it is quite funny to think about one of our Founding Fathers running around in his breeches), he was accidentally struck by an oncoming carriage, resulting in the injury and amputation of his leg. Which teaches us that even without cars, you should not jaywalk, or sleep with other men's wives.

While losing a leg might dissuade the less stubborn, Morris continued his long life of sleeping with other men's wives, so much so that fellow Founding Father John Jay once exclaimed that he wished Morris had lost something else instead.

But in 1809, this Evel Knievel of womanizing finally decided to settle down. And at the age of 57, he announced his marriage to Anne Cary Randolph, who was his 34-year-old housekeeper at the time. Besides being 22 years younger, Anne had earned a certain fame for a previous affair she had with her brother-in-law. The affair had resulted in a baby that mysteriously died just after he was born. Accused of the child's murder, Anne and the suspected father were detained and eventually brought to trial.

But after a particularly heated hearing, the case was ultimately dismissed due to lack of evidence. Apparently, the tawdry story that has been dubbed the first scandal of American history did not bothered Gouverneur and by all accounts, they were quite in love and spent the rest of their life happily married, despite her being a suspected infanticidal young bride and him being a known humanizer with a peg leg.

He landed a sweet job as the diplomat to France, which seems like a pretty comfortable gig, if it were not for the fact that during that time, Paris became the scene for most iconic act of civil unrest.
Unfortunately for Morris, the time he served as Minister Plenipotentiary to France went from 1792 to 1794, also known as the bloodiest years of the French Revolution.

Morris was often forced to face anti-aristocratic revolutionaries head-on, and according to historian Forrest McDonald was once forced to ward off a mob by literally thinking on his feet or foot, in his case. When riding in a quite ostentatious carriage, the distressed diplomat thrust his now wooden leg out a window in order to baffle the oncoming throng, his cries of "vive la révolution" confusing them enough to make a speedy getaway.

Being strongly and ironically opposed to the revolution, Morris even attempted to rescue Louis the XVI and Marie Antoinette from their inevitable fate.

Once the rescue attempt of the two royals failed miserably, he did manage to rescue and ship their personal furniture to his home in the Bronx, including an intricately decorated armchair that originally resided at Versailles. Just because you can't save your aristocratic pals, it doesn't mean you can't enjoy their aristocratic comfort anymore.

He readily enjoyed them in his family estate, 500 acres of land along the Harlem River that the Morris family had once purchased. This land would go on to become the residence of our one-legged, lady-loving constitutional creator. Named for his family, the neighborhood of Morrisania would become the home to Morris' estate expand to 2,000 acres. It is now known with its modern moniker of South Bronx.

This wasn't even close to the only influence the name "Morris" had on the city of New York, as Gouverneur went on to play a big part in the layout of modern Manhattan. Just for starters, Morris was one of the earliest advocates for the Erie Canal, his efforts establishing the creation of the Western and Northern Inland Lock Navigation Companies in 1792.

In 1887, Morris would be appointed to a group tasked with reforming the entire layout of the city. The commission rejected the European influence of old, opting for a grid system containing 155 streets and 12 avenues. Anyone faintly familiar with NY will recognize it as the modern and extremely convenient system we still have today.

Gouverneur Morris died the way he lived: getting in trouble on account of what was between his legs or, in his case, his leg. In November of 1816, Morris seemed to have trouble urinating. The problem was identified as a blockage in his urethra.

Historians would later diagnose this as a likely prostate cancer. To be more specific and way more grotesque, Morris thought that a piece of whale bone would a handy tool to get in there and treat the blockage. Yeah. That must have hurt. This very painful game of self-operation led indeed to internal injuries, infections, and inevitably, death.

For all his impact on the founding of America, diaries of the French Revolution, and contributions to New York City, it's almost comforting that Morris managed to stay weird and sex-crazed from the beginning to his very painful and uncomfortable end.

The perfect murder

Marguerite Alibert's story is a tale of gritty survival, lucrative sex work, and murder. Alibert was a formidable woman who pulled herself up from a world of poverty to the rarefied atmosphere of the France's elite, all the while accomplishing her goal of turning affairs into large sums of money.
For Marguerite love was a way to survive and thrive. She was first one of Prince Edward VIII's mistresses and then went on to marry an Egyptian royal. After it seemed shed had obtained everything she ever wished for, her story takes a murderous turn.
In the end, Marguerite went down in infamy as the princess who got away with murder.

The daughter of a taxi coach driver and a maid, Marguerite Alibert was born into France's middle class, that is to say, not quite dire poverty in the winter of 1890.
Her mother and father were, not to put too fine a point on it, total failures as parents.

When her younger four-year-old brother got run over by a lorry, and rather than going after the driver or at least carrying Junior down to the cemetery, the parents sent their naughty, brother-losing daughter to the Sisters of Mary for psychological torture. The nuns taught young Marguerite that if not for her sins, her four-year-old brother would still be alive regardless of the lorry.
With more help from the Sisters of Mary, Marguerite spent the rest of her guilt-ridden childhood cleaning someone else's house, only to lose both the childhood and the house to an unplanned pregnancy at 16.
They threw her out of the house to starve in the streets.

While Marguerite's "don't ask" baby went on to live on a farm, as they did in those days, Marguerite herself became a sex worker and was scouted by one Madame Denart, keeper of courtesans.
The Madame trained Marguerite to use her natural charm and beauty to make money instead of babies, which suited Marguerite just fine.
Marguerite had already learned from the sisters of Mary that she could only count on herself if she was to survive and flourish in any way.
She had also learned to sing there. Mezzo soprano, a handy skill in any quality courtesan's garter belt.
It seems she'd found a fulfilling career in which to put everything she'd gotten from her parents to good use.

Marguerite had a number of aliases, including Maggie Meller, taken from her first almost husband, a wealthy 40-year-old stable owner, Andre Meller, himself a married man. As we'll see soon, she was nuts for horses, money, and the name Meller.
While Maggie was never actually married to Meller, what with the laws of man and God and all, the 17-year-old liked the name and the money enough to take them for herself. We must admit Maggie Meller does have a ring to it, and it would soon become apparent to her that that ring was the only kind of ring she'd get from this fellow. Ironically, Andre, still married six years later, hung up his sugar daddy shingle because Maggie couldn't or wouldn't stay faithful to him.

Freed from the clutches of abject poverty and in possession of about 200,000 British pounds courtesy of Mr. Meller, Maggie got Raymonde, her "don't ask" baby, back from the farm and would later send her to school in London. It was the only really decent thing she's known to have done.

Prince Edward VIII, having recently borrowed a hooker from a friend to take care of his virginity problem, was just one of Maggie's many moneyed men, but he was also the Prince of Wales, heir to the British throne, and so here our story takes a fun turn.

Maggie was in her late 20s and an experienced Parisian courtesan at the time. Prince Eddie was a baby in comparison: 23, royal, freshly deflowered, and out on leave during his very first World War.
Their "frinedhip" was the good Queen Mother's worst nightmare.

Edward fell head over heels for Marguerite for about a year before he got bored, just long enough to write what he would go on to call "Oh those bloody letters." in a lament to his advisor Joey Legh.
But while the average parents might be embarrassed if confronted with the blathering of their firstborn in the spring of his first love, that shit could have ruined the royal family.
It may come as a shock that Maggie actually did settle down. Well, she got married anyway. In 1919 after a year of sending a regular stinker to Prince Edward VIII reminding him that she still had all those bloody letters, Maggie Meller married Charles Laurent.
He was handsome and boring, and he saved Prince Edward a lot of trouble. People, this is why boring exists. They divorced six months later netting Maggie a nice settlement to call her own. An apartment, 10 horse stables, cars, heaps of servants, and of course, a new name to use should the mood take her.

Maggie's new bae was actually a bey, or lord, not a prince. But that didn't stop people in certain circles from calling her Princess Fahmy when she married the hilariously wealthy Ali Kamel Fahmy Bey and settled down with him in Cairo.
The Egyptian, not a prince, received his title of bey from Egypt, and Egypt is an Islam-oriented nation. The strictly upright life of a bey's wife was not exactly appealing to thoroughly-established hedonist and probable dominatrix Maggie Meller, but she agreed to it on two conditions.

The first was that she be allowed to wear Western clothing.
The second, that she be allowed to divorce him. Prince Fahmy wasn't so into that, but he was willing to pretend it if it meant Maggie would convert. Just before the wedding, the clever bey slid the divorce clause off the table and replaced it with an edict that he be allowed to get himself more wives. Maybe they were true soulmates after all.
Why the bey thought this devilishly sexy twice-divorced Parisian prostitute he met while she was escorting a different rich man around an exotic country a year ago would ever become a proper Islamic wife, we have no idea. But apparently, he did, bless his heart.

Bey Fahmy and his princess fought more or less constantly, sometimes even carrying on with their rows in broad daylight in front of other people. He complained that her independence, insatiable sexuality, and general personality were utterly humiliating. This was, in fact, exactly what the bey had signed up for, but he seems to not ever have really figured that out.

Bey Fahmy had a certain reputation around Egypt as a closeted homosexual. Whether to perpetuate that rumor or to use it to her advantage, Maggie claimed to have been torn during unnatural intercourse. Considering her line of work, this coy, false-claimed innocence is pretty foul no matter what she meant it to do for her.

Those who knew her well enough suspected that she was working on getting another fat divorce settlement because this claim was one of many in a growing list of abuses she was collecting so soon after the marriage.
But wait, what about that last minute no divorce, more wives clause? Well, we'll never know how that battle might have gone, probably not great because it's perhaps a bit too perfect that the couple should have returned from a showing of The Merry Widow to have a violent fight in their hotel room that would make a merry widow of Maggie Meller on the night of July 9, 1923.
After a lot of shouting upon their return from the theater, the bey left.
He returned a few hours later and would never leave again under his own power. Around 2:00 that morning, three shots were heard.

Princess Fahmy was arrested, and an hour later, the bey was dead, shot by his wife in the back of the head with a .38 she'd been keeping under her pillow. It was rather neatly packaged as far as homicides go. There was no mystery. The murder weapon, the perpetrator, and the victim were all accounted for. There were no extra threads to untangle, witnesses present before and after the shooting, rounded the case out nicely.

But let's not forget about those bloody letters, because she certainly did not. Prince Edward VIII, who all things considered, got out of this lightly compared to Joey Legh.

Knowing that she was not born into aristocracy and that she might need to have a bit of insurance for rainy day, she had carefully kept 20 letters from Prince Edward VII, which were wildly indiscreet: he said things about the conduct of war that might have been misinterpreted, he made rude remarks about his father and there's a commonly sexual content to them as well. They're not the kind of letters you would have wanted the world to know about. Put all that together and you have the keys to a royal get out of jail free card. Maggie's mother's nuns didn't raise no fool. Her regular stinker of a threat letter to Prince Edward VIII about his letters was a refrain the former choir girl turned call girl was happy to sing again, only this time there was a lot more than 100,000 pounds on the line. Strings were pulled to protect the prince and his family's reputation.

Maggie's life as a lady of the night was never admitted into evidence and therefore couldn't be examined, thus taking care of those pesky letters and making sure no one would think less of Maggie for her work or Eddie for ever having been 23. This combined with some classic racism of the Roaring '20s ensured the defense could paint the picture they needed.

The late bey as the wife-beating, buying, swapping subhuman. Marguerite as the hapless white woman trapped in his savage brown clutches.

Guess how that turned out? Yeah, every decade has its trial of the century. This was one of them. People lined up around the building to see the action, or sent their servants to buy and/or save seats for them. Aside from the vicious slander of the victim, though, there wasn't much actual, well, action.

In September 1923, Bey Fahmy was convicted in the public mind of being an evil, depraved, racially inferior, perverted little monster man. Marguerite Alibert was acquitted of all charges.

Maggie returned to her native Paris to live a long, comfortable life of luxury. She continued her exciting lifestyle, but eventually withdrew from the limelight, supported by at least five different ex-husbands until her death at age 80 in 1971. Prince Edward's mistake is a cautionary tale to us all in the age of the internet. As for Maggie, we learned that a little extortion, a little imagination, and a lot of blackmail can make a very merry widow indeed.

The scandalous life of Jane Digby

Jane Digby led a wonderfully rebellious life, putting her freedom above everything else. She had countless affairs, several marriages, and a great deal of fun! She lived in the most lavish European courts and in caves. She spoke eight languages, adapted to every situation, and was an expert markswoman. She also contributed to the invention of the term "cad".

Jane Digby, born on the 3rd April 1807, died on the 11th August 1881. Jane was the daughter of senior British naval officer Admiral Henry Digby, who sailed under Admiral Nelson during the Battle of Trafalgar, and renowned beauty Lady Jane Elizabeth Coke.
Her family's fortune was acquired from the capture of the Spanish treasure ship Santa Brigida in 1799.
In 1824 when Jane was seventeen years old, she was married to a man twice her age, Edward Law, 1st Earl of Ellenborough. During their marriage, she had three affairs. One with herher maternal cousin, Colonel George Anson and on Austrian Statesman Prince Felix of Schwarzenberg.
In 1828, Jane had a son Arthur Dudley Law and despite some doubt about whether it was her husband or her cousin who fathered him, Edward acknowledged the child as legitimate.

It was around this time that Jane began her affair with Prince Felix and the two had a daughter named Mathilde in 1829. Due to the fact that Jane was still married to Edward at the time, she was sent away to be raised by Felix's sister. In February of 1830 Arthur died at just two years old and shortly after his death, Edward divorced Jane by an act of Parliament in what became a public scandal. Jane emigrated to Paris with Prince Felix, where in December of 1830 they had a son, also named Felix.
The child tragically died just weeks after his birth and Prince Felix abandoned Jane in Paris. It was from these events that the then derogatory word "cad" originated. The Prince's nickname was "Cad" after his favourite horse "Cadlands". After his desertion of Jane, the term became associated with ill-bred behaviour towards women.

After Paris Jane travelled to Munich where she became the mistress of Ludwig I, King of Bavaria.
While at court, Jane met Baron Karl von Venningen. They married in 1833 and went on to have two children together, a son Heribert and a daughter Bertha.

In 1838 Jane began an affair with a Greek Count Spyridon Theotokis and they had a son together named Leonidas in 1840. Upon discovering their affair, her husband challenged the Count to a duel in which the latter was wounded. Despite winning the duel, Venningen released Jane from their marriage, took care of their children and remained her close friend for the rest of their lives.

Even if she was not legally divorced from her husband until 1842, in 1841 Jane decided to convert to the Greek Orthodox faith and marry Theotokis. The newlywed couple moved to Greece where yet another strategy struck her in 1846 when their son Leonidas fell from a balcony and subsequently died.

Shortly after the child's death Theotokis divorced Jane and she soon became the mistress of King Otto of Greece, son of her previous lover Ludwig I, King of Bavaria.
While in King Otto's court she was introduced to Christodoulos Chatzipetros, a war hero from the Greek War of Independence and close advisor to the King.

Their affair, as well as Chatzipetros' various other sex scandals, lead to their dismissal from court and for a time Jane lived a nomadic lifestyle of riding horses, living in caves and hunting in the mountains. It was during this time that she gained remarkable equestrian and marksman skills.

Their relationship ended when Jane discovered his repeated infidelity and left him.

In 1853 at the age of forty-six years old Jane travelled to the Middle East and fell in love with a Syrian Sheik Abdul Medjuel el Mezrab, twenty years her junior. The two were married under Muslim law, highly unusual for the time, and it was reported that Jane became known as Shaikhah Umm al-Laban, meaning Mother of Milk or Milky Lady due to her fair complexion. Their marriage was a happy one; Jane adopted traditional Arab dress and learned to speak Arabic in addition to the eight other languages she spoke fluently.

They spent half of the year leading a nomadic life, living in goat hair tents in the desert. The rest of the year was spent in a luxurious villa Jane had built in Damascus. It was during her time there that she befriended the renowned British explorer Richard Burton and it was rumoured she may have contributed to his translation of the Kama Sutra. Her marriage to Abdul lasted twenty-eight years until Jane's death of fever and dysentery in 1881.

She was buried in the Protestant cemetery in Damascus and her grave bears a pink limestone footstone upon which is written her name in Arabic, written by her husband and hand carved. Jane was uncompromising in her pursuit of happiness and her many adventures spanned decades and across two continents.

The "coward, equivocator," and genocidal president

> President Andrew Jackson has a complicated legacy. On the one hand, he was a populist hero and a venerated war general. On the other hand, he was a slaving, genocidal maniac who drove the economy into the ground like a meteor shard.

Before he was a politician, Andrew Jackson was a military officer. And during the War of 1812, Jackson was shot in the arm.

The cure for bullet arm in those days was to chop off the whole thing and throw it in the nearest trash can. But Jackson wasn't having that. Jackson sought out a more holistic solution among the Cherokee. And it worked. And with that, Andrew Jackson went on to protect the people who generously saved his arm beneath the presidential mantle, providing them with civil rights under the law, and ushering in an age of peace, harmony, and culture. Just kidding.

Instead, one year into his presidency, Jackson authored one of the most twisted moments in American history. He signed the 1830 Indian Removal Act, which made it OK, legally, for the government to snatch native territories and herd residents westward into a new Indian Colonization Zone, which is government speak for internment camp. The ICZ was distinct from the US, so its people enjoyed no protection under the law. That zone is now called Oklahoma, home of Garth Brooks.

Under this act, the US army supposedly couldn't force indigenous peoples to hand their lands over. But the US army has never been good at not stealing from Native Americans, much like Andrew Jackson.

The first tribe to follow the trail, some double marched in literal chains as if armed escort wasn't enough, were the Choctaw, one of the five civilized tribes who adopted European customs to make their twitchy American neighbors less uncomfortable and still lost their homes.

The Supreme Court actually found that the state had no authority to pull this nonsense. But Jackson didn't let that bother him.

The forced march, made without food or supplies, claimed 4,000 lives. All told, over 70,000 Native Americans would be uprooted from their homes and driven westward to diminish, dwindle, and die.

Jackson was a man of many monikers. Political opponents called him King Mob for his ability to rile the electorate into a frothing ball of violence. And his election campaign was based largely in his being an experienced Indian fighter, a career that earned him the name Sharp Knife among the Cherokee he routinely slaughtered. Yeah, it wasn't a positive nickname.

After bitter fighting during the Creek War, Jackson oversaw the Creek tribe's terms of surrender. The terms were brutal. The Creek people had to surrender about 23 million acres of their land, which encompassed more than half of present-day Alabama and part of Georgia, to the federal government.

Then we had the Seminole War, the left sock of America's dirty laundry. Before Jackson got involved, Florida belonged to Spain and was home to a coalition of former slaves and Seminole Indians, an alliance that freaked Southerners out so much that they routinely sent armed posses of kidnappers over the border. Under secret orders, Jackson sent the US army into the Sunshine State, aiming to take it by right of conquest and crush the Indians and former slaves there.

He ordered his men to raise crops, abduct women and children, and deploy attack dogs. After the war, he proudly wrote to his wife, "I think I may say that the Indian War is an end for the present. The enemy is scattered over the whole face of the earth. And at least one half must starve and die with disease."

The official website for the Hermitage, a museum based at Jackson's Tennessee plantation estate, states, "in all reality, slavery was the source of Andrew Jackson's wealth." And that's in his museum. Jackson owned 161 slaves at the time of his death. While all previous presidents had slaves, Jackson also had a few fingers in the human trafficking pie.

He made his living in the domestic slave trade, which for him spanned from Virginia to New Orleans. When one of Jackson's slaves succeeded in a brave bid for freedom, Jackson offered a $50 reward and $10 extra for every 100 lashes a person will give to the amount of $300.

In 1821, he instructed his nephew to lash a woman called Betty should she continue "putting on some airs."
The fatal stabbing of a runaway slave named Gilbert supposedly humanized his approach.
But he would continue to peddle flesh until his death in 1845.

In 1806, attorney and famed duelist Charles Dickinson called the future president a coward, an equivocator, and his wife a bigamist over a horse racing argument. Jackson and his wife were technically bigamists, by the way. When he married her, she was already someone else's wife.

A butt hurt Jackson, never one to take a high road when his manhood was threatened, challenged Dickinson to a duel. Dickinson, an expert marksman, shot first and hit Jackson in the chest, shattering two of his ribs. And then, for his next act of manly chutzpah, remained where honor required him to stand, 24 feet from the wounded Jackson, who still had to take his shot if he could. Ironically, this took so long that Jackson's honor was impugned anyway. But he eventually managed to pull himself together enough to get off a fatal shot at his defamer.

Jackson would go on to engage in over 100 duels over the course of his life, nearly dying of a ruptured artery after he tried to horsewhip a man who would one day become one of his top allies in the Senate because that's how he rolled.

Andrew Jackson loathed the Bank of the United States. His actions against the bank would plunge the country into a nationwide economic depression. In 1832, Jackson shut down the Bank of the United States, opting instead to keep the nation's money in an underregulated pet bank, which loaned money to just about anyone who came asking. As any competent economist could have told him, this led to inflation.

Then Jackson had another on-brand idea: stop letting people buy land with paper money. He just didn't trust it, which no longer surprises us at this point. A specie circular, issued by Jackson on July 11, 1836, decreed that land could only be bought with gold or silver. Fairly naturally, this law slowed land speculation to a crawl, which led to decreased revenue for the states, which led in turn to the panic of 1837.

Near the end of the War of 1812, General Jackson arrived in New Orleans to find the city in disarray. Taking immediate command of the situation, Jackson put the city under martial law until the war was over, or so he said. He wouldn't actually lift the ban until months after the fighting had stopped.
When a Louisiana state senator wrote of his apprehension at the idea of an open-ended martial law, Jackson had the senator arrested. Then when one of those pesky district court judges demanded that the senator be charged or released in keeping with the Constitution of the United States, Jackson not only refused to do so, he ordered the judge jailed, and then kicked him out of New Orleans forever.

During his campaign, King Mob promised political positions to his key supporters. Then on the night of his inauguration, office seekers so crowded the White House that it became less a party and more a riot. Instead of ending corruption as his populist message promised, Jackson's administration had been credited with creating a spoils system in which Jackson purged federal employees in favor of those who had supported him.

At the start of his presidency, Jackson removed 919 government officials, a full 10% of all government employees, and dismissed 423 postmasters, many with long and credible records of service, within the first year of his tenure in office.
When abolitionist literature began to flood the American South, Andrew Jackson did exactly what a man who had recently established unlimited martial law would do. He banned it.

In the mid-1830s, abolitionists started what was probably the first direct mail campaign by sending its unsolicited materials to Southerners mailboxes. The Southerners did not appreciate this, as their livelihoods depended on them being able to pretend what they were doing was natural.
"I have read with great sorrow and regret that such men live in our happy country- I might have said monsters- as to be guilty of the attempt to stir up amongst the South the horrors of a servile war. They deserve to atone for this wicked attempt with their lives."
The Jackson administration would seek to ban all inflammatory abolitionist material from being delivered by the postal service.

It's worth noting that it was about this time that Jackson supposedly decided to see to it that his Hermitage slaves were treated with more humanity. If he ever read it, abolitionist literature would have informed him of just how pathetically fantastical the mask of the good master he crafted for himself really was.

Andrew Jackson had many issues with his first Vice President John Calhoun. And on one occasion, he literally threatened to behead him.
Jackson and Calhoun disagreed on the Nullification Crisis, leading Jackson to remark, "John Calhoun, if you secede from my nation, I will secede your head from the rest of your body." When Jackson agreed with the Supreme Court, like he did when the Court sided with him against South Carolina's federal nullification laws, for example, he said it was the country's ultimate power and must be obeyed.

Whenever Jackson disagreed with the Supreme Court though, he got pissy and outright ignored them. In Worcester versus Georgia in 1832, the Supreme Court led by Chief Justice John Marshall stated "Georgia laws that purported to seize Cherokee lands on which gold had been found violated federal treaties." Jackson, unapologetically set on taking said land and gold, reportedly responded, "John Marshall has made his decision. Now let him enforce it."
While historians are unsure if Jackson actually ever said that, they know that both he and the state of Georgia completely ignored the ruling and just stole everything.

When he was 16, Jackson inherited 300 to 400 pounds sterling from his late grandfather. It would be gone within the year, mainly because "Old Hickory" was as good at gambling as he was at finance. Just ask Charles Dickinson. When King Mob was inaugurated in 1829, massive crowds came to see him. At the time, the White House was open on inauguration day. And the first to arrive were Jackson's favorite toadies, most of whom were seeking an audience with the president to discuss the government positions he promised them for making it rain votes all over him, then came the actual mob.
Thousands of supporters guzzled booze, smashed furniture and china, and even mashed cheese into the White House carpets under their boots. We think the cheese was probably already on the floor. But it's not really safe to assume with this man.
One fancy society woman wrote, "But what a scene did we witness! The majesty of the people had disappeared, and a rabble, a mob of boys, negros, women, children scrambling, fighting, romping. What a pity. What a pity." Jackson seemed to agree. He escaped out the back window, leaving the White House to the raucous crowd, while he went on to whatever lunatics do when they get elected to high office.

He eventually used the event as an opportunity to get $50,000 from Congress to redecorate the White House though. One thing we can definitively say about Andrew Jackson the president: he really knew how to take a bad situation and exploit the shit out of it.

The fruitful life of the Fierce King

> **He killed an estimated 40 million people, he founded the Mongol Empire, he might have a little of his DNA in you. He is Genghis Khan.**

First things first, you heard his name 100's if not 1000's of times before, but there's a very good chance you've never heard it pronounced correctly. While most Westerners say Genghis with a hard g, that's incorrect. In Mongolia, the g is soft, so it's actually pronounced: Chinghis.

What does it mean? Well, there's no historical consensus, but Khan means ruler or King. And Genghis, or to be 100% accurate, Chinghis, is believed to mean stern or fierce. So, Genghis Khan means stern or fierce King. The confusion goes all the way back to spelling and pronunciation getting lost in European translation.
Since we're on the topic of names, Genghis Khan wasn't his name either, despite what you were taught in junior high and most, if not all, of high school.

The man who would unite the Mongol tribes was actually born to Mujin, meaning of or from iron, while Jin denotes agency. Thus, if you break it down Temujin means blacksmith. His name was said to have come from a Tatar tribesman who had been captured and brought home by the boy's father. The name Genghis Khan wasn't given to Temujin until 1206, when he was 44 years old, as part of this coronation as the King of all Mongols.

Our only source for the life of the young Temujin comes from the Secret History of the Mongols: an anonymous record of the early days of the United Konate.

According to that book, written for the Khan successors, Temujin was born sometime in 1162 on the banks of the Onon River. His father, Yesugei, was the chieftain of the Borjigin clan, the ruling class of the Mongol tribes. If you believe the legend, Temujin was born clutching a blood clot in his fist. An omen and that he was destined to be a great leader. Whether that's true is actually anyone's guess.

For someone who radically altered the world's population with his very own DNA (we'll get back to that in a bit) Temujin's first son may not even have been his.

It all started when his father arranged a marriage for him and delivered him at age 9 to the family of his future wife, in order to cement alliances between the Onggirat and the Mongols. Here's where things get messy.

On his way home after delivering his son to the Bortes, Temujin's father ran into the neighboring Tatars, who had long been Mongol enemies, and they assassinated him. When young Temujin heard about his father's death by poisoning, he returned home to claim his position as tribe's chief, but they denied the kid and abandoned his family leaving them without protection.

After several years of hardship and in slavery, Temujin finally married Borte, but the bad news kept coming. Not long after the marriage, Borte was kidnapped by the Merkit, a rival tribe, and she was reportedly given away as a wife. Temujin rescued her several months later and she gave birth to a son, Jochi, nine months after her rescue. The timeline of Jochi's birth was iffy at best.

Was Jochi Temujin's legitimate firstborn son or was Borte impregnated when she was kidnapped? It's something we'll probably never know.

But Jochi grew up to become a great military leader nonetheless, even though he was excluded from Genghis's line of succession. We know of Jochi, the son who may or may not have been the first son of Genghis Khan. We also know of eight other sons and daughters Temujin had with Borte, but that's not the extent of Genghis's offspring, not by a long shot.

While married to Borte, Temujin took a number of other wives, far too many to name here. While many of these women were taken as war trophies, at least one woman, Princess Qiguo was married to Genghis Khan as a gift of sorts, in exchange for relieving the Mongol siege upon Zhongdu. In short, it's uncertain which if any of these marriages were consensual.

Although it's certain his spouses bore him numerous children, including a number of daughters whose names weren't even recorded.

As famous and infamous as Genghis Khan is, very little is known about his personal or physical appearance. No contemporary portraits or sculptures of him survived and what is written about him at the time is practically revisionist history, the little we do know about Genghis Khan describes him as tall and strong with a flowing mane of blond hair, blue eyes, and a bushy beard.

But 14th century Persian chronicler Rashid Al Din claims Genghis had red hair and green eyes. Al Din never met the Khan in person, but these striking features were not unheard of among the Mongol.

You hear the name Genghis Khan and the first things your imagination conjures up are probably brutish acts of mass destruction, barbarism, and blood lust. All of those things are a big part of Genghis Khan's story but he was quite the innovator too.

He created the Yam route, which was an efficient postal system meant to send written orders to the far-flung outposts of his empire. He also adapted an official script in 1206 upon his election as Khan.

And while he was very likely illiterate, Genghis Khan kept written books of his laws. A complex and far reaching system of edicts called the Yassa.

Of course, for any good he did, he soured by destroying countless works of art, priceless artifacts, cultural sites, and other various precious objects. Chinese, Russian, Persian, and Muslim traditions of sculpture and painting were subjugated, and their masters almost always were killed.

While other Mongol leaders appreciated the cultures of the sedentary people they wiped out, the Mongols themselves left little in terms of cultural heritage and almost no written works.

Genghis Khan probably enjoyed the sight of blood but he was also a man of his word. Take for example, the time he honorably murdered the Mongol military and political leader, and childhood pal, Jamukha. According to the Secret History, Jamukha was eventually betrayed to Temujin by his followers in 1206. The first thing Temujin did was execute Jamukha's betrayers on basic principle. Among the Mongols, betrayal deserves the worst punishment imaginable. Then Temujin, despite not being really known for his generosity, offered Jamukha a renewal of the brotherhood and loyalty, but Jamukha refused. He kept insisting that if there was only room for one sun in the sky, there was only room for one Mongol lord. Jamukha had only one request: to be executed by dying a noble death, without any blood spilling. Temujin honored the request of his old friends, by having a soldier snap Jamukha's spine. It's said that Temujin then buried Jamukha with the golden belt that he had given to him when they had formed their bond of brotherhood. Pretty dramatic on the Khan's part.

Sounds like something a young George Lucas would have written in the mid-70s.

One of the great things about Genghis Kahn was that he had an eye for talent when it came to choosing people for leadership roles. Take for example, Jelme. During the 1201 Battle of the 13 Sides against the Taichuud tribe, Genghis got hit in the neck with an arrow. He obviously survived, and his army won the battle. But when he recovered from his wound he asked the soldiers of the defeated Taichuud tribe to reveal who shot his horse in the neck. Side note, either Genghis was using his horse's neck as a euphemism for his own injury, in an attempt to conceal his injury, or possibly to smoke out a false confession. Moving along, a soldier named Zurgadai voluntarily confessed and told Genghis, and I paraphrase: "You got me, I did it, but if you let me live I will serve you loyally".

Genghis was impressed. He valued skill and loyalty, so he pardoned and praised Zurgadai, making him an officer and nicknamed him Jebe, Mongolian for both arrow and weapon.

How's that for luck?

Jebe went on to become one of the Mongol's greatest field commanders during the expansion in Asia and Europe.

Just like most men in power who wield their force with little regard for their foe, Genghis Khan was a deeply religious man. He declared religious freedom in conquered lands and even granted tax exemptions for places of worship.

Despite their bad attitude, the Mongols actually had an exceptionally liberal attitude towards religion. While they subscribed to a shamanistic belief system that revered the Eternal Blue Sky, the step peoples also included Christians, Buddhists, Muslims, and others. No one was persecuted for their faith.

Genghis Khan also had a personal interest in spirituality. He reportedly prayed in his tent for several days before important campaigns and he often met with different religious leaders of the lands he conquered to discuss their faiths.

Genghis conquered the Western Xia and Jin empires as a matter of survival rather than blood-thirstiness.

He also had no intention of going to war with the powerful Khwarezmid Empire in modern day Iran, but it became inevitable after the Khwarezmian Shah executed Genghis's ambassadors to him and massacred a peaceful caravan. In a war lasting just three years, from 1218 to 1221, the Khwarezmid Empire was annihilated. With its population cold and its beautiful walled cities destroyed. Final defeat was inflicted at the Battle of the Indus River where 50,000 men, led by the Shah's son, were beaten and killed.

The Mongols exacted such a toll on the Khwarezmid Empire, that of its nearly three million people, at least one million were killed. Usually executed methodically using swords or axes. Of course, this is all a drop in the bucket in terms of Khan's body count.

Figures vary, but about 40 million people or 10% of the world population at the time were killed or died because of his attacks.

Famine and disease killed a large portion of the people but Ganga is wiped out any city or country that opposed him.

After destroying the Khwarezmid Empire, Genghis split his army into two units. One unit, which he led personally, headed back to Mongolia, but not before laying waste to northern India. The other unit, made up of two packs of soldiers, were led by Subutai and Jebe. They headed west, toward what's now Russia, pursuing the Kwarezmian Shah. They didn't catch him, but they made history anyway.

In a raid of so much power and destructiveness that it's never been equaled, two of Genghis's dogs of war sacked Georgia, Armenia, and defeated a gigantic Kievan Rus force at the legendary Battle of the Kalka River.

In keeping with Mongol tradition, the Russian princes who resisted were crushed to death under a platform, their blood never spilling. Because you, know, royal blood. Hundreds of thousands of Russian peasants were slaughtered and Russia itself would take centuries to recover from this Mongol invasion, and its geography was permanently changed.

It's only fitting that Kangas Khan's death is as shrouded in as much mystery as the basic details of his personal life. The common tale says he died in August 1227 during the sack of the western Xia capital, around the age of 64 or 65, after injuring himself from falling off a horse while hunting. Other sources list everything from malaria to an arrow wound in the knee, during the battle. One chronicle even says he was murdered by a western Xia princess he was attempting to add to his harem.

After his death, the traditional Kurultai tie was held. Meaning all Mongol conquests were put on hold. And all leaders met at the Onon river. Bypassing Jochi, whose parentage was never confirmed, they elected Genghis's third son, Ogedai, as the new Khan.

After his untimely and mysterious death, the Khan's body was returned to Mongolia and presumably to his birthplace in the Khentii Aimag, but we will probably never know for sure.

Genghis had left instructions to be buried without any markings or signs. But many assume his tomb is buried somewhere close to the Onon river. Of course, this was Genghis Khan's funeral, so there had to be some level of barbarism to it, and the Mongols came through in shocking style. According to historical evidence, 30,000 people participated in his funeral.

Of course, these 30,000 were killed by Khan's army to preserve the secret location of his tomb. But that wasn't enough, because Khan's army knew where the tomb was, they were killed by his traveling escorts.

And as Khan was taken to his final resting place by said escorts, all onlookers were murdered in order to keep everything a secret. When Khan's traveling escorts reached their destination and after they buried his tomb, they rode horses over his burial grounds to help conceal it, and they might even had changed the course of a river to go over it. Then his escorts killed themselves, taking the location of their leaders final resting place with them. And before you Google it, yes, numerous excavations have already been undertaken to find Genghis and the treasure said to be buried with him.

But even with satellite imaging used recently, its precise location is unknown.

AMAZING DISCOVERIES

Discovery and technological advancement is most often than none the result of genius, hard work, and years and years of failed attempts. But sometimes it is just an accident, a funny story, or an unresolved mistery.

The uncrackable manuscript

The most mysterious story is the one we can't read. The Voynich manuscript has been stumping linguists and cryptologists for centuries, and not even AI is able to crack it.

Deep inside Yale University's Beinecke Rare Book and Manuscript Library lies the only copy of a 240-page tome. The Voynich manuscript was recently carbon dated to around 1420. Its vellum pages are beautifully decorated with looping handwriting and hand-drawn images that might have been stolen from a dream.

Floating castles, real and imaginary plants, astrology diagrams, zodiac rings, bathing women, and suns and moons with faces accompany the text.
It seems like a pretty rad medieval manuscript that you should check out the next time you are in New Haven, right? But what is all the fuss about? After all we have the Lindisfarne Gospels in the British Library, the Westminster Abbey Bestiary, and the Vienna Genesis in the Austrian National Library (I really just wanted to show off my knowledge of medieval manuscripts!) Well, it turns out that the 24x16 centimeter book called the Voynich manuscript is one of history's biggest unsolved mysteries.
The reason why? No one can figure out what it says.

The name of the manuscript comes from Wilfrid Voynich, the Polish bookseller who reportedly came across the book at a Jesuit college in Italy in 1912. He was intrigued by the mystery and bought it from the Jesuits that at that time were a bit strapped for cash.
He was puzzled. Who wrote it? What was written in it? Where was it made? What was the meaning of the bizarre words and vibrant drawings? What secrets could it uncover?
He eventually brought it to the U.S., where experts have continued to argue over it for more than a century. The book has been the source of fascination for linguists and cryptologists alike; it is said that codebreakers from World War II worked on it to no avail.
According to the studies, the writing has all the characteristics of a real language, just one that no one's ever seen before.

The reason why the language is deemed real is that in actual languages, letters and groups of letters appear with consistent frequencies, and the language in the Voynich manuscript has patterns you wouldn't find from a random letter generator.
But so far, this is the only conclusion we have reached and what we can plainly see is that the letters are varied in style and height, some are borrowed from other scripts, but many are unique.
The taller letters have been designated as gallows characters.

The manuscript is richly decorated throughout with the embellishments typical of a scroll. It has been theorized that it has been written by two or more hands, with the paintings done by another author.

Over the years, three main theories have emerged about the manuscript's text.
The most accredited theory is that it's written in cypher, a secret code deliberately designed to hide a secret meaning. The second theory is that the document is hoax written in gibberish by a clever con man to make money off a gullible buyer, dating back to Medieval times. Others, that it was Voynich himself, although the carbon dating seems to have excluded this possibility.
The final theory is that the manuscript is written in a real language, but in an unknown script.

It is possible that medieval scholars were attempting to create an alphabet for a language that was spoken but not yet written.

Should this be the case, the Voynich manuscript might be like the rongorongo script invented on Easter Island, which is now unreadable after the culture that created it collapsed.

Even if no one has yet been able to read the Voynich manuscript, people have kept on guessing what it might say. The scholars who believe that the manuscript was the first and apparently only attempt at creating a new type of written language hypothesize that it might be an encyclopedia containing the knowledge of the culture that wrote it.

Other linguists speculated that it was written by Roger Bacon, the 13th century philosopher who attempted to understand the universal laws of grammar, or by the Elizabethan mystic John Dee, who in the 16th century practiced alchemy and divination.

There are also fringe theories that postulated that the book might have been written by a coven of Italian witches; and of course, it wouldn't be a true mystery if someone didn't think that it was written by Martians.

After 100 years of failed attempts and increasing frustration, scientists have recently shed a little light on the matter. The first breakthrough was the carbon dating.

Moreover, contemporary historians have traced back the provenance of the manuscript through Rome and Prague as early as 1612. From there it was most likely passed from Holy Roman Emperor Rudolf II to Jacobus Sinapius, his physician.

These historical breakthroughs are not the only discoveries we have recently made: in fact, comparative literature scholars have recently proposed the preliminary identification of a few words in the manuscript. The letters beside these seven stars might spell Tauran, the name for Taurus, a constellation that includes the seven stars called the Pleiades. The word Centaurun might be written right next to the Centaurea plant in on of the pictures. This are all very good guesses, but progress is slow.

The mystery remains, when we will finally be able to crack its code, what will we find? The dream journal of a 15th-century illustrator? A bunch of nonsense written by a wisecrack medieval con man? Or perhaps the lost knowledge of a forgotten culture?

The torturous past of the treadmill

> **The constant thud underneath your feet, the limited space, the sweat on your eyes, and the monotony of going nowhere. Certainly, hours must have gone by, but it's only been eight minutes, and you tell yourself, "This must be a cruel and unusual punishment." You would be right, that's exactly what it was.**
> **In the 1800s, treadmills were invented as a form of torture for English prisoners.**

In the 1800s the English prison system was bad, abysmally bad. The most common punishments were execution and deportation, and the lucky ones who were simply locked away in filthy cells faced hours of solitude.

Social movements led by philanthropies, religious groups, and celebrities, such as Charles Dickens, demanded changes to the dire conditions, in order to help reform the prisoners (which we might not even realize it now, but it is the ultimate goal of the prison system).

When their movement succeeded, the prisons were entirely remodeled and new forms of rehabilitation were introduced, amongst them the treadmill.

The original version was invented in 1818 by the English engineer Sir William Cubitt, and worked so that the prisoners stepped on 24 spokes of a large paddle wheel, the wheel turned, and the prisoner was forced to keep stepping up or risk falling off, similar to modern stepper machines.

Meanwhile, not wanting all that movement to go to waste, the rotation made the gears pump out water, crush grain, or power mills, which is why it is called the "treadmill."

These devices were seen as a genius invention that whipped prisoners into shape with the added benefit of powering mills that helped rebuild the British economy, which had been crushed by the Napoleonic Wars.

It was a win-win for everybody, except for the prisoners, of course.

Historians believe that the prisoners spent, on average, six or more hours a day on treadmills, which to put I in perspective is the equivalent of climbing 5,000 to 14,000 feet. And 14,000 feet is approximately Mount Everest's halfway point.

That was done five days a week with little food.

Since prisoners didn't have a voice in the matter and everybody else was patting themselves in the back for such a brilliant idea, Cubitt's treadmill quickly spread across the British Empire and the U.S.. Within a decade of its invention, more than 50 English prisons were fitted with treadmills, and roughly the same number in the U.S. as well. Unsurprisingly, the physical exertion combined with poor nutrition caused many prisoners to suffer breakdowns and injuries.

The prison guards did not seem to care, they were actually quite enamored with the horrid contraption. For example, in 1824, a New York prison guard James Hardie credited the device with calming down his rowdier inmates, and wrote that the "monotonous steadiness, and not its severity...constitutes its terror," a quote I might still agree with.

The treadmills lasted in England until the late 19th century, when they were banned for being excessively cruel under the Prison's Act of 1898.

But as we now, the torturous contraption hadn't took his last victim yet: this time it would target the unsuspecting public.

In 1911, a treadmill was patented in the U.S.

By 1952, the forerunner of today's modern treadmill had been invented. When the first jogging craze hit the U.S. in the 1970s, the treadmill was marketed as an easy and convenient way to improve aerobic fitness, and lose the extra pounds, which, in all fairness, it's pretty good at doing.

The machine has maintained its popularity, its torturous history long forgotten.

But the next time you voluntarily subject yourself to what was once a form of torture, be grateful that you can control when you'll hop off. Or else you might use your newfound knowledge as a way to justify yourself for not doing it (not that I ever did it!)

The ha(z)y history of Dippin' Dots

The Dippin' Dots: a summertime staple. But this confectionery treat didn't start as, well, ice cream: it was meant to be cow feed.

Dippin' Dots were invented in the 1980s and not by an ice cream brand as you might think, but by a microbiologist, Curtis Jones.
Curtis Jones had specialized in cryogenics and in 1987 was working for a bio-tech company in Kentucky, trying to figure out how to pack and distribute food for farm animals more efficient.
His big breakthrough came when he flash-froze cattle feed at 350 degrees below zero, which produced small pellets of frozen hay.

Luckily enough, Curtis loved making (and eating) ice cream. Quite pleased with his freezing technique, he started using liquid nitrogen to freeze ice cream at extremely low temperatures and ended up with small beads of it. When eaten, the heat of the mouth would melt the beads and so the Dippin' Dots was born.

A year later, he formed what would become the Dippin' Dots company out of his parent's garage in Illinois. But there was a problem: Curtis had nowhere to sell the product. Dippin' Dots have to be stored at such low temperatures that it made it impossible for grocery stores to store them.
He got creative once again and decided to market his product to alternate locations.
Now, they're sold at amusement parks, festivals, zoos, and other summertime destinations. But whether or not they really are the ice cream of the future, we'll just have to wait and see.

The not-so-cheesy history behind fondue

Fondue. It's a wonderfully delicious thing we do with cheese: we melt it. We dip it. We eat it.

In the '70s, it became super popular. But that didn't just happen by chance. There was an ominous force behind it, the Swiss cheese mafia.

100 years ago, cheese was a hot commodity in Switzerland. It was exported at high volumes and played a major role in the Swiss economy. But that all changed after World War I. European countries, devastated by the war, could no longer afford to buy expensive, imported cheese, which was bad news for Switzerland.

So, the government stepped in, and they formed The Cheese Union.

Basically, it was a cartel, and it worked like this. The first thing they did was force every dairy farmer and cheesemonger to fix the price of cheese, eliminating competition, meaning everyone could stay in the game. The cheese cartel also told them exactly how much cheese to make and limited the varieties.

So instead of making thousands of different kinds of cheese, they only made seven.

Every producer who dared defy them and produce a cheese outside of the Swiss Cheese Union approved list was condemned to the vacuum-packed destiny of the mass produced supermarket cheese. If it didn't get the Union's stamp of approval, it wasn't Swiss cheese

It worked. The cartel controlled the cheese supply for decades. By the '70s, they got greedy and wanted to expand their cheese racket globally.

So, they introduced the world to a dish already popular in the freezing cold Alps, fondue. In the rest of the country it wasn't all that well known, but Swiss Cheese Union declared it a national dish nevertheless.

By marketing cheese for fondue, the cartel was able to sell more. After all the "original" recipe called for equal parts of Gruyère and Emmenthal, which were the two most marketed and protected cheeses on the Cheese Union list.

But, as with most cartels, things got shady. Money went missing. Some people were scammed, other took kickbacks, and in the end, some went to jail. And by the 1990s, the Swiss Cheese Union was dismantled.

So, there you have it: the reason we know and love fondue is because of a shady government program that convinced the world to consume massive amounts of melted cheese.

The loneliest plant

Encephalartos woodii is tall, tough, and handsome. Yet, it has been all alone for centuries. Will this lonely plant ever find a partner?
This is a story of a plant that long ago ruled the world. A plant that, today, is the very last of its kind.

Encephalartos woodii, *E. Woodii* for friends, was named after John Medley Wood, the British botanist who discovered it growing on a hillside on the coast of South Africa in 1895.

A tall, handsome plant caught his eye, and, as botanists do, he carefully removed a small branch of it and shipped it all the way to the Kew Gardens in London, where it's been grown and has lived for the last 117 years.

But Woodii's history dates much, much further back.

The *Encephalartos woodii* is a cycad.
Cycads have been around for over 300 million years. As the millennium came about, cycads flourished providing a perch for pterodactyls, shade for triceratops, and a tasty snack for brontosauruses.

It is estimated that at one point, during the Jurassic, cycads made up 20% of all plants on Earth, and were distributed in every corner of the globe.

But good times don't last forever. A comet came, probably, and the dinosaurs went extinct.
Ice ages came and went.

New modern, fancier plants, such as conifers and fruit trees, started pushing the old, tired cycads out. The once proud population of *E. Woodiis* was slowly, but steadily reduced until there was only one left (possibly).

A single solitary *E. Woodii* kept growing quietly on a hillside in Africa, which is where John Medley Wood found him. At that time, he had no way of knowing just how rare his discovery was, but expedition after expedition, year after year, in search of other E. Woodii have proved fruitless.

The problem is that cycads are dioecious, which means that you need separate male and female plants to create a new one, and our Woodii happens to be a male, a lonely bachelor.

If a female mate cannot be found, it really will be the last of its kind.

To this day, researchers are still looking. After all, it's a big world, there might just be a chance. Plenty of trees in the woods!

The heroic recipe for a war-winning bagel

> If you ever saw a Guang-Bing, you might have just mistaken it for a bagel; after all it's shiny, it's round, it's got a hole in the middle, soft on the inside, crispy on the outside. But it is also a legendary bread helped China win a war 500 years ago.

So how can bread lead a country to victory in battle you might ask?
It was 1563, China was struggling to defend itself against Japanese pirates.
Each night, the Japanese pirates would sneak off their boats and take whatever they could from general Qi's army. Before the army even noticed the Japanese had vanished. Somehow the pirates knew exactly where the General's army was stationed every time. It turns out it was the campfires used to cook their meals.

General Qi noticed that the Japanese didn't have the same problems because they ate sushi (it's not a joke, they actually brought onigiri as rations), but since raw fish wasn't to the general taste he invented his own strategic snack: the Guang Bing are cooked in an underground clay oven. So, the soldiers could make food without giving away their location.
What about the hole in the middle? That was so that the soldiers could string out the bread to carry around their necks. That's right, a bread necklace. This created a portable food that wouldn't slow them down during an ambush.

Now, military tactic to win a war has become a beloved snack in Fuzhou: you can have it as a breakfast sandwich with eggs, with pork fillings, for lunch, or simply with green onions and beansprouts for a nutritious snack. Whatever you choose it's delicious on its own too.

The joy of cooking instant ramen

Some people associate instant noodles with broke college students, but instant ramen wasn't created for a bunch of hungry 20-year-olds. The man who invented them was much more ambitious: he wanted to solve a hunger crisis in Japan.

Just after the end of World War II, food shortages were plaguing Japanese cities.
The U.S. supplied wheat flour and encouraged the Japanese to make bread; but Momofuku Ando didn't understand why Japanese would make bread instead of noodles, which was something that was already part of their culture, contrarily to bread.
Ando decided to take matters into his own hands and invent a new ramen, which was made to last.

He spent over a year trying to figure out how to best preserve the noodles. He needed a tasty and easy, and most importantly nonperishable recipe. But it was quite challenging to maintain the unique texture and robust flavors that most people were used to. One night, while he and his wife were making dinner, he had a breakthrough: he threw some noodles in a bowl of hot tempura oil and realized that flash frying the noodles was the answer he had been searching for.

This method not only dehydrated them, but most importantly left small perforations that allowed the noodles to recook quickly. And that is how instant ramen noodles became an instant success.

His products gained more and more notoriety when he introduced the packaged ramen in the 1950s and in 1978 when he marketed Cup Noodles. Momofuku Ando's company began selling over 40 billion units every year, and he became a culinary icon in Japan.
Next time that you feel guilty for heating up a cup of instant noodles, remember, you're also slurping down a little piece of history.

The most beloved snack

The creation of the potato chip is a rather snarky, surprising, and idiosyncratic story.

As soon as French fries arrived in America, they became a restaurant mainstay. Many restaurants even served French Fries as their signature dish. French Fries were actually considered very hoity-toity once, if you can believe it.

In 1853, George Crum was a chef at the Moon's Lake House in Saratoga Springs, New York. Their signature dish was none other than Moon's Fried Potatoes, or as the aristocrats would say: "Potatoes served in the French Manner."

On a day like any other, a customer who might have been Cornelius Vanderbilt himself ordered fries. Upon being served, Cornelius sneered at Moon's potatoes, and had them sent back. They were soggy and not crispy enough, he said.

Vanderbilt sent back the second plate of fried as well, and the third, and the fourth, and continued a few more times until Crum lost it.

He really lost it, the stereotype of the angry chef is not just a modern tropos.

He decided to show Vanderbilt, cut the potatoes paper-thin, and fried them up.

In 1853, as you might imagine, eating with your hands was a major faux pas, which made Crum's revenge even more diabolical. By cutting the potatoes paper-thin, there would be no way that Vanderbilt could use his fork and he would have been forced to use his hands.

Crum's Mean Girls style plan backfired, because the patrons dug in with both hands, and loved them: the Saratoga Chips were born. Not only did they became a Saratoga dining staple, but within a few years, they took the world by storm. Crum himself opened his own restaurant with baskets of chips displayed on each and every table.

The fishy origins of Ketchup

Ketchup: it's so American, that the red in red, white, and blue, is from the tomatoes the ketchup is made from. But that wasn't always the case. The first recorded recipe for ketchup comes from China. And for more than a thousand years it wasn't even made with tomatoes. It was made with fish guts. –

Fish intestines, stomach, and bladder mixed together with salt, then sealed and heated in the hot summer sun for 20 days. That was the original ketchup. The fermented fish paste that dates back to 6th century China became very popular throughout Southeast Asia and British and Dutch settlers who arrived in the 1600s loved it.

Over time, they brought the precursor of the ketchup home to Europe and decided to add their own modifications including beer, walnuts, oysters, mushrooms, peaches, and strawberries.

By the mid-1700s, ketchup was a mainstay on every British dinner table and when colonists went west, it also made its way across the Atlantic.

That's where tomatoes come in. They're native to the Americas and it's even rumored Europeans once believed they were poisonous and used them with reluctance.

In 1812, James Mease, a Philadelphia horticulturalist and scientist, introduced tomatoes into the mix and subsequently published a tomato ketchup recipe that was the beginning of a new crimson era.

From there, many different iterations were concocted and by the end of the 18th century, The New York Tribune called tomato ketchup America's national condiment that was on every table in the land.

Tomato ketchup is here to stay and I, for one, don't miss the fish guts.

The immortal cells of Henrietta Lacks

Imagine something small enough to float on a particle of dust that holds the keys to understanding cancer, virology, and genetics. We are lucky enough that such a thing exists in the form of trillions of trillions of lab-grown human cells called HeLa.

Since it became possible to do so, scientists grow human cells in the lab to study how they function, understand how diseases develop, and most importantly test new treatments without killing patients.

To make sure that they can repeat these experiments several times and compare the results with those of other scientists, they need huge populations of identical cells that can duplicate themselves identically for years, but until 1951, all human cell lines that researchers had tried to grow in a lab had died after a few days.

That year a John Hopkins scientist by the name of George Gey received a sample of a strange looking tumor: dark purple, shiny, and jelly-like. It was a special sample: some of its cells kept dividing, and dividing, and dividing, with no end in sight. When individual cells died, generations of copies took their place and thrived. The result was an endless source of identical cells that's still around today.
The very first immortal human cell line.

Gey labeled it "HeLa" after the patient who had died from the unusual tumor, Henrietta Lacks.

Henrietta Lacks was born on a tobacco farm in Virginia and lived in Baltimore with her husband and five children. She had died of aggressive cervical cancer a few months before her tumorous cells were harvested, and she never knew about anything about it.

What is so special about the cells from the tumor of Henrietta Lacks that lets them survive when other cell lines die? The short answer is: we don't know.
Normal human cells have built-in control mechanisms, which literally works by committing suicide. They can divide approximately 50 times before they self-destruct in a process called apoptosis.

This prevents the propagation of genetic errors that creep in after repeated rounds of division. Cancer cells ignore these signals and divide indefinitely, crowding out normal cells. Even so, most cell lines eventually die off, especially outside the human body. The HeLa cell line, though, is still alive, and thriving, and dividing, and that's the part we can't explain, yet.

Regardless of why we have them, when Dr. Gey realized he had the first immortal line of human cells, he sent samples to labs all over the world. Soon the world's first cell production facility was churning out 6 trillion HeLa cells a week, and scientists put them to work in an ethically problematic way, building careers and fortunes off of Henrietta's cells without her or her family's consent, or even knowledge until decades later.

The polio epidemic was at its peak in the early 50s. HeLa cells, which easily took up and replicated the virus, allowed Jonas Salk to test his vaccine. They have been used to study diseases, such as measles, mumps, Ebola, and HIV.

We know now that human cells have 46 chromosomes because a scientist who worked with HeLa discovered a chemical that makes chromosomes visible.

The HeLa cells themselves actually have around 80 highly mutated chromosomes.
They were the first cells to be cloned. They have traveled to outer space. Telomerase, an enzyme that helps cancer cells evade destruction by repairing their DNA, was discovered first in HeLa cells.

Thanks to HeLa, we now know that cervical cancer can be caused by the HPV virus and we have vaccine for it.
HeLa was the basis for discoveries that have filled thousands of scientific papers.
HeLa cells are so resilient that they can live on almost any surface: a lab worker's hand, a piece of dust, invading cultures of other cells and taking over like weeds; which means that countless cures, patents, and discoveries were all made thanks to Henrietta Lacks, probably more than we know.

On the amazing properties of gunk

Isaac Asimov phrased it best: "The most exciting phrase to hear in science, the one that heralds new discoveries, is not 'Eureka!' but 'That's funny…'"
In the long history of science, many major discoveries came by accident. Perhaps they came from recognizing potential in an unexpected result or even a failed recipe's waste. Accidents turned into serendipity.
The inception of the entire modern chemical industry can be attributed to accidental discoveries that started with garbage.

In the 19th century there we had to tackle a new kind of waste that was floating around: coal tar. It was the sticky, stinky, awful muck leftover from turning coal into all those pretty gaslights.
Before we figured out that we could pave road with it, it was pretty much useless, worse than that it was kind of annoying to dispose off.

So, August Wilhelm von Hoffman, the head of London's Royal College of Chemistry had an idea: he noticed that some bits in the chemical composition of coal tar were similar to the bits in known medicines.
If he got the chemistry right, the world would have affordable, easy, and mass-producible cures for disease.
In 1856, he assigned 18-year-old William Perkin to the project Team Coal Tar.
Perkin's goal was to try to turn the gunk into quinine.
Quinine was used to treat malaria, but the drug had to be extracted from tree bark, which was annoying and time-consuming. Perkin knew that quinine and coal tar had similar chemical formulas.
Easy job, he thought, let's take some of the stuff in coal tar that is kind of similar to quinine, add some other things that look a bit like of quinine, remove the pesty, useless byproducts, and there you go, right? Not so much.

His first attempts produced a reddish-black powder instead of the off-white quinine crystals.
Never matter, he would try again; he made a couple changes and tried again with a different coal tar starting ingredient, and though that a simpler formula would do the trick.
Wrong again: instead of off-white he got an even darker powder.
He washed it out with a little alcohol ready start over.
But when he added the alcohol, the black powder produced a breathtaking purple.

Perkin was struck by inspiration. He figured out the amazingly purple stuff would make a pretty cool dye silk: he saw dollar signs (or rather, pound sterling signs).
At the time, purple-dyed fabrics were made using exotic crushed snails, so only the very wealthy could afford to wear purple. Crushed snails were a thing of the past, Perkin just made a purple dye out of bloody garbage!

Perkin called it "mauve" after a French flower, because "trashy purple" wouldn't make for a good marketing campaign. Dreaming of broad profit margins, Perkin did what many entrepreneurs did: he quit and started perhaps the first artificial dye factory.

Within a few years, mauve had influential fashion fans: Queen Victoria and Napoleon III's wife, Empress Eugénie. The fashion craze, called "mauve measles" spread like, well, like the measles. Suddenly the middle class could afford a color beyond grey, drab brown, or off-white.
Perkin made a killing with the mauve measles, amassed over 100 million in today's dollars, and retired at the ripe old age of 36.

If you think that coal tar can only produce one happy mistake, you would be wrong. Another discovery was made by a careless chemist of a coal tar factory.
In 1878, Constantin Fahlberg brought his own gunky coal tar work home with him i.e., he forgot to wash his hands. At dinner that night he discovered that his bread tasted incredibly sweet.
Fahlberg and his lab-mates realized that the source of the sweetness was a substance derived from a coal tar residue they called saccharin, the most common artificial sweetener.

The most mysterious island

I know this is a chapter about funny stories about accidental discoveries, but how about an "un-discovery"?

Sandy Island is a beautiful, warm, and uninhabited island part of the French overseas territory of New Caledonia. It sits only about 650 miles north-east of Australia in the Coral Sea. This island was likely first discovered in 1774 by Captain James Cook, who, fun fact, was never actually a Captain, but Sandy Island was formally mapped in the late 19th century after being spotted by a passing whaling ship.

Sandy Island, being a sunny piece of paradise, would probably be the perfect place to live if not for one small problem—it doesn't exist.

The French Service Hydrographique et Océanographique de la Marine, also known as the guys that make the ocean maps for France happened to notice in the 70s that sea depth data showed the ocean being between 5,000 and 7,000 feet deep where Sandy Island was supposed to be which was puzzling.

The French definitely wanted to figure out whether the island the size of Paris that they assumed was part of their country actually existed so they fired up a plane, flew over, and surprise: it didn't.
I'm sure that was a bit of a bummer but, no harm done, the island was removed from all official French maps in 1979 and the word was spread about Sandy's nonexistence but it wasn't spread enough.

It was around the time that Sandy Island was first un-discovered that mapping organizations worldwide were converting their data from analog to digital and one of them, then called the US National Imagery and Mapping Agency, was doing just that but it just happened that their analog maps had sourced their information from maps that sourced their data from the original maps that included Sandy Island and they didn't get the message from France.

They've since published the beautifully named Global Self-consistent, Hierarchical, High-resolution Geography Database which is essentially the definitive data-source for where the world's coasts are since it's freely available.

Its data is used by a good majority of modern digital maps including Google Maps. You can even download it yourself but it's not very exciting. That's why Google Maps showed the small island on its maps. It does not, however, anymore.

By the year 2012 some maps showed Sandy Island existing and some did not depending on their data source. A team assembled by the University of Sydney was in the area doing unrelated research on the RV Southern Surveyor when they happened to float by Sandy Island and notice its distinct lack of existence.
Having all the equipment, the Southern Surveyor then surveyed the area, recorded the accurate data, and undiscovered Sandy Island for the last time.

After publishing their findings, Google Maps, along with every other map, removed Sandy Island from existence. But this still leaves two big questions: why was Sandy spotted in the first place and why could you see it on Google Maps satellite view until 2012?
The first question has a plausible but unconformable explanation. The whaling ship that first mapped Sandy Island probably did see what looked like land. You see, when underwater volcanoes erupt they often spurt out pumice—a type of rock that actually floats on water.

Typically, this rock will float densely together and look like land creating what's called a pumice raft. Ocean currents have been known to bring pumice rafts to the area of Sandy Island making it seem probable that that's what Sandy Island's discoverers saw.

Now for the second mystery. We've thoroughly established that Sandy Island doesn't exist so why did Google's satellite view show it? Well, it turns out that a lot of their satellite view isn't actually satellite imagery. You see, when you image ocean from satellite you don't actually get the images that drive you directly to your favorite ice-cream shop. They get bathymetric data—surveys of the ocean floor.

There isn't actually a completely straight line between Australia and New Caledonia—just a streak of higher resolution data from one ship sailing a straight line and collecting bathymetric data.
Where there's land Google will switch to using full satellite imagery so where Sandy Island was supposed to be their systems expected to have ground satellite imagery but didn't since the island didn't exist so instead, until Sandy Island was undiscovered definitively in 2012, the satellite map just showed an island shaped black void instead.

A not-so-secret building

The fact that a skyscraper in Manhattan doesn't have any windows is a highly classified government secret—a secret we only know because of leaked NSA documents and investigative reporting.

The skyscraper in question is known by two names: some call it The Long Lines Building, , while others call it simply 33 Thomas Street, in the Tribeca area of New York.
It stands 550 feet or 170 meters tall, has 29 stories and, just like Apple's headquarters or a coffee shop in Brooklyn, has no windows at all.

Until recently, not much was known about the building. The only real publicly available information was that it was built between 1969 and 1974 by AT&T, designed by an architect named John Carl Warnecke, and that it served as a telephone switchboard hub, mainly routing AT&T's long-distance phone calls.

It's easy to forget now that everyone has a cell phone that they protect as if it's their own child, but phones used to all be connected by physical cables—and landlines still are. For the whole system to work, the cables all have to connect to each other, and 33 Thomas Street is one of the places where that connection happens.
33 Thomas Street's job is to change which cable is connected to which based on who is trying to call who.

There used to be actual people who did this called telephone operators who would actually answer your call, ask who you wanted to talk to, and then switch the cable by hand, but after a while, we figured out that not only did everybody hate talking to strangers on the phone, but also that that system was incredibly inefficient, and so the telephone operators were replaced with machines, just like we all will be in 50 years.

I mean, once bots learn to read quickly and write bad puns, it's over for me.
These phone switching machines require intense security and they have to run no matter what—after all, if the machines stop working, the phones stop working.
Even in a disaster scenario, the machines need to stay operational—the only thing worse than an hurricane is a sharkicane, but the only other thing worse than a hurricane is an hurricane that knocks out the phone lines, so people can't communicate and get help.

That everything-proofness was the public justification for the lack of windows at 33 Thomas Street—the architect claimed he was told that he needed to design a building that could survive a nuclear blast and still keep the phones working.
The only way to do that was to build it without windows, so that's what they did.

But recent reporting suggests that's convenient for another reason. According to reporting from The Intercept, 33 Thomas Street is much more than just an AT&T phone switching hub. With more efficient modern equipment, AT&T had some empty floors so they were kind enough to lease these out to the NSA. Given the convenient location the NSA made it a surveillance site, to tap into and monitor phone calls, faxes, satellite transmissions, and internet data.

In 2013, an NSA subcontractor named Edward Snowden released a massive trove of classified documents revealing that the US had secretly been running several global surveillance programs.
Believe it or not, back in 2013, the fact that the government was doing a bunch of sketchy, illegal surveillance was considered surprising news.

Among the leaked documents there was frequent mention of a mysterious surveillance site called TITANPOINTE, but its location was so classified that even Snowden didn't have access to it.

In 2016, though, journalists were able to piece together a series of different clues in Snowden's documents, combine it with their own reporting, and prove that 33 Thomas Street is, in fact, the mysterious TITANPOINTE.

Here's how: One document disclosed that TITANPOINTE was in New York City. Another said that the site was supervised by LITHIUM—which we know is the NSA's codename for AT&T.
Yet another said part of TITANPOINTE's surveillance work was intercepting satellite communications and there's only one place in New York City, run by AT&T, that has satellite ground stations—33 Thomas Street. You can even see its satellite dishes in the satellite imagery of its roof.

There was other evidence too—for example, one document said that to get to TITANPOINTE, you should first head to the FBI's New York office, which is only a block away from 33 Thomas Street.
Plus, another document said that TITANPOINTE had several pieces of equipment that AT&T employees have confirmed are used at 33 Thomas Street, and of course, the final piece of evidence was that 33 Thomas Street is a freaking skyscraper that doesn't have any windows, which is about as suspicious as a sign that says, "NORMAL BUILDING, NOT A SPY CENTER AT ALL JUST A TOTALLY NORMAL BUILDING, NOTHING TO SEE HERE."

The first meme

We are in the golden age of...memes. Every generation likes to believe that they invented something, a generation had the steam engine, another had cars, the 60s had the sexual revolution. We have memes.

What it really comes down to with memes is formatting. A lot of memes are just captions on an image, and let's be honest there is nothing inherently unique about the idea of captions on an image.

Political cartoons have been around for centuries. They were especially popular in Britain and France during the 1800s. Peanuts, Garfield and Marmaduke have all been staples of the cartoon section for decades.
Even caption contests such as the one in the New York Times have been running for almost 100 years.

However, all the way back in 1921, the University of Iowa satire magazine "The Judge"

How you think you look when a flashlight is taken. How you really look.

which is a great name for a satire magazine, printed what has the potential to be the first meme.

A witty caption, check, a dopey image, also check. So, we got a meme, right? Well, no.

Not according to Richard Dawkins. Why is he the meme authority you might ask? Well, he invented the word. The word meme was first used in 1976 in Dawkins' book, *The Selfish Gene*.
By Dawkins definition a single image cannot be a meme. Instead memes are, "Culturally transmitted entities that spread from person to person such as hearing a song that gets stuck in your head." The meme goes through variations and mutations as it spreads. It literally goes *viral*.
A meme starts out as something that's sort of funny and then people will recognize that, change it, and it mutates into something else which is then funny only because you recognize the first thing and then it continues to get "memer" and more mutated.

As the name of the book implies he compares these memes to genes, you know like DNA and only the most culturally dominant carry on. Now if that's sounds familiar, it's the exact same theory as Charles Darwin's Survival of the Fittest. That is until PewDiePie used them at which point they're artificially dead.

The book itself has nothing to do dank memes on the internet, it's actually about boring stuff like biology and altruism, but it's message remains relevant. The best memes get spread to the most people. However, when most people think about memes, you don't think about some old school thing, you want to know about what was the first internet meme.

In 1986, 3D animator Michael Girard and his company Unreal Pictures, were contracted to develop a program for animating 3D CGI characters. They built a skeleton that could be loaded unto a number of different characters. In the skeleton rigging we control the character's movements. This step is very standard these days, but it was pretty revolutionary back in 1996. Around that same time another contractor, ViewPoint Data Labs, built a number of different character skins for the program.

Some of these skins included a clown, a dinosaur, and everyone's favorite, a baby in a diaper.
The program shipped out to customers with a number of demos preloaded including one doing a complex cha-cha dance. Eventually the program landed with a developer at LucasArts, Ron Lussier.

Lussier turned the dancing baby into a gif and emailed it out to some of his friends.
You know how it goes? They tell two friends, who tell two more friends, and before you know it, it was a viral sensation.

At one point dancingbaby.net experienced so much web traffic they need to revert to text only web page. Which kind of defeats the purpose.

Girard believes the big reason why it was so popular is because of how unsettling it was. The chubby little baby was sitting just outside the uncanny valley where something looks almost human, but not quite, and people were sharing the gif not because they thought it was cool, but because they thought it was hilariously creepy.

Despite its massive popularity in the 90s Girard is not a fan of the dancing baby, and has gone on record to say he 100% regrets creating it. Apparently, the writers of Ally McBeal were big fans. In the show Ally and the baby are dancing together to the music of *I gotta a feeling*.
The music got added to the original animation and that became the most popular animation of the meme.

Memes have changed a lot since the dancing baby gif. In the early to mid 2000s memes started to be a little more relatable in a global sense. Think of stuff like the success baby, or the awkward penguin, Like a boss, or things that make you cringe like the Delta safety videos from a couple of years ago.

Nowadays the shelf life of a meme is short because they are mostly reactive to something the people are talking about during the time that they're actually relevant.
Their relatability lasts about as long as the source captures the internet's mind.

Elon Musk thinks that the dead deer at the bottom of a pool is funnier after he finds out it's a real picture? Meme. Will Smith's genie looks like it was created using an Nintendo 64. Meme!

The creepiest melody

Remember when Mufasa died? Or when Luke Skywalker's aunt and uncle were killed? Or even when George Bailey decided he couldn't bear to live anymore? These are some of the most grim, tragic moments in film history, and they have something else in common: just four notes. Once you start paying attention, the melody you have heard in these movies is everywhere. We've been associating it with death for almost 800 years.

What you are hearing in those movies is called the "dies irae," A Gregorian chant created by Catholic monks in the 13th century for one specific mass: funerals.

"Dies irae" means "Day of Wrath" in Latin.
That's the day Catholics believe God will judge the living and the dead and decide whether they go to heaven or hell for eternity.

The musical material and the text combine together to create an ominous sense of dread.
The influence of the Church grew steadily in the next few hundred years, including its cultural influence, which is why the Day of Wrath started showing up in composition outside the church's domain, like Mozart's 1791 symphony "Requiem," which was influenced by the music of funerals.

But it was Louis-Hector Berlioz, the French composer, who took the dies irae's cultural capital to a new level, in 1830.
In his "Symphonie fantastique," he used the melody but left out the words.
Moreover, the story of the symphony isn't set in a church or funeral: it's about an obsessive love, in which the main character who has killed his lover dreams that the victim has come back as a witch to torment him.
The movement is called "The Dream of a Witches' Sabbath." It's set at midnight in a graveyard and Berlioz wrote in several pieces of creepy spooky music, including the dies irae.

What better piece of spooky music to play? After all it was a piece of music that already had these connotations behind it.

Taking their cue from Berlioz, other composers added versions and parts of the dies irae to their works. Hungarian composer Franz Liszt's included it in the Totentanz, or Dance of the Dead, inspired by a medieval painting depicting suffering and death, and Giuseppe Verdi's wrote it in the Messa da Requiem.

But this melody is so familiar to our Western ears, that it couldn't be confined to just music.
In the early silent films, the dies irae was extracted even further and used as a sort of sample or reference to dark, ominous actions that were taking place on screen. They couldn't be exactly subtle since the music created the whole atmosphere.
Silent films were accompanied by full orchestras, which played compositions that helped propel the soundless stories along. A vivid example is 1927's Metropolis, a silent German sci-fi about a dystopia full of robots, hot chicks, and destruction which uses the dies irae in particularly dramatic moments.

When movies started incorporating sound, the dies irae maintained its use as a shorthand for something grim, malicious, and frightening. From It's a Wonderful Life to Star Wars: A New Hope.

But its most iconic use might be in The Shining. After all, The Shining is a horror film and that's the perfect signifier for the dies irae.
The dies irae has come a long way from 13th-century funerals to scary movies. But clearly there's something about those four notes that makes us feel uncomfortable.

So, why is the music so universally dreadful? The chant is in what's called Dorian mode — and we don't have to dig into all the ancient modes like that — but today if you would play those first four notes you would say that that's in a minor mode. Minor music has always had a connotation of sadness and darkness.

If you look at the music sheet and know how to read music, you'll see that F and E are half steps apart, right next to each other: our ears are trained not to like those sounds together. To make matters worse, the notes descend, getting deeper as the phrase progresses.
Musical lines that descend are sad whereas music that ascends, that rises, is much uplifting.
Combine these three things together and you've got an inherently spooky song, even if you don't know about all the fire and brimstone.

If you start listening, you'll realize that the dies irae is everywhere: the phrase has become so culturally ingrained in our consciousness that even a modified version such as the theme to The Exorcist, or a shortened version, such as the Nightmare Before Christmas score can imbue as with the same sense of dread and anguish.

How nuclear bombs killed the art forgers

Han Van Meegeren might be the most famous art forger of the 20th century. He had mastered the technique of making fakes look really old: he added aging chemicals to his paints, baked the finished piece and used a rolling pin to crack the paint. He once tricked Nazi leaders into trading 137 priceless paintings for one forgery.
Han's forgeries have become works of art in their own merit and are on display in Amsterdam's Rijksmuseum.
So, how can you detect a world-class forgery from a world class artist?
Historians typically rely on their eyes and their knowledge, but even so they've been fooled many, many times.
Still, if you want to be the next master forger, you have a bit of a hurdle to go through. There is a new scientific tool that make it virtually impossible to sell a forgery and weirdly enough, it wouldn't have been possible without the nuclear arms race.

Starting in the 1940s, over 550 nuclear bombs were exploded above ground, which meant that the atmosphere choke full of two radioactive isotopes that didn't exist on Earth before 1945, because they can only be created by fission reactions.

Since then they've travelled around everywhere in miniscule amounts and show up in almost anything; from our bones and brains to pigments and painting supplies.

Any forgery made after 1945 will almost certainly contain just a pinch of these isotopes. So, now we can test anything, from old wine bottles to woodcarvings to tell if it was made after 1945.

But what if someone forged a Leonardo in the 1800s? We would need a different trick: carbon dating.

Carbon-14 is a heavier, radioactive isotope of carbon that's much rarer than ordinary carbon.
Everything that eats, such as plants, and everything that eat things that eat air, have a small fraction of this heavy carbon in their cells alongside all their normal carbon. Carbon-14 is constantly decaying, but gets replenished when they eat.
The moment something dies, the carbon-14 stops being replenished, and slowly, very slowly, decays away. The comparison between the radioactive carbon to normal carbon gives us the date of the material.
Canvas, wood, even the oils used in paints are all plant-based and can be carbon dated.

This method proved that a Fernand Léger painting bought by collector Peggy Guggenheim was actually painted in 1959, four years after the artist's death. In fact, what is under a painting can be just as informative as the art itself, if not more valuable. In the days before Amazon free shipping, canvases were hard to get, so artists often painted on top of other paintings.
X-rays revealed that Van Gogh's "Self Portrait with Glass" was painted over a woman's entire portrait and Picasso's "Old Guitarist" was originally a half-finished canvas.

A clever forger nowadays knows that to make a good fake, you have to paint over an old painting. "Portrait of a Woman" attributed to Goya, was proven to be a fake when the x-rays showed a portrait by a completely different artist underneath. So, you should really paint over something that matches, as well. Technologies really don't make life easy for art forgers!

If these other methods fail, the paint holds one more clue, like blood at a crime scene.

Paint has three main ingredients: pigment, the color itself; a binder, which holds the paint together; dissolved in a solvent, either water or oil. the perfect palette for a forensic investigation.

Since different pigments were used in different places over the different centuries, they can give us an idea when and where a painting was made. If you zap the paint with electromagnetic radiations and look at the light it emits you can tell all the exact components. These spectra of lights are the fingerprints of specific atoms. For example, they can show if a red is made from cinnabar or rust.
If just one element doesn't belong, the painting is probably a fake.

For instance, for most of history, white pigments contained toxic lead (as Elizabeth I learned all too well), which was later discarded in favor of other white pigments. When investigators examined a painting attributed to Frans Hal and discovered a white pigment containing zinc, which was not invented until after Frans' death, the confirmed the forgery. Too bad, they didn't find out until after it was sold for over $10 million dollars.

But, let's get back to Van Meegeren; what made him so excellent? He actually beat the atomic forensic methods by making his own authentic 1500s paints, with old pigments like cinnabar red and lead white.

But despite all his tricks, he was caught. How?
The chemicals formaldehyde he added, to harden and 'age' the paints was too modern. Even with authentic paint and canvas, and a master's touch, the one thing he couldn't do was make his paintings look the right kind of old. There's just no substitute for time.

HARROWING SURVIVAL STORIES

Are you looking for nail-biting stories? Look no further, here are the most exciting and absurd survival stories you will ever read!

Living underwater

Usually waking up because you have to go to the bathroom is annoying. But using the bathroom in the middle of the night was the decision that saved Harrison Odjegba Okene's life.
29-year-old Harrison was the lone survivor of a boat sinking at sea, but he shattered the record for being the only known person in the world to have survived on the sea bed for nearly 3 days and all thanks to a midnight tinkle.

The Gulf of Guinea is rich with petroleum laden layers of sedimentary seabed, which is why many offshore oil rig drilling operations set up shop along this stretch of the African coast.
On May 26, about 20 miles off of Escravos, Nigeria, three tugboats were fighting against the choppy sea as they performed tension tow functions on a Chevron oil tanker that was filling up at Single Buoy Mooring #3.
Shortly before 5 am, the tugboat Jascon-4 capsized. Because the Gulf is plagued by piracy problems, the security protocols on the tugboat required the 12-man crew to lock themselves in their rooms while sleeping.
But this rule unfortunately slowed down the Jascon-4's crew when they tried to escape.
The crew members had to unlock themselves out of their cabins, with the exception of the vessel's cook Harrison, who had gotten up to use the bathroom in his underwear.

When the boat keeled over and the water rushed in, Harrison had to force the bathroom's metal door open against a pounding wall of water. But, the pressure of the water was so strong that Harrison was unable to follow his colleagues to the emergency hatch.
He helplessly watched as a surge of water killed 3 crew members and swept them out of the boat into the raging sea.
Then the water pushed Harrison down a narrow hallway into the bathroom of an officer's cabin.

He was dazed, cold, and bruised, but still alive, he managed to keep his head above water by using an overturned washbasin in the 4 feet square bathroom.
The boat sank approximately 100 feet, stopping only on the seabed, upside down.

When the tugboat capsized, a rescue operation was immediately launched with the help of other boats in the area and a helicopter. The diving crew located the wreck and marked the location with buoys.
They dived and banged on the hull of the boat, and Harrison hammered back, but they didn't hear him.
The divers were not prepared to deep dive, they were only able to stay at the depth of the wreck for a limited period of time. Since they saw no evidence of survivors, the search and rescue team was called off.

After almost a day stuck in the bathroom, Harrison decided it was time to leave his little air pocket. In the darkness of the ocean surrounding him, he swam and found his way into the engineer's office. Luckily, there was another air pocket here too, approximately 4 feet high, according to Harrison's estimation.
Once he had solved the immediate problem of having air to breathe, Harrison could focus on other problems.

The first one was that he was cold, really cold. In May, the average surface temperature of the east Atlantic is a balmy 81.9°F. But unfortunately, Harrison was 100 feet down! He was shivering, wet, and wearing only boxer shorts. He was going into hypothermia: his body was losing heat faster than he could produce it.

Very carefully, in total darkness, Harrison felt his way around the cabin. He found some tools and managed to use them to strip off the wall paneling. With the material from the wall and a mattress, he was able to build a makeshift platform to sit on. The platform helped Harrison to stay afloat, since it lifted the upper half of his body out of the water and allowed him to reduce heat loss.

He was hungry, thirsty, still cold, and stuck in complete darkness. He was also understandably terrified. He was a deeply devout man, so he tried to think about his family and prayed and call on Jesus to rescue him.

With each passing hour, the sea water began to corrode the skin from Harrison's tongue.

He could smell something rotting all around him and realized it was the decomposing bodies of his former shipmates.

Every sound in that immense darkness was increased ten-fold: he could hear the banging of wreckage and the water against the walls, the creaking of the hull, and most horrifically, the splashing and eating sounds of the fishes nibbling at the corpses.

On the surface, the Lewek Toucan, a dive support vessel, had arrived to the area of the sinking.
West African Ventures, the parent company of Harrison's tugboat had hired a deep sea salvage diving team to retrieve the bodies of the lost crew members; they did not expect any survivors at that point.

The 6 divers, deck crew and technical staff of the Lewek Toucan knew it was going to be a grueling and saddening mission. Not only the work of recovering the dead was heartbreaking, but the boat had sunk upside down into soft mud, shaking up fine silt and creating extremely poor visibility.

Moreover, because of the aforementioned security protocols the boat was latched from the inside.
The second dive team consisted of Nico Van Heerden, Andre Erasmus and Darryl Oosthuizen supervised by Colby Werrett on the ship, who helped guide the divers via microphone while watching the dive through a camera worn by Nico.
The team spent over an hour breaking through an external watertight door and then a second metal door to get into the sunken boat. Once inside it was extremely disorienting with the ceiling being on the bottom and the floor overhead.

The murky waters were filled with all sorts of hazardous objects, including furniture and equipment. Slowly and painstakingly, the divers explored the capsized boat.
They had already recovered four of the twelve corpses, when Nico went up the stairs to the main deck: a tight squeeze wearing the diving gear.

Trying to get through, he suddenly felt something reaching out of the dark waters and touching him…

Harrison had nearly given up hope when he had heard the familiar sound of an anchor dropping.

Then he heard hammering on the hull of the boat; it could only have been divers! He banged fruitlessly on the wall, but they couldn't hear him.
Finally, Harrison saw the light from one of the diver's head torches, swimming through the hallway past the cabin. Unfortunately, the diver was too quick and left the area before Harrison could reach him.
But then came the magical moment. If you haven't yet, you should see the surreal, amazing rescue footage from Nico's video when he sees what he believes is another dead body: he touches the corpse's hand and the hand unexpected squeezes his.

Nico had time for a brief freak-out, as his supervisor Colby yells through the microphone "He's alive, he's alive!"
Colby tells Nico to comfort Harrison by patting him on the shoulder and giving him a thumbs up sign. The divers were amazed to find Harrison alive. But his ordeal wasn't over.

The maximum depth for recreational diving is 130 feet. Generally, recreational divers don't stay at 100 feet for more than 20 minutes.

Moreover, a person inhales roughly 350 cubic feet of air every 24 hours. Because the boat was under pressure on the ocean floor, scientists estimate that Harrison's air pocket had been compressed by a factor of about four. Which means that in terms of the air pocket, the divers had reached Harrison just in time.

If the pressurized air pocket was about 216 cubic feet, it would have contained enough oxygen to keep Harrison alive for approximately two-and-a-half days. Harrison had been underwater for about 60 hours.

An additional danger to consider carbon dioxide buildup. CO_2 is fatal to humans at a concentration of about 5%. As Harrison breathed in air, he exhaled carbon dioxide, slowly increasing the levels of the gas in the tiny space. Thankfully, CO_2 is absorbed by water. By splashing the water inside his air pocket, Harrison had inadvertently increased the water's surface area, heightening the absorption of CO_2 and helping to keep the gas below the 5% level.

The divers described Harrison as having CO_2 poisoning: he was short of breath and delirious when they found him. He wouldn't have lasted much longer.

To begin, the divers used hot water to warm Harrison up, then put an oxygen mask on. Meanwhile, on the surface, the dive support crew was in contact discussing how to best help the survivor with medical and diving experts. After all, it was something that no one had ever encountered before.

Harrison had yet another problem: the bends.

The bends, decompression sickness (DCS), or Caisson disease occurs when nitrogen bubbles form in the blood as a result of changes in pressure.

If Harrison ascended directly from 100 feet underwater to the surface of the ocean, the bubbles in his blood would cause in the best-case scenario joint pain and rashes and in the worst-case scenario paralysis, neurological issues, cardiac arrest, or even death.

It was quickly decided that Harrison would be treated with the same protocols meant for the saturation divers coming up after a dive.

Therefore, Harrison spent about 20 minutes getting used to breathing through the mask. After that, the divers put on him diving helmet and harness. They were worried he would panic as they got him out of the boat and endanger the dive, but Harrison continued to be cool under pressure.

Harrison was taken from the boat and brought to a diving bell which finally took him to the surface.

He arrived topside at 7pm on Tuesday, the 28th of May. Extremely disoriented, Harrison thought that it was Sunday evening and he had been trapped for 12 hours at the most. He was shocked when he learned that he had been underwater for over 2 days.

After being rescued, Harrison was moved to a decompression chamber where he stayed for 2 and ½ days while his body decompressed to the surface pressure.

The only survivor of the tugboat Jascon-4, Harrison made a full recovery and returned to his hometown of Warri, Nigeria.

He wasn't present at the funerals of his colleagues because he feared their families' reactions.

Some rumors had started to spread that Harrison saved himself through black magic; but aside from superstitious beliefs, Harrison was also plagued with survivor's guilt. Since the incident Harrison has experienced and never fully recovered from PTSD.

Since then he has taken a cooking job on dry land and vows to never again take a position on a boat. Unlike our next survivor, the woman who survived three sinking boats, Ms. Jessop.

The unsinkable Violet Jessop

You may have heard the name Violet Jessop as one of the Titanic's survivors, but did you know that she didn't just survive one sinking ship, but three?

Violet Jessop, "Miss Unsinkable", enjoyed incredible "luck" from a young age.
She was born in 1887 in Argentina to Irish immigrants. When she contracted tuberculosis as a young child and was given just a few months to live, she managed to fight the disease and went on to live a long, healthy life. When her father passed away, her mother decided to move to Britain, where she took a job as a stewardess on a ship.

While her mother was at sea, Violet attended a convent school. Unfortunately, her mother became ill, violet had to provide for her siblings. So, she decided to follow in her mother's footsteps and become a ship stewardess herself.

The first hurdle of a complicated life was finding a ship that would take her. She was 21 years old at the time and most women working as stewardesses in the early 1900s were middle-aged.
Employers thought that her youthful good looks would be a disadvantage to her, because it might "cause problems" with the crew and passengers. (She did get at least three marriage proposals while working on various ships, including one from an incredibly wealthy first-class passenger.)
Violet solved the issue by making herself look dowdy with old clothes and no make-up. After this transformation, she had more successful interviews.

After a brief stint aboard a Royal Mail Line steamer, the Orinoco, in 1908, she was hired by the White Star Line. Violet started out on the Majestic and switched to the Olympic in 1910. Despite the long hours and meager pay (£2.10 every month or about £200 today), she loved working aboard the massive ship.
She initially had some concerns about the crossing the Atlantic, but she reportedly liked that the Americans were kinder to her while she served them.

But just one year later, the troubles started.
In 1911, the Olympic collided with the HMS Hawke, which was a ship designed to sink ships by ramming them. Both ships were considerably damaged: the Olympic had his hull breached just below the water line, but miraculously didn't sink. They made it back to port with no harm done, and Violet disembarked without a scratch.

A couple of years later, the White Star Line was looking to hire crew to cater to the VIPs aboard the notoriously unsinkable ship, the Titanic.
Friends and family convinced her that it would be a wonderful experience, so Violet eventually decided to take a job on board the ship. As you know, the Titanic struck an iceberg and sunk, killing more than 1500 people. Violet escaped the disaster on lifeboat 16.

In her memoir, she recalls, "I was ordered up on deck. Calmly, passengers strolled about. I stood at the bulkhead with the other stewardesses, watching the women cling to their husbands before being put into the boats with their children. Sometime after, a ship's officer ordered us into the boat first to show some women it was safe." As she jumped on the lifeboat, she was handed a baby to care for.
When they were rescued by the Carpathia, the baby's mother found her and whisked the baby away, grabbing the baby out of Jessop's arms and running off. Let's hope it was indeed his mother!
Violet had lived to sail another day.

The thing she missed the most after the Titanic sank was her toothbrush that she'd left on board.
You and I would probably stop getting on ships at this point, or at least Olympic class ships, but not Violet.

Just before World War I, she decided to serve as a nurse on board the Titanic's other sister ship, Britannic, which operated in the Aegean Sea.
Given her track record, you can probably guess what happened next. It's like inviting Angela Lansbury to a Murder Mystery Dinner Party.

The Britannic slid over a mine that had been planted by a German U-boat. The ship was substantially damage and quickly and predictably started sinking. This time, Violet wasn't lucky enough to jump into a lifeboat as the ship was sinking too fast. She just jumped overboard.
In her own words, "I leapt into the water but was sucked under the ship's keel which struck my head. I escaped, but years later when I went to my doctor because of a lot of headaches, he discovered I had once sustained a fracture of the skull!"
She joked that she only survived because of her thick hair, which softened the blow. This time at least she remembered to grab her toothbrush before evacuating, unlike with the Titanic.
Even this latest disaster was not enough to stop Violet.

After the war, ships became a more and more popular form of transport.
Violet left the White Star Line for the Red Star Line and worked on a ship doing world cruises for several years. Luckily for Violet and everyone traveling on the ships she was aboard later, no such vessel she worked on ever sustained significant damage again. She tried out a clerical job for a while after World War II, but went back to working on Royal Mail ships before she retired at the age of 61.

After surviving the sinking of the sister ships the Titanic, the Britannic, and the Olympic, she ultimately died in 1971 of congestive heart failure at the ripe old age of 84.

The original castaway

Despite popular belief Tom Hanks wasn't the first man stranded on an island.
Thomas Musgrave shipwrecked on a tiny island and instead of waiting around for 4 years, he built a dinghy and sailed 400 miles to rescue within a year.

If you've seen the movie Castaway, you are obviously an expert on how to survive on a deserted island in the middle of the ocean. First, you do some recon to see if anyone else is on the island and if there's anything to eat, like bananas conveniently dangling from trees or any wandering animals. Nothing; it seems you'll have to fashion a spear so that you might do some shallow water fishing. Well, that turns out to be more difficult than you thought. At least you managed to collect some rainwater after a shower, using a large leaf as a receptacle.

You're also well aware that if you don't find something head-shaped and proceed to draw eyes and a nose on it you might lose your mind. You call him, "Rocky." If it's a girl, you might call her, "Coco" or "Shelly." In reality, the chances of you surviving on an uninhabited island for a long time are slim. If you got washed up without any tools you might find yourself in a bit of a pickle. Even if you did find the most important thing, drinkable water, you're still going to have to build a shelter, make a tool for hunting, and actually be able to hunt. Indeed, if there is anything available to kill.

But some people have survived, and now I will introduce you to one Captain Thomas Musgrave, a man whose story is nothing short of amazing.

He was born in England in 1832, but at the young age of 16 he set out to sail the seas for the first time. His whole life was in and around ships, but when the Grafton, his latest ship, left Australia on 12 November 1863 to search for mining and sealing opportunities, his life would change forever.

He headed off with a crew of five to Campbell Island, which is part of New Zealand's subantarctic islands. It's in the middle of nowhere, but it was believed that there would be tin to mine and so off the six went.

They had a back-up plan, because if tin wasn't found they could at least resort to seal-hunting and on their return sell the furs and oil. But after they reached the most remote and unwelcoming place on earth, not only did they not find any tin to mine, but not even the seals hadn't turned up for the hunting party. They couldn't afford to go back empty-handed: explorations were not cheap.

They decided to head to Auckland Island and explore there. It was a Thursday, on December 31, 1863, a bad day for a sailor.

Strong winds battered the ship; the water broke in all directions and a thick fog surrounded the vessel. These bad conditions remained, but on New Year's Day the men got sight of the island. As they approached the island, they saw a large number of seals, which lifted the men's moods, before the bad weather started to batter the ship again. They managed to drop both anchors but in the strong winds, heavy rain and rough seas, they couldn't steady the ship. At around midnight a violent gale blew the ship against rocks. The water rushed into the ship and in no time the ocean was spilling onto the deck. The men abandoned all hope of pumping the water out and instead gathered as many provisions as they could.

The ship was wrecked; it was a lost cause. The wreckage was close enough to the island to get their things and leave the ship.

They were alive, but none of them could imagine what awaited them. They had some food, tools, as well as a gun and gunpowder. They used bits of the ship including the sails to build a shelter. After a week the men hadn't been able to get much done due to awful weather and vicious winds, but when things cleared up they got work on the shelter.

With timber from the boat as well as cloth from the sails, it wasn't that hard to knock-up a shelter. It helped that one of the crew members had experience in this and he at least had a combination hammer, something similar to an axe and a drill. In time, they had a stable cabin to live in. Soon it would have a chimney so they could have a fire in the place and let the smoke out. It had a table, and to sleep on the men made what looked like stretchers. As the weeks passed, the provisions were running out, but the seals were virtually everywhere. The men could hear them roar as they slept, which was like music to their ears.

In fact, when they woke up there'd be seals right outside their shelter, so the closest one got it, and ended up seal meat. Living on only seal meat wasn't exactly the best diet and the men didn't want to come down with scurvy, so they started looking for other food sources. Luckily, around the island there were widgeons, which are kind of like ducks. Those were very tasty. The guys discovered that older seals tasted horrible, but ia cub that had never even been in the water it was delicious. When he ate it for the first time, Musgrave remarked, "It tastes like lamb!" The seals didn't much like those two-legged animals taking their cubs, and put up a fight. They were soon scared off when the men fired a gun.

It wasn't always seal for dinner, though.
The guys also ate a lot of fish and crabs. As deserted islands go, it wasn't all that bad. Nonetheless, as months passed, the men started to wonder how long it would take for an expedition to find them, or if anyone was looking for them at all. The fact was, those guys had long been thought of as dead.

Two months had passed, when Musgrave wrote in his diary: "I am in exceedingly low spirits today, and I know that one loved one in Sydney is so also; for I have no doubt but by this time they have given me up for lost, and what is to become of my own dear wife and children? May God, to whom only they can now look for comfort, watch over and protect them, is my constant and fervent prayer. I shall never forgive myself for coming on this enterprise."
What could they do to pass the time? Well, they worked on that house of theirs and with all the timber they needed they made it a pretty decent abode. It kept out the cold, had an area for working, a kitchen area, and a warm fire. On top of that, they had managed to keep the mosquitoes out, that had been an annoyance.
Some seal clubbing days, things didn't always go to plan.

In fact, on one particular day a tiger seal had taken offense to the clubbing of his young friends and one of the men had to hide up a tree until the others came to his rescue. What Musgrave would call "pitched battles" with seals had become quite a regular occurrence. But as the months passed on, their major battle was with misery. The days were long, the weather was horrible, and the men had lost all hope of ever leaving the island. They played games and made their own dominoes, but there was only so much they could do to keep their spirits up. Their spirits were lifted considerably when one of the men made a huge breakthrough.

What was that you might ask? The answer is the man had successfully made his own "hooch", a kind of prison beer that didn't taste so bad. He made this from a flower that grew all over the island, which he then fermented. They now had beer on tap for as long as they wanted, and it also became another part of their mixed diet. After a few months and a lot of drinks they had also taught the parrots they had to talk, which was some amusement for them. On May 15, Musgrave wrote: "Oh, my God! How long is this to last? Oh, release me from this bondage! Night and morning, day and in my dreams, I offer up my prayers to Thee."
They had developed better fishing techniques, but in June the seals disappeared and so did their main food source. The water was warmer and the seals spent most of their time in the water: hunting them became almost impossible. They had to deal with hunger again.

The warmer months passed and the seals returned. The men had food again, but the hope of ever seeing a ship sail close to the island was gone from their hearts.

In October, Musgrave wrote: "It would be impossible for me to convey to anyone an idea of my present state of mind. I am anything but mad; if that would come it would very likely afford relief." It was that month the men realized that they had to get off the island. Food wasn't always available and there were periods of terrible hunger. Their health was affected; some had been injured while out hunting and surveying. Things weren't looking good. Building a ship to sail through rough waters isn't quite as easy as the movies showed us. Musgrave wrote that the idea of just making a ship that wouldn't sink in a second without any expertise seemed farcical to him. Nonetheless, the men collected as many parts of the wreckage as they could and discussed how they'd build this thing. If anything, they had time in the day to think and build. In spite of the bouts of hunger, the men started putting something together that looked sea-worthy.

Musgrave wrote: "I hope we may succeed. It is quite true that by energetic perseverance men may perform wonders, and our success would by no means constitute a miracle. The men are all very sanguine, and I have no doubt but we shall be able to make something that will carry us to New Zealand." Sanguine means "positive", in case you didn't know that.

A year had passed and there had been more than a few failed attempts to launch their home-made boat. Some days were spent fixing it, others were spent in hunger and looking for grubs to eat. Musgrave didn't write for months, and then in Spring he started again: "The men are in what he calls a deplorable state, skinny and dressed in rags. They face "grim starvation" at times and almost want to gnaw on their own hands."

In June Musgrave wrote: "We were all seized with a violent attack of dysentery about the same time. This we have all recovered from; but I am left with rheumatic pains and cramps, which will in all probability cling to me through life. But it's time to launch the boat, even though they accept there is little probability of success. They will not survive much longer on the island, but the thought of drowning also weighs heavily on their minds."

One thing that did lift their spirits was the discovery of a cat, which stayed with them while they finished their vessel.

On 27th June they launched the boat, which was so frightening some of the men wanted to return to the island. After attempts to sail were made, it was clear that five men were just too heavy. It was decided that two men would be left behind and if the others made it home they would send out a ship to collect them. The three finally managed to sail to Stewart Island which was inhabited. There they met a Captain Cross, the first human they'd seen in 18 months. Musgrave wrote: "When we landed I could not stand, but was led up to that gentleman's house, where something to eat was immediately prepared for us, of which I partook very sparingly; for I felt very ill and unable to eat." Weeks passed, but the men and Captain Cross eventually made it back to the island where they hoped the two that were left behind were still alive.

This is Musgrave's description of the joyous meeting: "One of them, the cook, on seeing me, turned as pale as a ghost, and staggered up to a post, against which he leaned for support, for he was evidently on the point of fainting; while the other, George, seized my hand in both of his and gave my arm a severe shaking, crying, 'Captain Musgrave, how are ye, how are ye'"

What's more incredible is that four months after those men had been shipwrecked on that island, another ship had been destroyed and another group of sailors were trying to survive on another part of the island. Both groups had no idea the other was on the island.

On that other ship only 19 of the 25 men got to shore and the others drowned. They didn't have the same luck and there was less to eat, and in the end only three survived when they were seen by a passing ship. Some died of starvation; others were abandoned. In their case, it was every man for himself, rather than the collaboration Musgrave enjoyed with his men. One of those three survivors said things were grim and at one point two men got in a fight and one killed the other. The next morning the winner of that fight was eating the loser.

The terminator of World War I

Adrian Carton de Wiart fought in some of the 20th century's deadliest battles and endured everything from losing limbs to receiving bullets to his noggin. That probably sounds terrifying to most rational people, but for the man they called the Unkillable Soldier, he actually had a pretty good time.

In 1880, Adrian Carton de Wiart was born to a wealthy privileged family from Brussels. He spent a good part of his childhood in Cairo and then got his education in England, with the expectation he would become a lawyer. But Carton de Wiart had another calling, that of the soldier. When the Second Boer war broke out in 1899, Carton de Wiart was a student at Oxford.
Being a Belgian national, he didn't really have a personal stake in the struggle between Britain and South African Boers. But he really wanted to fight anyway. Using a fake name, age, and nationality, he enlisted in the British army, all this behind his father's back.

Carton de Wiart would later write that this was the moment he knew war was in his blood saying, "I didn't know why the war had started and I didn't care on which side it was to fight. If the British didn't fancy me, I would offer myself to the Boers."
Before the conflict was over, he would take bullets to his groin and abdomen. But it didn't kill Adrian's enthusiasm for war one bit.

Serving in the Boer War convinced Carton de Wiart that combat would be his life's work. With the battlefield as his canvas, Adrian would become a warrior artist.

But he was nearly derailed. In 1902, he sought out and received a position in British India fighting with the Irish Dragoon Guards.
During this stint, Adrian nearly lost his commission for firing his gun at another person, because he found that man annoying.
Adrian had been recovering from some cracked ribs when a local laborer started bothering him. Carton de Wiart first threw some stones at the man, but the target simply moved out of range. This might've ended the whole thing. But once he was safe from the stones, the laborer turned around to laugh at the convalescing soldier. That was a bad idea. As Carton de Wiart tells it, "it was too much for my temper and I promptly put up my gun and peppered him in this tale." The laborer reported him and he was put under arrest the following morning. Carton de Wiart was punished with a heavy fine, but did not ultimately lose his commission over the incident.
Life lesson? Never turn your back on an Adrian, especially if he's holding a gun.

Britain entered World War I in 1914. And Carton de Wiart was really enthusiastic about being a part of it. Eagerness, however, isn't a bullet proof vest. And he quickly had one of his eyes blasted out during a skirmish. One would think his chief concern would be survival or maybe keeping his sight, but it wasn't. He was only worried the last guy would compromise his ability to fight, saying "people imagine the loss of a hand to be far more serious than the loss of an eye, but having tried both, I can say sincerely that it is not my experience."

By most accounts, World War I was a nightmare. And 1916 was a particularly bad year. It brought Verdun and The Somme, two of history's deadliest battles, in which millions were killed. Adrian Carton de Wiart, however, saw things a bit differently. Despite losing both a hand and an eye, Adrian rose all the way up from being a captain to being the youngest brigadier general in the Allied army. As such, he considered 1916 the luckiest year of his life.
Years later, Carton de Wiart would write that he truly enjoyed his experience in World War I and wondered, "why do people want peace if war is so much fun?"

In 1915, Carton de Wiart was commanding troops on the Western front. The enemy fought with both guns and gas. So, serving in the trenches was especially dangerous Despite this, Adrian was happy to be there. War movies typically show us soldiers running through such battlefields dodging bullets and shells. But Adrian didn't bother. He found the gas didn't affect him.
As for the shells, he thought they were terrific, though he wished more of them were coming from his side.

On one occasion, his second in command even scolded him for not ducking out of the way of the shells. Carton de Wiart however considered himself a fatalist and believed that there was no point in dodging, because when your number was up, there was nothing to be done. Before he could speak, however, the two heard another shot coming. His second in command ducked out of the way, while Adrian stood his ground. The shell hit. Carton de Wiart was thrown some distance. And when he picked himself up, he immediately noticed a hand on the ground. When he inspected it closely, he realized it was wearing the glove of his second in command. The rest of that man's body was 30 or so feet away. When it's your time, it's your time.

During a battle in 1915, Adrian Carton de Wiart severely injured his hand. He would describe the injury as a ghastly sight. Two fingers were dangling from a bit of skin. And his palm, along with most of his wrist, had been shot off. Complicating the matter was that his watch had been fused to the remains of his wrist. He asked the doctors to remove his dangling fingers, but they refused.
So, he pulled the fingers off himself. Yeah. Adrian said he felt no pain doing it. Unfortunately, Adrienne's hand didn't heal and he had to have it amputated, a procedure he described as no worse than having a tooth out.

If you think having only one hand kept him from returning to the war, well, you clearly don't know Adrian Carton de Wiart. During World War I, Carton de Wiart received a serious head injury and doctors ordered him to return to London to recover. As a war machine, Adrian got bored easily if he wasn't on the battlefield. And that could sometimes lead to trouble.

While visiting an elite gentlemen's club called Whites, he was approached by a fellow club member and offered the chance to serve as the second gun in a duel. The club member explained that he wanted to duel with another man who was paying undue attention to a lady he liked. Most of us would probably decline the chance to get shot over someone else's romantic conflict. But Carton de Wiart thought it was a perfect way to resolve matters of the heart. So he happily accepted. Adrian then went to talk to the man they intended to duel. He explained the situation and said that they were happy to fight with any weapons the man should choose. The other fellow however found the whole thing ridiculous and it took some time for Carton de Wiart to convince him that he was serious.

Needless to say, the man didn't want to duel and argued it would get all of its participants into trouble with the law, especially if someone was hurt or killed. Adrian, however, felt that with war on, no one would care. He suggested holding the duel in a secluded spot and then using gasoline to cremate the loser. If that plan sends chills down your spine, then you're not alone. The man was so freaked out, he immediately signed an affidavit swearing to never speak with a lady again.

Adrian loved guns. However, he also knew he had a considerable temper and he feared that if he lost it, he might end up shooting at his own people. To guard against this, he refused to carry a revolver and instead chose to arm himself with a walking stick. Such was the case at the Battle of the Somme, where he led troops into combat. Being armed with nothing but a stick would hamper the effectiveness of most men.
But Carton de Wiart wasn't most men. He fought with such dauntless courage, he was given the highest award of the British honor system, the Victoria Cross.

Carton de Wiart may have fought like an action hero at the Battle of the Somme, but he didn't escape unscathed. He actually took around to the head. In his memoirs, Adrian would recall that the doctor verified his skull was still intact, ordered him a bottle of champagne, and then explained that by some miracle a machine gun bullet had passed right through the back of his head without touching a vital part. In fact, the only after effect of the wound was a tickle he would feel whenever he got a haircut.

In 1918, World War I finally came to an end. Adrian, however, had long since decided he was a soldier for life and went off in search of another conflict to fight in. He found it in Poland, where the British military was aiding the Polish in their struggle against the Soviets.

It was there that, in 1920, Carton de Wiart was traveling on a train that was overrun by the red Russian cavalry. Not being the kind of guy to take a thing like that lying down, Adrian snatched up a revolver and proceeded to light them up. He stood his ground and single-handedly fought off the invaders.

In 1939, World War II broke out and there was no way Adrienne Carton de Wiart was going to miss it. He had 30 years of military experience under his belt and the government knew they needed him. No less than Winston Churchill himself asked Adrian to lead the British military and diplomatic efforts in Yugoslavia.

While traveling there in 1941, his plane crashed at sea and was discovered by Italian soldiers. Carton de Wiart was detained and became a prisoner of war. Despite being 60 years old at that point, Carton de Wiart was still tough as nails. And he attempted to escape at least five separate times. He never made it, but he caused a ton of trouble for his captors and finally got his freedom in 1943.

After being released from the Italian POW camp, Carton de Wiart was a hero. Winston Churchill, who considered him a model of chivalry and honor, made him a British representative to China, where he worked alongside important officials like Chiang Kai-Shek.

He did not, however, get along with Mao Zedong, who was, at the time, the leader of China's communist party. Carton de Wiart considered Mao a fanatic. Most diplomats would probably keep that to themselves. But Carton de Wiart was fearless. On one occasion, he even went out of his way to insult Mao by claiming that Chinese troops hadn't really contributed much towards defeating the Japanese.

After leading one of the most reckless and dangerous lives imaginable, the last major injury Adrian Carton de Wiart suffered was, ironically, a pretty boring one. While visiting Rangoon, Burma, he slipped on some coconut matting and broke his back. The recovery was long and difficult. But as usual, he toughed it out and would live another 10 years, finally dying in 1963 at the age of 83.

The tragic life of an enlightened man

Forty-one years after his debut in the "Guinness Book of World Records," Ranger Roy Sullivan continues to hold the dubious distinction of being struck by lightning more than any known person. Not twice. Not three times.

Seven times.

The National Oceanic and Atmospheric Administration tells us that lightning will hit the tallest object with a positive charge from the negatively-charged cloud where it begins.

So, maybe the worst thing you could do would be to stand in a swimming pool during a thunderstorm holding a very tall metal rod.

Lighting often hits trees, but in a wide-open space such as a golf course, it could be you. But what are actually the chances of being hit by lightning and what will likely happen to you if you do get hit?

There is data available regarding exactly how many lightning deaths there are year-by-year in each country. According to the National Lightning Safety Institute, if you are Mexican, beware.

That data tells us that Mexico is way out in front of lightning deaths, with 223 last time they did the count.

Thailand was second at 171 deaths, South Africa third with 150 deaths and Brazil fourth with 132 deaths.

Then there's a big drop off to Romania, in fifth place at 75 deaths. The USA is quite high, in ninth place with 50 deaths. Perhaps data wasn't available in many countries, but according to that report most of the world sees no lightning strike deaths each year, but in most countries people will be hit.

If you come from the USA you have a 1 in 171,000 chance of being hit, which might be long odds but not that long. That is just one year, though, if you live until you are 80 and are American your chance of being hit is around 1 in 14,600, according to the National Weather Service.

By comparison, CNBC said that the odds for winning the Powerball grand prize is about 1 in 292.2 million.

1 in 171,000 for this year might not quite give you peace of mind, and if you are Mexican or Thai we suggest you stay off the golf course on a stormy day.

But what is the chance of instant death if you do get hit?

Well, 90 percent of folks that are unfortunate enough to be the recipient of a lightning strike actually survive. All is not lost, except perhaps a bit of hair and some brain function. Yes, that's the worst part.

Lighting can carry up to one billion volts of electricity, and if that smacks you when travelling at an average speed of 200,000 mph (300,000 kph) it's bound to have a profound effect under the hood, so to speak. Experts tell us that the good news is people are very, very rarely hit by a direct strike.

You might also pick up the phone and get a blast to head as the lightning travels to you, and this is called a "contact strike", but one of those is not surprisingly super rare too.

Most of time when people are hit by lightning what we actually mean is that the lighting hit something and then the current travelled to you.

For instance, if the lighting hit the ground anywhere as far as 60 feet away you could literally get the shock of your life. It might hit the ground, travel to you, go up one leg and down another, all the while stopping your heart and lungs from functioning. The more power that goes through you, the more likely you are to die or suffer some serious damage.

You might even get what's called a "side splash", which means the lightning jumps from an object and onto you. That object could even be your friend, which was a particularly distressing fact for the star of today's show. Let's say you do survive- what are the odds of coming out of it smiling? Well, it's likely that strike will change you.

The nerve damage could have an effect on your memory, your personality, or it might give you regular headaches or even epilepsy.

If that isn't bad enough, the strike itself can severely burn you.

With all this in mind, how on Earth did someone survive 7 strikes?

His name was Roy Sullivan, and he died in 1983 at the ripe old age of 71.

The former U.S park ranger has a place in the Guinness Book of Records for most hits by lightning. His nickname was the, "Human Lightning Conductor." When you hear that, it's kinda funny.

It's even more amusing that many of his friends stopped hanging out with him outside because of their perceived risk of being hit while near him.

The least funny part of the tale is that when he was lying in bed next to his fourth wife he shot himself in the head. That was the end of old Roy, and his 41-year old wife had to deal with the mess.

It seems nature couldn't get this guy, and he got himself in the end.

Roy was first hit in 1942, and suffered burns but no brain damage. You see, his job meant working in the Shenandoah National Park in Virginia, and as we know such places can be dangerous places to be during thunderstorms.

It wouldn't be until 1969 until he was hit for a second time, and that time he was driving in his truck.

The lightning hit the truck and knocked poor Roy unconscious, but all he suffered were injuries to his vanity. The strike took his hair, eyebrows and eyelashes.

He was hit again a year later, and he just brushed that one off. In '72 he was hit again, and again went the hair. As you can well imagine by this point Roy was getting rather paranoid. Let's hope he wasn't taking any of that LSD that was everywhere in those days. He started to think that some kind of powerful force was out to get him, and so stayed away from crowds just in case he provoked the wrath of this mighty lighting-God again and others got hurt.

On a more practical level he started carrying around a can of water, likely a bit ruffled by the fact he been made bald against his will on two occasions.

The hippy era had not been very loving for this man, and things were about to get even worse. In '73 Pink Floyd released "The Dark Side of the Moon", which is perhaps where Roy thought he belonged. He was hit by lighting again that year, and this time said that the cloud had definitely been following him. He had tried to get away, but to no avail. He had driven from the cloud, and then run from his truck, and boom, it got him. This time he was able to put his burning hair out. He said about the strike, "When my ears stopped ringing, I heard something sizzling. It was my hair on fire. The flames were up six inches." Roy then had a good run of three whole years of not being hit, although he still kept away from clouds.

But on June 5th 1976 there was a particular fast cloud he apparently couldn't escape from and it got him. "I actually saw the lightning shoot out of the cloud this time, and it was coming straight for me," he later said.

This time he had no can of water at hand and again he lost most of his hair.

He was hit for the last time almost exactly a year later while he was fishing. Yep, there goes the hair again, but he also suffered more severe burns this time and the loss of hearing in one ear. On his way back to the car he was confronted by a bear, if things weren't bad enough.

That was his final hit, although his wife also got one when she was with him. She'd been hanging out the washing with Roy nearby, but this time the lightning God chose the spouse.

Now, all this sounds kind of sketchy. Was Roy looking for attention? Did he have a habit of self-harm by setting fire to his hair? He was always alone when hit, so we may wonder if he really had been doing too many drugs or was just a bit crazy.

But all his hits were confirmed by the superintendent of Shenandoah National Park, R. Taylor Hoskins.

What's more surprising than merely surviving is the fact he didn't seem to suffer any long-term mental injuries. At the same time, the fact he blew his brains out could mean he wasn't exactly in the best frame of mind.

You might now be thinking, what are the odds of being hit seven times. Well, it works out at 4.15 in 100,000,000,000,000,000,000,000,000,000,000. Maybe Roy should have played the lottery.

The woman who fell from the sky

On December 24, 1971, LANSA 508 from Lima to Pucallpa, Peru was struck by lightning. Now considered the deadliest lightning strike in aviation history, it caused a crash that ultimately led to the demise of everyone onboard, except for one 17-year-old girl: Juliane Koepcke survived a plane crash and 11 days alone in the Amazon.

Koepcke's hazy disjointed recollections of the flight and the crash are nothing short of pure nightmare fuel. It was the day after her senior prom and just a few hours after her high school graduation ceremony. She was flying with her mother between Pucallpa and Lima so they could celebrate with her father. Along the way, the plane encountered a storm.

The sky became pitch black all around them. And lightning was constantly flashing outside the windows. While her mother was concerned, Juliane, who loved to fly, didn't think much of it. Suddenly, there was a bright light on the wing. And her mother said, now, it's over. The engine roared. People screamed. The plane plunged sharply towards the ground and began to break apart.
Juliane's mother was thrown from her seat.

Finally, Juliane, along with her seat bench, was sucked from the fuselage and out into the sky. Koepcke says she felt a calming wind as she plummeted toward the thick forest canopy, which she later recalled as resembling green cauliflower or broccoli. Her seat, which she was still belted to, rotated like a helicopter blade. She suspects this may have played a role in slowing her descent and that the seat itself must have cushioned her fall. Yeah, think about that the next time a flight attendant reminds you to buckle up. Juliane blacked out before impact. And due to a concussion, she retains no memory of the next 20 hours or so.

She suspects she must have awakened during this period and removed her seat belt because it was off by the time she fully regained consciousness. It was 9:00 AM the morning after the crash. In fact, she could tell thanks to her watch, which at this point was still functioning. It was also pouring rain. Koepcke was soaking wet, dirty, and partially underneath her seat bench. She crawled fully under to escape the rain while she regained her strength.

According to Koepcke, it would be a full day and a half before she was able to get up and walk. Juliane could tell her collarbone was badly broken. It was a sharp break that was overlapping beneath her skin but luckily had not punctured through. She also had a deep laceration on her calf. But because she was in shock, it wasn't bleeding too much. Another cut on her arm had become infected with maggots. She feared that this might mean the arm would eventually have to be amputated. But at this point, there was nothing she could do about it. Doctors would later discover she also fractured her shin, strained her vertebra, and tore her ACL.

Likely due to the effects of adrenaline, she didn't feel any of those things until much later after she had reached a hospital. Once she felt strong enough, Juliane forced herself to her feet. Most people would probably be terrified to find themselves alone and injured in the middle of a jungle teeming with snakes, crocodiles, and all manner of poisonous flora and fauna.
But Juliane Koepcke had a very unique childhood.

Her mother, a world-renowned ornithologist, and her father, a famous zoologist, worked at a research station in-- would you believe it-- a Peruvian rainforest. Yes, Juliane had been raised in a very similar area. And her familiarity with the types of terrain was a major factor in her survival. It also meant she never became overly afraid of her situation.
Juliane wasn't afraid for herself, she was afraid for her mother.
Once she was able, Koepcke began to scout the area immediately around her crash site for other survivors and resources.
She was careful to leave a trail since she knew how easy it was to get lost in the jungle.

On the fourth day after the crash, she heard a sound she recognized as a king vulture landing in the forest. She knew from her ornithologist mother that this particular type of vulture only landed when carrion or rotting flesh was in the immediate vicinity. Following the sound, she discovered the remains of three other passengers. Still strapped to their seats, they had impacted the ground with such force that they were buried 3 feet deep with only their feet remaining visible. One of the victims was a woman. And Koepcke initially feared it might be her mother.

However, poking her with a stick, she was able to discern that the woman had painted toenails, which her mother did not. During those first few days, Koepcke would occasionally hear the sounds of rescue planes overhead. Because the forest canopy was so thick, she wasn't able to see them. More frustratingly, she could not get their attention. Eventually, the sounds of the planes disappeared. And she realized they were no longer searching for survivors. She would later describe these as her most hopeless moments.

She realized she would have to rely on herself if she was going to escape the rainforest alive. Finding water was as simple as licking droplets off leaves. But finding food was no easy task. She didn't have the tools necessary to fish or hack at edible stems and roots. And she knew a great deal of what else grew in the rainforest was poisonous. Though it wasn't much, Koepcke had been lucky enough to discover a bag of candy near where she landed. That candy would be her only sustenance. And she rationed it carefully, eating just a couple of pieces each day. Once it was gone, she experienced extreme hunger.
At one point, Juliane briefly considered trying to catch and eat some wild frogs she had spotted but discovered she was too weak and slow to get them. This ultimately turned out to be a good thing since she later learned they were venomous dart frogs that likely would have ended her.

Juliane searched the area she landed and for other survivors. But she didn't find any. She did, however, find a small well. It reminded her of some advice her father had given her as a child. He told her if she was ever lost in the jungle, she should follow the water sources to find rescue. The idea was that each tiny stream would lead to a bigger one and eventually to one big enough to be a water source for potential rescuers. Juliane has stated that had she found other survivors, she probably would have stayed put and waited with them. In hindsight, she realized that likely would have costed her her life.

Without anyone else to wait with, she decided to start at the well and follow the water. Progress was slow and difficult. Koepcke was wearing only a short sleeveless mini dress, which made the nights very cold for her. Her watch had also stopped working, which meant she had to keep a close eye on the sun to tell time. She was also missing a shoe, which was particularly worrisome, given that she knew there were snakes that liked to camouflage themselves among the leaves on the forest floor. Complicating things even further was the fact that she had also lost her glasses in the plane crash.

Taken together, all this meant that she had to constantly use her remaining shoe to probe the path ahead of her before she could take even one step. Eventually, the creek she was following became deep enough to walk in.

Despite the fact that Koepcke could see crocodiles slipping in and out of the water, she knew they seldom bothered humans and that by traveling by water was ultimately safer than traveling by land. As she followed the water, Koepcke noticed that the way was often blocked by logs-- a sign that the area wasn't well traveled and might not lead her to rescuers.

Blocking these discouraging thoughts out, Juliane continued on.

Then on the 10th day after the crash of LANSA flight 508, Koepcke spotted a boat. At first, she thought she was hallucinating. But she moved toward it and found herself actually able to touch it. Once she determined the boat was real, her adrenaline kicked in.

Near the riverbank where she spotted the boat, Koepcke saw a path leading up into the forest. Assuming her rescuers had gone in that direction, she tried to make her own way up the path. By this point, she was so weak she could only crawl. Even worse, the maggots that had infected the cut on her right arm were causing her intense pain, as they tried to burrow further into the wound.

Luckily at the top of the path, she came across a small hut that had a can of gasoline in it. She recalled that in her childhood, her father had used kerosene to treat a dog who had a similar wound. Juliane sucked the gasoline from the can and applied it to her wound. The pain was intense, but it worked. She removed 30 maggots herself. Her rescuers would later remove another 50. But thanks to this quick-thinking action, she never had to lose her arm.

With no one else in sight, Koepcke tried to sleep in the hut under a tarp but found the ground too hard. She returned to the riverbank and spent the night there. In the morning, she returned to the hut. This time, she was discovered by three Peruvian men. They were confused by her presence and frightened by her bloodshot eyes and blond hair.

Luckily, Juliane spoke fluent Spanish and was able to explain her situation to them in their own language. The next day these men took her downstream in their boat to a nearby town where she was able to get treatment at a local hospital. Juliane was the only survivor of LANSA a flight 508. But it's interesting to note the crash almost claimed one more. Film Director Werner Herzog was almost on the flight. But a last-minute change in plans caused him to cancel his reservations. Inspired by this twist of fate, he would later create the documentary Wings of Hope to tell the incredible tale of Juliane Koepcke's survival.

A life without a head

When you read survival stories, you might expect stories about well... people, but despite the fact that I have blathered on about the resilience of the human body and soul, the prize for the most amazing survival story goes to Mike the Headless Chicken.

There's an old urban legend that a farmer in Colorado cut the head off a chicken with an axe, but instead of bleeding to death and being ground into chicken nuggets, the chicken survived, headless, and just kept running around.

It sounds pretty crazy, but it's just crazy enough to true, and it actually did happen at least once, in 1945. Not only did the chicken survive, it went on to live another, very famous, 18 months. So, do chickens not actually need their heads? Well, frankly, not most of it.

When Mike the chicken had his head lopped off, the axe missed two very vital parts: the jugular vein, and the brain stem. It also missed one of his ears but that wasn't particularly important to his survival.

So, while Mike was missing pretty much every part of his higher brain centers; the lower part, which regulates things like breathing and heart rate, was still mostly intact and with a blood supply to keep it going.

There were some things Mike wouldn't be able to do, like math, but since the brain stem attached directly to the spine, in both chickens and humans, it could react to stimuli and keep the body in homeostasis, and well... not dead.

He went on to live the glamorous life of sideshows, contending with the fame of a two-headed baby. His picture ended up in Life and Time and earned $ 4,500 per month (equivalent to $51,525 in 2019) for 18 months. See, you don't need a brain to get ahead (pun intended!)

However, one fatal day chomping down on his hard-earned kernel corns, Mike choked to death in his motel room. You might ask, how was he able to eat it at all?

Well, his owner Lloyd Olsen of Fruita, Colorado (which still celebrates a Chicken Mike Day in May), recognizing his potential as a sideshow star after the failed decapitation, fed him with drops of water and milk with an eye dropper, tiny worms, and small kernels of corns, by dropping them in his open throat, which ultimately proved fatal.

As a brief excursus, please allow me to clarify that simply not having a head doesn't mean you're immediately dead.

Back when people got their heads cut off by guillotines, when France was cool, there were anecdotal stories about body-less heads able to move their eyes, open their mouths as if to speak, and blink for up to 30 seconds.

The brain really only has a few seconds after being removed from the body, and thus a source blood and oxygen, before falling into a coma and dying. Any action after those few seconds is most likely a muscular reaction. The same happens in chickens.

It's not uncommon for a headless chicken, even one missing its brainstem, to run around for a little while after decapitation. The headless chicken's muscles can continue to contract for a short while without a brain telling them to do so.

But the animals best suited to cheat death and haunt us as zombies are cockroaches, because they're designed differently from us.
When a human or chicken heart beats, it pumps blood around the body to give it the energy and oxygen it needs; and one of the many things that happens when you're decapitated is you lose a lot of blood, and your blood pressure drops, and your heart can't keep up.

But cockroaches don't rely on blood pressure. Cockroaches and many other invertebrates have something called an open circulatory system, where instead of going through blood vessels, the blood floats just around in the body cavities and makes direct contact with the internal tissues and organs. That means that when a cockroach is decapitated, the threat of the loss of blood pressure is not that big of a deal.

Moreover, the roach can keep breathing with the brain entirely. Roach breath comes in through holes along the body segment called called spiracles, that send air to the cells that need it. And because they don't need to eat as often as humans, roaches they can survive weeks without a head.

You might have living, breathing, headless cockroaches that you thought you had killed running around your house right now while you are reading your book in bed.
Good night and happy dreams!

CONCLUSION

I hope you have enjoyed this book as much as I've enjoyed writing it.
Thank you for enduring my terrible puns and jokes and if you have found the stories interesting and would like to spread the word like the HeLa cells, please leave a review on Amazon!

Made in the USA
Monee, IL
19 December 2020

54057328R00090